For Su Proebster, with love and gratitude.

First published in 2021.

Copyright © 2021 Martin Baynton

ISBN 978-0-473-57165-8 (paperback)
ISBN 978-0-473-58088-9 (hardback)
ISBN 978-0-473-57166-5 (epub)

Any references to historical events, real people, or real places are used fictitiously. Some names, characters, and places referred to are from the works of Lewis Carroll, their use is gratefully acknowledged by the author. All other names, characters and places are products of the author's imagination.

The quotations opening each chapter are from
Alice's Adventures in Wonderland and *Through the Looking Glass.*

12 11 10 9 8 7 6 5 4 3 2 1   1 2 3 4 5 6 7 8 9 / 2

Cover art by Martin Baynton based on drawings by John Tenniel.
Book design: Smartwork Creative, www.smartworkcreative.co.nz

www.takingwonderland.com

TAKING WONDERLAND

The Secret of Safe Passage

BOOK ONE

Martin Baynton

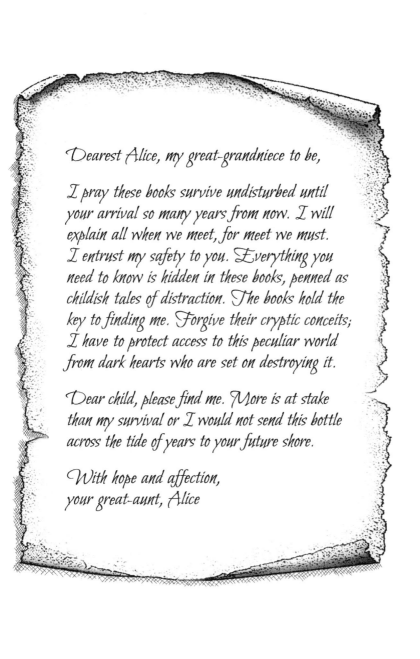

Dearest Alice, my great-grandniece to be,

I pray these books survive undisturbed until your arrival so many years from now. I will explain all when we meet, for meet we must. I entrust my safety to you. Everything you need to know is hidden in these books, penned as childish tales of distraction. The books hold the key to finding me. Forgive their cryptic conceits; I have to protect access to this peculiar world from dark hearts who are set on destroying it.

Dear child, please find me. More is at stake than my survival or I would not send this bottle across the tide of years to your future shore.

With hope and affection,
your great-aunt, Alice

CONTENTS

4 JULY 1862

FOLLY BRIDGE, OXFORD, ENGLAND

She felt a little nervous about this;
'for it might end, you know,' said Alice,
'in my going out altogether, like a candle.
I wonder what I should be like then?'

Thunder rolled in the distance, a summer storm brewing off to the west. They would have to finish the picnic and leave, but Alice wasn't ready. This would be their last outing together and she had to make them understand. Everything depended on it.

'Sit down, Alice. It was a wonderful tale, but you've not had a single bite since you began.' Emily pushed a plate of sandwiches towards her. Alice looked at her friend and their chaperones, the Reverend Thomas and Mr Dodgson.

'Sorry,' she said, and sat down on the blanket. Alice had been pacing as she'd read the story to her small audience. They all seemed engaged, yet none grasped the purpose of the story, how it was more than a tall tale constructed for their amusement. How could they?

'I liked the tea party best,' said Emily, 'though all that business about time getting stuck at teatime was a bit odd, don't you think?'

'It might appear so on first reading,' said Alice. She looked across the river to the meadow beyond. The simplicity of the setting, the normality of it, tore at her heart. Could she really keep all this safe? Was she prepared for the price it would exact? Summer light was casting dappled gold on the world around her, on the towpath, the arched bridge and the distant church. She scanned it all, her back straight, her neck stretched, like a creature of prey on high alert. Nothing caught her eye. Yet she knew they'd be coming for her. The Men of the Rose.

'I will eat if you make me a promise,' she said, taking a cheese sandwich.

'Name it,' said Emily.

Alice fixed her attention on the bespectacled writer, Mr Dodgson. 'I want you to arrange for the book's publication.'

'Publication?'

'Yes, and exactly as I have written it here, Mr Dodgson. Not one word can be changed. Not for any reason. Can I rely on you? Please?'

The group seemed a little stunned by the request.

'Alice,' said Mr Dodgson, 'the tale is engaging, certainly. Imaginative, quite definitely. But no publisher would commit to such a flight of fancy, not one penned by a young and unproven writer, no matter how talented.'

'I quite agree,' replied Alice, 'which is why you shall publish it under your own name.'

'Me?' Dodgson appeared flattered and confused in equal measure. 'If it is to be published, it must be in your name. You must take full credit.'

'Then use a nom-de-plume, some blend of us both. My middle name would do – you could write as Mr Carol.'

Alice had been reading her story from four thick school-books, every page covered in her own meticulous writing. She stood and placed the volumes into Mr Dodgson's hands.

'Mr Dodgson. As you rightfully point out, my age would be a barrier. So, I entrust this to your care. There are a few pages of instruction at the back. But please, not one single word of change. The text has been constructed to both mask and to reveal. There are keys buried within anagrams. There are riddles designed to obfuscate and there are entire phrases where the number of letters themselves will guide the reader on how to step through these puzzles. So not one word of change, Mister Dodgson. May I rely on you?'

'I will do my best, young lady. That, at least, I can promise.' Alice knew this would have to do. For safety, she had made three handwritten copies, but having it published was far safer; there would be multiple copies, hiding the secrets in plain sight. Others would need it one day if she was ever to be rescued.

It began to rain, and they scrambled for cover.

The downpour obscured everything as the carriage pulled up. A bolt of lightning cracked and lit the face of the manor house as Alice stepped down and raced for the front door. She glanced back up the driveway and saw no sign of pursuit.

For three weeks, she had sensed the Men of the Rose

closing in, and last weekend her encounter in a small Charing Cross Road bookshop allowed for only one explanation – they knew her identity. She had turned over too many stones in her search for the true history of the young boys. How cruel that an act of charity might lead to their deaths. Yet she might still save them, even at this late hour – two innocent boys and all the melancholy folk she had come to love.

Stepping into the hall, Alice shook the rain from her cloak. She must go tonight, without any farewells. It would be unforgivably cruel on her parents, but if she looked at their loving faces, her resolve might crumble.

'Alice?' Her mother had been waiting. Of course she had. There would be supper laid out. They would want to hear about her picnic, and there would be cards and laughter. The little things that made life so precious.

'Hello, mother. What a storm!'

'Straight from the Old Testament. The puppies have tun-nelled under the hearth rug.' Light from the library spilled into the hallway behind her mother, a theatrical backlight that made her seem ethereal, almost translucent, as if Alice's decision to leave was already draining her life.

'We're taking supper in the library. You're soaked!'

'A little. We were a band of pirates keeping ahead of a storm. Mr Dodgson was all but spent at the oars when we finally made it to the boathouse.'

'Splendid!' Her mother clapped her hands in delight. 'Come and tell us all about it and with as much embellishment as possible. Your father had a testing day in the city and would welcome the distraction.'

It was too much. Alice ran forward and threw her arms around her mother.

'Goodness, what's this about?' Her mother returned the

embrace, but her body had stiffened. Alice looked into her eyes; there was nothing but love there, loved wrapped in the steel of a woman ready to absorb whatever bad news her daughter might deliver.

'You know I love you. And Father. You know that, don't you?'

'Well, of course. And we love you. Unconditionally. Do we need him here or is this a conversation best kept between women?'

'What?'

'If you've fallen for the ancient Mr Dodgson, no amount of brandy would brace your father for that news.' Alice almost exploded with laughter.

'Mother! That is beyond naughty – how dare you.'

'Then what?'

'I just wanted to tell you, that's all. I love you both more than you will ever know. Whatever happens, you must remember that.'

'Whatever happens? This is very theatrical, even for you.'

A violent crash of thunder shook the house, rattling the windows and toppling a vase from its stand near the front door. They turned to see it strike the tiled floor, but Alice hardly noticed – she'd seen movement through the glass panels, the distorted image of a black carriage pulling up outside.

She ran up the stairs without another word.

'Alice!' Her mother followed, alarmed now, as a bolt of lightning struck an ancient oak that towered three stories high in front of the house. The tree ignited like a torch, its light shivering on the faces of three men as they stepped from the carriage. They wore long black coats and sported white roses in their lapels. They had put the pieces together. They had come for her.

Alice took the stairs two at her time, cursing herself for

leaving it so late. She ran to her room and slammed the door behind her. Her mother reached the bedroom door a moment later and hesitated.

'My darling, what is it? Please tell me. Whatever it is, we'll face it together.' She opened the door and pushed inside, her heart beating in her throat.

The room was awash with light from the tree burning outside. There was no sign of her daughter. Then her eyes settled on the large antique dresser they had bought for Alice's tenth birthday.

There was Alice, in its mirror, waving goodbye; her face wet with tears, her image fading even as her mother reached out to it.

CHAPTER 1

DAY ONE

NEWTON UNBOUND

———————

'Oh, you can't help that,' said the Cat, 'we're all mad here.'
'How do you know I'm mad?' said Alice.
'You must be,' said the Cat, 'or you wouldn't have come here.'

'Yes, but something must be outside the bubble. Got to be. If the universe is expanding like a bubble it must be expanding into somewhere.' The boy was sitting two rows across from Ali; he had a chin like pink nougat and was getting all worked up. He seemed genuinely interested in the debate. And stupid.

'Dickhead,' sighed Ali. It was painful listening to feeble-minded crap from the other students, all locked in their Newtonian straitjackets. She turned her attention back to her forearm where she was inking a fake tattoo with a blue pen. The face of a cat, grinning.

'There is no "somewhere" for the universe to expand into.' The teacher had started to pace in front of his desk. 'I know this is hard to picture, that's why we need maths to describe it. The universe isn't expanding into anything because the universe *is* everything. There's nothing outside of it, so there's nothing for it to expand into.'

'So, it's just making it up as it goes along?' Nougat Chin again.

'Not really.' The teacher smiled as he tried to find the right words. Ali liked him, Mr Kepler. The poor fart meant well, and he was still enthusiastic; he still liked to teach. Not like the rest of the staff, sleepwalking to their retirement.

'But if it's an expanding bubble, sir, then it must have an edge, must have a border,' said a second boy, no smarter than Nougat Chin. 'And if there's a border, there must be something outside that border.'

Ali shook her pen – almost empty. Her cat needed one last eyebrow. She would draw it arched. Amused disbelief.

'How about your border, newbie?' A whispered challenge came from behind her. Ali didn't turn. She knew it was the flathead with biceps for brains, the one who called himself 'Beef.' He'd been poking her in the back for a few minutes now, the courtship of a pre-schooler in a sandpit. 'Cross your border anytime, just text me.'

Ali disengaged, letting the voices fade to a background buzz, like summer insects. A teacher at her last school had shown her how to do it – a way to keep calm and stop the anger from grabbing hold. She could focus on her breathing and withdraw into silence, letting the world drift along without her. Mostly.

Through the window she watched a rabbit nibbling a fringe of lawn by the tennis courts. It was a good school, so she would try to make it work, try to keep her anger at bay and give her dad a break. He deserved it.

'Alice,' Mr Kepler's voice pulled her back.

'Sir?'

'Help me out here, any suggestions?' Ali looked down at her tattoo. Why had she doodled a cat? She didn't even like cats! Schrödinger's Cat, maybe? Her subconscious having an emergent moment.

'Like you said, Mr Kepler, you can't explain it with words. Just with maths.'

'Try.'

'Okay. The big mistake is to picture space without thinking about time.'

'And?' Mr Kepler smiled encouragement.

'Well, no one has a problem picturing tomorrow as empty space, do they? That's because tomorrow hasn't happened, so there's nothing there. Right?'

'Right,' said Nougat Chin, nodding slowly as if pretending to understand.

'Go on, Alice.'

'Well, the universe isn't an expanding bubble of space; it's an expanding bubble of space AND time. So, there's nothing beyond the edge, there can't be, because it hasn't happened yet. Out beyond the expanding edge of the universe it's always tomorrow.'

'Excellent.' The teacher beamed at Ali. 'Thank you.' Faces turned to look at her, the new girl they'd been warned about, the one with the temper. Another jab in the back.

'I like brains,' Beef whispered behind her, 'legs and brains. Real turn-on.'

'Can I steal that explanation for future classes,' said Mr Kepler, 'use it and claim credit?'

'Knock yourself out,' said Ali, 'just don't ask me to explain String Theory anytime soon.' Beef grabbed the moment to make a play for centre stage.

'Sir. I have a string theory. I think newbie girl here can tug my strings any time she likes.' He got his applause and stood to take a bow.

Ali stood as well, heating like a kettle towards the tipping point of her anger. 'Mr Kepler, sir?'

'Yes, Alice?'

'Permission to teach the dipshit behind me one of Newton's Laws?' She turned and explained to Beef how a moving object keeps moving until it meets an opposing force. It was more a demonstration really. One moving fist coming to a stop when it met the opposing force of one grinning face. The face stopped grinning and started to bleed. Excellent.

'Did you understand that okay?'

Suspended. Again. Ali sat in the principal's office cursing her temper, and life in general. Her last councillor had called it Life Rage, rage in search of a new target because the old one was out of reach. She could kick and scream all she liked – her mother's ghost wouldn't hear.

'I have no choice,' the principal was saying. 'Your teacher's explained the provocation,' she glanced at Mr Kepler, who was sitting beside Ali, 'however that young man's behaviour does not excuse violence. I have no wriggle room here, you see, not for a charge of assault. Suspension is mandatory.' The woman seemed genuinely sympathetic, she even smiled when the school's nurse came and confirmed that the victim's nose was broken.

'We've sent your father countless phone and text messages asking him to join us here, but apparently …' She frowned at a scribbled note. '… he is working in a lead box some miles under Wales. Is that even possible?'

'Sure,' said Ali. 'Always around when I need him.'

'Ali's father is on the UK HERT team,' explained Mr Kepler, 'a new facility at the bottom of a coal mine under Cardiff.'

'In a lead box?' The principal seemed to find this rather peculiar.

'Don't even go there,' said Ali.

'I'm sorry, go where?'

'There's nothing weird about Dad's work.'

'I never said there was, Alice.'

'You were joining dots. Weird work and poor parenting. And it's not a lead box, it's a Faraday Cage. He's measuring cosmic radiation. It's weak, so you have to screen out everything else. The equipment has to be shielded inside a Faraday Cage, named after the bloke who first built one, way back.'

'Good to know,' the principal looked down at her notes, 'and presumably that explains why your father isn't getting our calls?'

'Bingo.' Ali sighed. Her dad was going to be pissed off. She'd promised she'd make it work this time. Three schools in four years. Letting him down was all the punishment she needed. Ali reached up to a silver pendant hanging round her neck, a nervous gesture she did in moments of stress. The pendant had belonged to her mother, a Saint Christopher inscribed with a boy's name, Jack. Her Dad wouldn't tell her who Jack was. Maybe he didn't know. A boy from her childhood? An old flame?

'I'm sorry, it won't happen again. I'll apologise to that dipshit.'

'Good. But not today. Today you leave the college grounds.'

'He was assaulting me!'

'Verbally. You punched him.'

'But before all this, he was stabbing his stupid finger in my back. And that's not just assault, that's inappropriate contact.'

Ali glowered at the woman. 'So, I stand up for myself and hit some bully because I won't let people shit on me, and you side with him! That's great girl power right there. Go figure!'

'You're not helping.'

'You want me to roll over? Not going to happen. I want to press charges. Assault. So call the police.'

'They were called, by his parents, he's the one doing all the bleeding.' The principal sat back in her chair. 'You will be given a complaints form, and I encourage you to make whatever complaints you see fit. The boy is a spoilt brat with spoilt parents to match. But in the meantime, you must leave the premises and undertake your suspension back with your family.'

'Bit tough, that. Right?' Ali stared at the thick file on the desk. It was all in there, the story of what happened to her mother. It had made headlines, how she had died on a UNESCO mission negotiating the release of child hostages. Thanks, Mum. What about *this* child?

Ali focused on her breathing. She retreated and let the world drift into fog. She could see Beef's grinning face, her fist connecting in slow-mo, she could feel the bruise on her knuckles – a good bruise, a bruise she could see and touch.

'And then, if that fails, the next step is expulsion.'

'Expulsion?!' That brought her back.

'Yes Alice, the two-week suspension is a chance for serious reflection, a family intervention where ...'

'I don't have family. Just my dad. That's it. Me and Dad against the world.' Ali almost laughed; did she really say that out loud? Embarrassing.

'Not according to your enrolment papers. After your father, your next of kin are an aunt and uncle on your mother's side.'

'Never met them.'

'Perhaps, but they are your sponsors, Alice – good people by all accounts, who've been funding your education. We couldn't reach your father so we called them. They've agreed to host you for the two weeks of the suspension.'

'I don't believe this shit!'

'That language isn't helping your cause, Alice. They will host you and they will monitor your attitude. Their view will go a long way to informing the board's final decision.'

'Serious? I go and stay for two weeks with some oldies I've never met, and they get to decide if I get expelled?'

'Good. You are listening. Any questions?'

'About a billion.'

'We'll keep calling your father.' The principal closed the thick folder of papers, 'Mr Kepler has kindly offered to drive you. He can fill you in on the details as you go.'

Ali followed her teacher from the office.

'This is bullshit!'

'Just grab your things, Alice, we'll meet in the carpark.'

Ali headed down the corridor. Her locker was in a different wing on the far side of a garden courtyard. She marched outside, still seething with indignation, and there was Beef, yelling at a man in a dark suit. The man spotted Ali and ushered Beef away, manhandling him across the yard. Beef's father?

'See you in court!' Beef turned and gave her the finger.

'Or hospital,' Ali yelled back as the man bustled the boy through a door and out of sight. Something fell from the lapel of the man's dark suit. Ali crossed and picked it up.

It was a flower. A white rose.

CHAPTER 2

DAY ONE

GREY MANOR

———————

'I'll see you safe to the end of the wood,' said the White Knight,
'and then I must go back, you know; that's the end of my move.'

The apartment was a small second-storey affair overlooking a city park. Her teacher stayed out in his car while Ali went in to grab what she needed for the next two weeks.

A few months ago, when Ali and her father had moved in, Ali had asked for the front bedroom, which looked straight out onto the park. From her bed, all she could see were the trees – London disappeared completely. Her father had given in without a fight; in fact, he preferred the back bedroom, it was quieter, no street traffic. She went to his room now, pulled a suitcase from his wardrobe, then sat down heavily on the bed.

'Stupid fracking idiot.' She smacked her face with one hand, then smacked again, harder. Her dad had worked so hard to get her into that college, even moving here, so she could bike in every day. The place must eat half his salary in rent, two bedrooms by a park in central London.

Now she'd messed up, and he wasn't even around to be angry about it, or to listen to her side of the story. He was down in his rabbit hole unlocking more secrets of the universe. Ali pulled out her phone and thumbed a text. At least he should hear it from her, an apology of sorts, when he surfaced.

He would ring of course, he always did, the moment he was out of the cage. But at least a text showed she was thinking of him. Better than nothing.

'Please don't blow this. You're the brightest student I've got.' Mr Kepler said as he drove. Ali was sulking, and for the first fifty kilometres neither had spoken.

'You've not been with us long, but you've changed the dynamic already. Made the others all sit up. You've got a real head for science, and I can see you love it too.'

Ali continued to ignore him.

'I've read your file. I know what you've been through.'

'Doubt it.' Ali pulled her woollen beanie over her eyes and slid down in her seat. This was not a conversation she cared to engage in.

'Look, Alice ...'

'Stick to science, Mr K, you don't cut it as a counsellor.'

They stopped for fuel. Mr Kepler bought a coffee and paced the courtyard while he drank it, a five-minute break from the intensity of his student's brooding silence. It didn't help, and he slammed the door when he got back in the car.

'That's the way, Mr K. Let it all out. Bang the car up a bit, makes you feel better. Always does it for me.'

'Yes, so I've read. How many assault charges is it now?'

'Stopped counting.'

'The paperwork doesn't. You do this when you hit sixteen and they'll lock you up.'

'Great! So I still have a few months to punch some idiot faces then.'

'In what universe is that funny?'

'Take your pick. The way Dad sees it there's an infinite number of them.'

Another ten kilometres of silence.

'You're like a black hole, Alice, you know that?'

'Ha!'

'You think that staying silent makes you invisible. Doesn't work. You're one giant gravity well, affecting everything around you. More energy than you know what to do with.'

'I see what you're doing. Way too obvious.'

'Really, and what's that?'

'You think some geeky science talk will get me chatting up a storm. Sorry, not happening. I get more science talk on weekends with Dad than you can shake a quark at.'

'Interesting.'

'Not really.'

'I just got to you.'

'If it makes you happy.'

'It does. You threw quarks back at me, a little counter jab. Yes, I got to you. I think I'd make a pretty decent counsellor.'

He grinned, and Ali grinned back. And then they were talking. Not student and teacher. Science nerds. Equals. It made the journey bearable for them both, a hundred miles of science talk.

It ended abruptly when he explained the ground rules for her suspension.

'No phone?! Are they serious? No fracking way!'

'It won't be seclusion if you can wall-to-wall chat, now would it? So there's no phone, no internet. And no swearing.'

'Fracking isn't swearing. It should be - should be the worst fracking thing you can say given it's such a gross fracking assault on the fracking planet.' A few kilometres later they came to the small village near Cambridge where her relatives lived. Mr Kepler stopped to ask an elderly man for directions. He told them, then gave a description of the place, a large manor house invisible from the road behind broken gates. Then he complained about the building's neglect.

'Shameful, no other word for it. Amounts to vandalism, beautiful place like that going to rack and ruin.'

'Yes, well, I'm sure you're right,' said Mr Kepler. "It must be a bottomless pit trying to maintain an old building these days.'

'Then they should move out and sell the place to those who can look after it properly. You expected?'

'Yes, and we're a little late, so if you'll excuse me.'

'Not with the other folk, are you, those two women?'

'Two women?'

'The ones looking after the old couple.'

'No,' said Mr Kepler. Ali listened with growing impatience as her teacher tried to disengage. But the local villager was relentless, his questions growing more and more intrusive.

'So what business have you got there? Up from London, are you?' Ali felt the familiar pumping of blood that came when her anger was triggered. She had to shut this man up before she lost it completely and jumped out to punch him. She leaned across to the open window.

'Excuse me, could you step into the road, please?' she gave the man her very best and brightest smile.

'Sorry?'

'Step into the road. I need to run you over to stop all your stupid talking.' Ali continued to smile her bright smile as the old man stared back at her, open-mouthed, unable to form a reply. Then he turned and marched off, grumbling under his breath.

'The luxury of youth,' sighed Mr Kepler, as they set off again.

Neither of them noticed the blind woman step from the doorway of a small bookstore as they drove past. They didn't see how she craned her head to peer into the car; how she fixed her blind eyes on them till they were lost from view around the next bend.

The directions to the manor house proved accurate. The place was hidden from the road down a sweeping gravel drive where impressive wrought iron gates were rusted open. Weathered statues topped stone pillars on either side, their form and detail lost to erosion and moss.

'Spooky shit,' said Ali as drove through. Formal gardens with box hedges lined both sides of the driveway.

'You sure this isn't a film set?'

'Feels like one,' agreed her teacher, 'especially that thing!'

Up ahead a white lightening-tree stood centre stage at the head of the drive. The face of the building, three stories of ivy and red brick, was a dull backdrop to the dead tree.

They parked the car, hauled out their bags and approached the house. The front door swung open and a large woman greeted them. She was at least a foot taller than Ali and twice as wide. She had a white uniform, small eyes, big teeth and a massive head.

'Welcome to Grey Manor.' The expression on the woman's face suggested they were far from welcome. 'Your rooms are ready,' she said, taking their bags and lifting them as if they were feather pillows. 'Tea in the parlour in fifteen minutes. Follow me.'

Ali watched the woman's huge back as they followed her up the staircase to the first floor. Her teacher raised an eyebrow and grinned. Ali grinned back, but it was forced. Mr Kepler wasn't going to be stuck here with this weightlifting freak. The woman was a mass of solid muscle.

'I'm Nurse Potts. People call me Potty – but only the once. You will refer to me as Nurse Potts. Yourself?'

'Alice.' Only friends called her Ali. And she wasn't about to tell this woman her other nickname – Newt. Only her mother had used that. Ali had fallen down a set of steps and scraped her knees when she was three; between her tears she'd asked why everything fell down and never up?

Her mother had smiled and called her Newton. In time it became Newt.

'Promise me you will never stop asking such wonderful questions,' she'd said.

Ali never had.

They were shown to their rooms. Mr Kepler thanked Nurse Potts and told Ali he would see her downstairs for tea. Her own room was a depressing blend of cream walls and brown furniture, and it perfectly matched her mood. The only relief came from an oil painting of bluebells; a woodland scene with slender birch trees and a carpet of flowers. Everything else was a triumph of boring.

Ali flopped down on the bed and closed her eyes. It could have been worse – it could have been girl central, all frills and lace and pink ponies.

'I'm NOT going to survive this shit hole.' She lay back and began thrashing her legs up and down, her heels battering the mattress like hammers; a trick her mother had taught her for letting off steam.

'Take it out on the bed darling. Like this.' They had lain

down together on her parents' mattress and thrashed like a pair of amateur swimmers until Ali's dark mood had been transformed by laughter.

'It's just energy in the end, Newt. Tears of rage or tears of laughter. So best we choose laughter.' Ali did it now. Hammering her heels as the tears welled up and the frustration washed out across her cheeks.

CHAPTER 3

DAY ONE

NURSE POTTS

---

*The table was a large one, but the three were all crowded
together at one corner of it: 'No room! No room!' they cried
out when they saw Alice. 'There's PLENTY of room!' said Alice
indignantly, and she sat down in a large arm-chair at one
end of the table.*

Twenty minutes later she was heading down to the parlour.
Nurse Potts had said fifteen minutes, so Ali waited an extra
five. The rules on engagement had to be established. Her
rules, not theirs. It was time to meet her jailers ... if she
could find the right room. The Potts woman had mentioned a
parlour, whatever that was.

'There she is – come in, young lady. Let's have a proper look
at you.'

The parlour turned out to be a large and sedately furnished
room halfway down the hall, and the greeting came from an

elderly woman in an antique wheelchair with brass fittings and faded leather arm rests. She was elegantly dressed, her arms covered by delicate lace gloves.

'Yes indeed, get yourself in here,' said a silver-haired man sitting beside her, the Times newspaper on his lap, open at the crossword. He was stout, with a full head of hair and a thick white beard. He stood as Ali entered the room and there was a warm twinkle in his eyes.

'Lovely to see you again, Alice.'

'Again?' She looked from one to the other, studying both faces. Nothing. She had never seen these people before. She was sure of it.

'It was many years ago. You came here with your mother when your father went off to that place in the Alps.'

'Cerner? The Particle Accelerator?'

'That's the fellow. We had a family gathering of sorts. Your mother came to show you off.'

Ali did the maths. 'I would have been three when Dad went there.'

'Yes, just a toddler,' the elderly woman gave a short laugh, 'but you had a temper even then – we had to keep the vases out of your reach.' She extended her gloved hand. 'Come and sit, the cake is far too dry. Shop-bought. We might as well eat the box it came in …'

Ali didn't sit nor take the offered slice. She was not going to be sucked into domestic chitchat that easily.

'… and the tea's cold. Making a point of being late is a young lady's duty. I myself was never very good at it, but there are always consequences. Cold tea is the least of them.'

Good, they'd registered her small protest. Ali looked past them to a set of French doors. Outside, the garden was bathed in late-afternoon sunshine giving it a picture-book intensity.

'Can you see them out there?' asked the old man.

'See who?' said Ali.

'Our two girls got bored and took your teacher for a tour of the garden.'

'Girls?' Ali turned. 'There's more than just me interned here?'

'Interned!' the old man gave a chuckle. 'What a splendid word. No, you're our only guest. I was referring to the staff. You met Nurse Potts, and there's Miss Waxstaff, our house-keeper.'

'They both seem very taken with your teacher,' said his wife. 'Rather a handsome fellow, don't you think?'

'Mr K! Serious?' Ali didn't think any of her teachers were the least bit cute. 'So, what do I call you?' How are we related?'

'To the point, good. I think I like you.' The old man beamed at her.

'Dad never mentioned you. Ever. This is all a bit weird. One minute it's just Dad and me, and now … this.' Ali gestured at the room.

'Quite,' said the old man. 'Two old farts come popping out of the woodwork. Formal introductions then. We are Lord and Lady Grey, the last of the Greys.'

'On the direct line, at least,' added his wife, 'given the archaic patriarchal system of lineage we are forced to sub-scribe to.'

'Still got all her marbles,' laughed Lord Grey. 'Can't keep up with her some days. We have no direct heirs, no males on either side. But I had two sisters, both of whom have passed on, bless their socks. The eldest, Kitty, was your grandmother.'

'Granny Kitty?'

'Yes, Kitty died in her twenties when your mother was just a baby. We've always kept a weather eye on your mother since then.'

'Did a crap job then, didn't you?'

'Ah! Right.' Lord Grey glanced at his wife and stroked his beard. He looked so uncomfortable, Ali almost regretted her little jab.

'No. We did not,' said his wife, looking at Ali with a directness and intensity she found unnerving. 'Do sit down and try not to be so vulgar, Alice. It ill becomes you, and your mother would not have been impressed.'

Ali sat, surprising herself, and reached for a slice of the cake.

'Good. Your mother had a bold spirit and enough heart for ten women. She was selflessly dedicated to her work, she wanted to save the world, nothing less would have done for her. Should we have dissuaded her?'

'Yes. Once she had me, once I arrived. I should have been enough; she didn't have to save all those other kids and abandon me. Seems to me she was being pretty fracking selfish.'

'Very possibly, and your father agrees with you.'

'He does?' This surprised Ali.

'Certainly.'

'Well, enough skeletons for now ... need to pace ourselves.' Lord Grey smiled and attempted to move the conversation along. 'You have her eyes. Doesn't she have her eyes, Martha?'

'Yes, eyes and attitude – both.'

Ali turned away, feigning interest in the room. 'I don't see any photos of Mum ... or Granny Kitty. Or anyone. Bit weird if you're so proud of her, feels more like you've disowned your whole tribe.'

'There are photos aplenty,' said Lord Grey, 'just not on the walls. We're not ones for parading memories. Letting the past clutter up the present is indulgent and morbid.' He glanced across at his wife, as if checking this was a shared view.

'We have them pasted into scrapbooks,' said Lady Grey. 'We can dig them out after supper. Until then, why don't you explore the grounds?'

And that was it. Ali realised she was being dismissed. She got up and headed for the door, then turned and pointed to the newspaper.

'It's CHARM, by the way.'

'What is?'

'The answer to that last clue.'

'Really?' Lord Grey frowned at his paper, mouthing the letters as he filled in the squares, his brow creasing even further, 'I'll be damned – it fits.' He read the clue aloud, *Five letters, an offensive little thing.* How the deuce did you get CHARM from that?'

'Put the silly man out of his misery, would you?' Lady Grey beamed at Ali, clearly enjoying her husband's discomfort.

'A charm's a subatomic particle, so a little thing, right? There's a bunch of them, all with weird names. The clue said it was an offensive little thing, so like a charm offensive. Rather obvious really.'

Ali was good at puzzles, always had been. Puzzles, like how come two relatives she'd never heard of before knew so fracking much about her.

The gardens turned out to be equally puzzling. Ali couldn't put her finger on it, but there was a sense of 'wrongness' about them that nagged at her. On the surface everything seemed normal enough, if a large garden estate could be considered normal in modern England.

'Bloody hell, I'm gentry!' Ali almost laughed as it dawned on her. Was she going to inherit this one day? There were lawns fringed with flower beds and box hedges, pine trees with skirts of rhododendron, greenhouses and a sprawling herb garden, potting sheds, stables, and a tennis court where weeds had been the only players for years. Encircling it all was a ribbon of woodland that bordered the estate. All very pretty, all very neglected.

It might have been the theatrical effect of the late afternoon sun, but the gardens felt like a set that had been dressed too quickly. There were no garden tools stuck in the beds, no wheelbarrow of weeds from a job half done. None of the tell-tale mess of real life.

And no gardeners, she thought as she looked into the stables and potting sheds. A place this big didn't look after itself. Where were all the hot young gardeners with their shirts off? How was she going to survive two weeks with just the old couple and Nurse Potts?

'Dad – this place would have been cool when I was a kid. I'm pissed off with you for keeping it a secret.'

CHAPTER 4

DAY ONE

THE BARN

---

*Alice opened the door and found it led into a passage, not
much larger than a rat-hole. She knelt down and looked
along the passage into the loveliest garden you ever saw.
How she longed to get out of that dark hall, and wander
among those beds of bright flowers and those cool fountains.*

One side of the main lawn was bordered by a brick wall with
an archway half concealed by a curtain of ivy. Ali pushed
through and found a neglected orchard on the far side, its
trees wrestling for light, their unpruned branches a tangle
of limbs. In the middle was a clearing with a barn that looked
as old as the house itself. It was a solid affair of rough-sawn
planks weathered to a dull grey.

'Ha! Look at you.' Ali laughed when she saw it. The sensa-
tion of stumbling onto a filmset had gone up a notch. Stable
doors were rusted in place across the front and a small door in

the side was secured by a sliding bolt and a padlock. Ali found a window, wiped a gap in the grime and peered inside.

The barn was empty except for a stack of storage boxes and a few sticks of furniture covered in dust sheets.

'Alice. There you are!'

Mr Kepler came around the side of the building with Nurse Potts and a second woman dressed completely in black, from her tight-fitting jacket to her skirt and laced shoes.

'Hi, Mr K, nice escort.' The woman in black was incredibly thin, almost a walking skeleton, and she seemed to stumble as she approached, reaching out a hand to Nurse Potts for support.

'Steady.' Mr Kepler took the woman's other elbow.

'I'm fine,' the thin woman said. She dropped her eyes, took a deep breath and stared at the ground as if intent on studying the grass. Then she stepped forward and looked up, straight into Ali's eyes.

Frack! Ali tried not to flinch, but it was hard – the woman's gaze was cold and intense, her eyes blazing with something Ali had never experienced before; not directly, not personally. It was hatred; raw and undisguised. How was that possible? They'd never met.

'What?' It was all she could think to say. She wanted to look away but forced herself not to. It was like holding shards of ice in her bare hands.

'So here we are,' said the woman. It was barely a whisper, her face hardly moving, the skin stretched tight across her skull. She tilted her head to one side, like a bird inspecting some bug it was planning to eat. 'You, very obviously, are the Greys' niece.'

'Yes,' Mr Kepler answered for Ali, breaking the tension. 'Alice, this is Miss Waxstaff, the housekeeper. I've been getting the grand tour – the place goes on forever.' He gestured up at the old barn. 'What's this, another stables?'

'Barn,' said Nurse Potts, 'far as I know.'

'It was a coach house,' the housekeeper corrected her.

'Whatever.' Potts shrugged. 'His Lordship calls it the old barn.'

'It's magnificent, whatever it is.' Mr Kepler walked over to the door and peered through the small window. 'Can we go inside?'

'No,' said Potts, her voice dull and business-like. 'Barn's off limits.'

'Fair enough,' said Mr Kepler, turning back to them. 'Shall we keep going? Love to see more. So good to be walking around after that drive.'

'Off limits?' said Ali, finding her voice. 'Why's that?'

'Don't know,' Potts shrugged her giant shoulders. 'I was told you can go everywhere else, just not the barn.'

'Yeah, but why?'

'Ask your uncle,' replied the housekeeper, who hadn't moved the whole time nor taken her eyes off Ali.

'I will.' Ali almost groaned at herself. *I will?* How lame was that? But it was hard to find a snappy comeback with a skeleton woman beaming hatred at her.

She felt for the pendant round her neck, the talisman she would rub like a lucky token in times of stress.

Waxstaff's reaction was instant. She rocked backwards, the muscles of her face moving for the first time, her features pinching into a scowl.

'What have you got there?'

'Saint Christopher,' said Ali, holding it out as far as the chain would allow. For a bizarre moment she thought the housekeeper would shrink away from it, like a movie vampire cowering from a crucifix. She didn't.

'Very pretty,' she said curtly. 'Dinner is at six o'clock sharp, please be on time,' and she turned away, striding off though the orchard with Potts hurrying to keep up. Ali stared after her, then tucked the St Christopher back out of sight.

'They for real?'

'Pretty odd,' Mr Kepler agreed. 'Quite chatty though.'

'What was with my pendant? Like she'd seen a ghost.'

'Who knows, maybe a convent girl thing. Took a beating from her teachers and blames it on the church.'

'So who are they? My jailers or my entertainment?'

'Choice is yours, Alice. The world is what you make it.'

'And they want to make *you*, Mr K.'

'Meaning?'

'They fancy you.'

'Kill me now.' He shook his head as if trying to clear the image. 'Come on, let's get to the house and prep for dinner.'

He led the way across the orchard, dipping and bobbing his way between the tangled branches.

'So, what did you learn?' Ali asked.

'Not much, they were asking all the questions. Waxstaff's been here a while. Potts more recent. Your aunt fell and broke her hip a few months ago. It was either a live-in nurse or go into a rest home.'

'Crappy deal.'

'Beats crawling under a hedge.' They came to the archway in the brick wall and pushed back through the ivy. 'So, let's talk about you.'

'Let's not.'

'No choice.' Her teacher brushed a cobweb from his hair as he stepped out from the ivy. 'I have to walk you through the rules of your suspension. I head back in the morning, and need to know you're taking this seriously.'

'I'm not, it's a joke.'

'Not for these relatives of yours. As I understand it, they've been funding your education for three years.'

'And I should be grateful?'

'That would be the normal way of things, yes.'

'I shouldn't even be at school.' Ali's teacher was outpacing her, but she made no effort to catch up. 'I've learnt all the science I need, I'm ready for uni.'

'And who will pay for that?'

'I could do a year's internship at some research lab, pay my own way.'

'You're too opinionated and too smug – no one would hire you.' He stopped and turned to Ali. 'You know a hell of a lot about science and bugger all about yourself. When the school couldn't get hold of your father, they called the Greys to tell them you were being expelled. It was your aunt who argued for a short seclusion instead. Two weeks of soul searching.'

'Soul searching! Wash your mouth out, Mr K.'

'Just an expression. I don't mean the Christian soul.'

'Language pollutes with old ideas.'

'Very eloquent.'

'One of Mum's. The concept of souls and an afterlife really pissed her off. Which means I can't disrespect her by thinking she might still be fluttering about like an ethereal spirit even if I really, really wanted to. So, no soul talk.'

'I'm sorry.' Mr Kepler suddenly looked uncomfortable, and Ali almost felt sorry for him. 'It was a poor choice of words.'

'Yes it was, there's no room in science for religious fairy tales.'

'I was improvising, Ali – your aunt never said "soul searching," she said you might need a few weeks of proper grieving.'

'What!?' Ali glared at him. 'What would she say that for, I'm not six! I don't have to take this shit.'

'No, you don't, and you don't have to *be* a little shit either! Life fell on you from a great height, no question. But you aren't defined by what happens to you – no one is – you're defined by how you choose to react to it.'

'Seriously! No way did you just say that out loud.' Ali almost laughed, her anger evaporating. 'What bumper sticker was that off?'

'It was a fridge magnet.'

CHAPTER 5

DAY ONE

SUPPER AND SCIENCE

———————

'If you knew Time as well as I do,' said the Hatter, 'you wouldn't talk of wasting Time. We quarrelled last March when I sang for the Queen and she bawled, "He's murdering the time." Now Time won't do a thing I ask!'

Ali arrived fifteen minutes late for dinner. Waxstaff and Potts were seated at one end of the table with Mr Kepler, while her aunt and uncle sat side by side at the other. Ali felt Waxstaff's cold eyes on her the moment she entered the room. She sat opposite her relatives and made no attempt to engage in the small talk that was underway. Mr Kepler was entertaining the room with an explanation of Einstein's general theory of relativity. She listened for five painful minutes as he tried to explain the concept in kindergarten terms.

Despite their age, her relatives seemed a lot smarter than the two staff. Ali couldn't believe how little Potts understood basic science. There was no way anyone, even her teacher, could explain cosmology to a person who thought a galaxy was like a solar system, only bigger. Waxstaff didn't appear to know much more, but at least she was smart enough to keep quiet about it.

'I don't see the point of it,' said Potts, 'why would anyone study time? I mean, what for? When it's gone, it's gone. Can't live in the past, can we.'

'I can,' laughed Lord Grey, 'I do it every day.'

'We all do,' said Mr Kepler. 'Everywhere we look, we're looking back in time, even that wall across the room is a little further back in time than you are.'

'Poppycock,' said Lord Grey. 'There's a damn clock hanging on it. Same time as my watch. Ah, no! A bit behind actually. Rather spoils my counterpunch.'

'It's why relativity is hard to explain,' said Mr Kepler. 'Light takes a fraction of a moment to travel from the wall to your eye, so the wall you see was the wall of a moment ago. The further away an object is, the longer it takes for the light to reach your eye. When we look at distant galaxies, we see them as they used to be, millions of years ago.'

'About when you were born, Bertie dear,' said Lady Grey.

'Quite so, my darling. Which is why I'll sleep in the village tonight, watch you through a telescope, and see the pretty filly I fell for all those years ago.'

'Bravo,' said his wife, 'and I dare say we shall both sleep the better for it, because sound, even snoring, travels a great deal slower. Does it not, Alice?'

'It does, Lady Grey.' Ali smiled at her aunt and held her gaze for a long moment. There was a lot going on behind those old eyes.

'As for you, young lady, we have been given to understand

that you have an excellent head for science.'

'She does,' said Mr Kepler. 'My best student.'

'Then tell us, my dear,' said Lady Grey, 'what's hot at the moment? What has been exercising your scientific curiosity?'

'What's your money paying for – is that the question?' Even as she said it, Ali wanted to kick herself, to take the words back. Too late for that.

'No, that wasn't the question.' Her aunt looked across the table and fixed Ali with an expression she couldn't read. 'But I'll answer it, if it's important to you. Would we have been better spending our limited finances on something a little more tangible, like a new roof? Is that your question?'

'Maybe,' said Ali. Waxstaff muttered something under her breath and exchanged a shake of the head with Nurse Potts.

'Do you plan to be rude like that,' asked Potts, 'or does it come naturally?'

'Just being honest, that's all,' said Ali. 'They might get better value from fixing the house.'

'There you are,' laughed Lord Grey, 'our niece agrees with me. Mend the damn roof! I've said it a hundred times. Does anyone listen?'

'Gravity waves,' said Ali.

'Come again?' said Potts.

'That's what's I'm studying at the moment. Gravity waves and ideas that spin off it, like extra dimensions.'

'Glad to hear it,' Lord Grey waved his fork at her. 'If you can beat the Times crossword, then it's money well spent.'

'Extra dimensions,' Nurse Potts was shaking her head. 'The nonsense they talk about these days. What happened to algebra?'

'Not the fault of the kids,' said Miss Waxstaff, 'they're easily impressed, they eat up any nonsense that catches their attention. I blame your profession, Mr Kepler, filling their heads with crackpot notions.'

'Crackpot?' Ali stopped eating and glared at the woman.

'Yes, of course.'

'I see,' said Ali, ignoring the warning looks her teacher was throwing at her. 'You have a solid grounding in theoretical physics, do you? You feel qualified to venture that opinion?'

'No,' Waxstaff glared back at her with her narrow bird eyes, 'but I have a solid grounding in spotting bullshit when I see it.'

'I like this,' beamed Lord Grey, and clapped his hands, 'ladies fighting at the table, nothing better. Bullshit indeed. What do you say to that, Alice?'

'Nothing,' said Ali. Her teacher let out a long breath, clearly relieved.

'Heh!' snorted Miss Waxstaff.

'I've nothing to say to Miss Waxstaff, it would be a waste of breath.'

'And now she resorts to insults.' Miss Waxstaff sighed and shook her head. 'The last refuge of the ignorant mind. Lose the argument and stoop to insults. You warned us she had a temper, but vulgar too? That's very disappointing.'

'To be fair,' said her teacher, 'you did throw the first insult, you tried to diminish her field of interest, and the latest insights around gravitational waves are far from bullshit.' He looked down the table at Ali, his eyes pleading with her.

Ali sighed, put down her knife and fork, and turned to Lord Grey. 'But it'd be different if *you* are interested in hearing about it?'

'I am, if I can keep up.'

'Physicists like my dad want to know why gravity is so weak compared with the other forces. Some think it's leaking off into other dimensions. And to explain how gravity and quantum effects work together, you've got to have extra dimensions for the maths to make sense. And now they've found gravitational waves, ripples in space-time caused by massive objects. It's all very cool.'

'It's garbage,' Nurse Potts said, shaking her head, 'and the government wastes our taxes on this nonsense.'

'Hardly nonsense, Miss Potts,' said Mr Kepler, getting animated again, 'it helps explain how everything works. Gravitational waves ripple through the universe, stretching and compressing space.'

'Lost me already,' said Lord Grey.

'It's simple.' Ali tapped her plate. 'Imagine there was a huge jelly on this plate. Tap the jelly with a spoon and the waves distort it as they jiggle through it. It's the same with the universe and gravitational waves.'

'Got it,' beamed Lord Grey. 'Good to know I'm not senile after all. And good to know you love science. Would it be irritating to suggest this is inherited from your talented father?'

'It would. A girl likes to take credit where she can.'

'Eloquence too! Bravo, child. We shall get along splendidly.'

'Just because I like science doesn't mean I live in a nerdy bubble – I read Jane Austen as well as Stephen Hawking. I might split an atom, but I would never split an infinitive.' Ali was astonished when her aunt applauded.

'Delightful!' Lady Grey was beaming at her. 'It's been years since our table was graced with anything resembling repartee. These next two weeks might feel like an imposition to you, but I suspect they will be a tonic to Bertie and myself.'

'Good to know,' was all Ali could think to say. The housekeeper pursed her lips and said nothing, but Nurse Potts was bursting to express an opinion.

'In my experience, if we tolerate bad manners – we encourage them.'

'Duly noted,' said Lord Grey, 'and no more talk of gravity. Let's talk sport … who followed the cricket on the radio today?' He looked round the table, his hopeful smile quickly fading as it registered a complete lack of interest on every face. 'Right, no cricket then.'

That night, Ali lay in brown and white linen in her brown and cream room and listened to the buzzing of her brain as it tried to crunch through all the new data. It was how she saw her brain, a complex computer that continued working in her sleep as it sorted the day's experiences, sifting the critical from the dross.

'Figure out the house,' she said aloud, setting a mental search engine in motion that would spend the night playing detective, 'then work out why Dad kept all this a secret. To stop me dwelling on Mum? Embarrassed that someone else was coughing up for my education? Or is it something darker – a skeleton?'

She gazed up at the cream ceiling and tried to disengage, tried to let her brain freewheel. It was something she'd practised for years after her dad had told her how Einstein liked to stare into a fire and let his mind drift.

Newt, the best ideas come when you stop thinking, she told herself now. Einstein would fill his head with the facts he thought important for some new idea, then he'd stare into his fire and disengage, let his brain drift off and do its thing while he watched the flickering flames.

Sometimes she could do it. But not tonight. The day had stirred up so many emotions, including the warmth she'd felt so unexpectedly over dinner – warmth for a couple of old wrinklies. How disconcerting was that?

And there was something else … Ali couldn't put a finger on it, but another emotion was in the mix; a foreboding, as if she'd wandered from the path and was moving into a dark forest. She sat up and looked around at the oppressive room.

'Colour. I need more colour.' There was no relief from the endless cream and brown except from the painting of the bluebell woods. She went down to the dining room and grabbed one of the candlesticks that made up the centre piece of the long table.

'Perfect, you'll do.' It had three candles. She used the embers of the fire to light all three, carried the candlestick up to her room and set it on a small side table below the picture so the bluebells were centred in the upward spill of light.

'Better.' She dropped back on the bed and lay on her side, staring at the picture. A draught from the window played across the flames, their wavering light giving the trees and bluebells the illusion of movement. And as she drifted off to sleep, it seemed to Ali that the scene in the picture was far more real than the bedroom around her.

CHAPTER 6

DAY TWO

THE LIBRARY

And so she did: wandering up and down, and trying turn after turn, but always coming back to the house. 'Oh, it's too bad!' she cried, 'I never saw such a house for getting in the way! Never!'

'You snore like a donkey.'

'What?' Ali frowned across at her teacher, who was helping himself to toast. They were eating alone on the garden terrace in early morning sunshine.

'Like a donkey. My room was right across the landing. I thought it was old plumbing rattling about, but no – it was you.'

Ali didn't argue; she knew she snored. Obstructive sleep apnoea the specialist had called it, first diagnosed when she was seven.

'Who's Jack?' Mr Kepler pointed to the small St Christopher hanging round Ali's neck. 'Boyfriend?'

'It was Mum's, I think some old flame gave it to her.'

'And she wore it? Your dad didn't mind?'

'Don't know, they never discussed it. When do you leave?'

'Soon as I've eaten, I need to be back in class this afternoon. I said my goodbyes to your folk last night – your patrons.'

'Stupid word.'

'It's what they are. Though I guess you'll be calling them Uncle Bertie and Aunty Martha,' he grinned, and Ali laughed.

'Who'd have thought? My own little fiefdom of rellies. Going to grill Dad on this when he climbs out of his hole. Why the crap did he never mention them?'

'Ask your aunt, you'll have plenty of debates over dinner if last night was any indication.' Mr Kepler reached into his jacket and took out Ali's cell phone. 'Want to try your dad again before this comes back with me?'

'You're taking it?'

'We went through this, Ali, it's hardly seclusion if the whole world is on tap.'

'I'll go mad.'

'You mean bored, not mad.'

'Bored out of my mind!' Ali almost snatched the phone as her teacher passed it over.

'Boredom is the incubator of new ideas.'

'No lectures, I'm suspended.' She scrolled for her dad's number.

'Not a lecture, merely an observation. No one does original thinking anymore, they just go online and paddle about in the collected wisdom of the past.'

'Now *you're* being boring.'

'Boredom's good, it forces you to think for yourself, to entertain yourself, gets your brain talking to itself instead of the faceless masses online.'

'Well you talk to yourself all you want, Mr K, my faceless masses are science chatrooms full of people like me' – she hit dial – 'smart people who know stuff, unlike the Salt and Pepper Sisters.'

'Who?'

'Potts and Waxstaff, they look like a pair of salt and pepper shakers.'

'That's rude.'

'And funny.'

'Yes, and funny. But don't be so arrogant – they don't know much science but they're far from stupid. Too much going on with those two.'

There was no reply from her father, just the voicemail message. It was always the same when he was down in his lab, nothing she could do but send him texts. She used to make them short and angry, little yelps for attention.

'I can leave him a text, right?'

'Of course.'

She tapped in a long one, doing her best to keep it light and cheerful but still putting pressure on him to come and visit the moment he surfaced.

'Done,' she handed the phone back, thought for a moment and then gave her teacher the passcode. 'Trust you not to read back over my texts.' Mr Kepler said nothing, he just raised an eyebrow.

'Someone has to answer him when he texts back.'

'And?'

'He's going to worry. Paint a good picture, tell him all that ego booster stuff you told me about being your best student.'

'He knows you're smarter than both of us. It's all we talk about.'

'He calls you?'

'Now and then. We were students together. He leaned on me to get you into the college.'

'What!' Ali stared at her teacher.

'I thought you knew.'

'No!' Ali couldn't decide if she was pleased or pissed off. Her teacher got up from the table and looked round at the garden.

'It's bloody lovely here. Hard to go back to London.'

'Drive safe.'

'Try to have fun, Alice, you need to make it work here. The Greys seem to like you, and they were impressed with all that Jane Austen talk. Showed another side of you.'

'What side? Drama queen?'

'No. It was genuine, the real you, peeking out from the bunker. I knew you were smart, but last night you sounded intelligent.'

'Shall I curtsey now?'

'And then she's back with a predictable petulant jab. Boring.' Mr Kepler headed inside, leaving Ali to kick herself.

She spent the morning exploring the house and failing to avoid Waxstaff and Potts who kept appearing at her shoulder. They never prevented her from going anywhere, but they always seemed to be hovering close by. They would be crossing a hallway behind her, entering a room as she was leaving it, or simply passing her on the stairs. They would ask if she needed anything, and that was all, like they were keeping tabs on her – and not very discreetly.

'Have you cloned yourselves?' she asked Nurse Potts as they bumped into each other in the kitchen doorway.

'Cloned?' said the huge woman, who seemed to fill the doorframe.

'You're everywhere, there has to be more than the two of you.'

'You tell me – you're the clever one. Oh wait, maybe we're busy just doing our jobs, maybe life doesn't revolve around you. There's a novelty.'

'Nice jab,' said Ali, stepping back to allow Potts through the door. Her teacher was right, this woman wasn't stupid at all, that was a smart comeback.

The house had three stories. Many rooms were mothballed, white drapes covering their furniture. Every room on the ground floor was in use, though the old couple only seemed to use two of them: the dining room and a parlour where a glass conservatory looked out over the main lawn.

Then Ali found the library.

'Holy crap, awesome.' She knew immediately this would be her room. It was like a gentleman's club from some Dickens novel, a place where old men sat in leather armchairs, sipping brandy and talking gibberish. One wall was covered in bookshelves, and a scuffed wooden ladder ran the entire length of the room, suspended from a brass rail.

'Oh, I have to do this.' Ali rode the ladder back and forth a few times. She felt ten years old again and laughed at the idea of doing this with her dad when he came to get her. They could have a duel with walking sticks, like musketeers.

She checked out the room as she swept back and forth. There was a fireplace, its red brick mantle hosting a row of stuffed creatures in glass display jars.

'Look at you lot!' There were field mice and ferrets, ravens and rats, even a badger, every glass eye sparkling with the illusion of life. It should have made the room feel cold, even spooky, but it didn't; the stuffed creatures made it feel lived in, as if the room was their sanctuary.

'Well, here you are.' Lady Grey came squeaking through the door on her chair, pushed by Nurse Potts. 'I see you've found the library.'

'Sorry.' Ali grabbed the bookshelf, bringing her ladder to a sudden stop.

'Don't be. I spent hours riding that thing when I was a girl. Did you see the scrapbooks of photos in your fly-past?'

'No.' Ali stepped down, trying not to look sheepish in front of Potts.

'Far end of the second shelf. The pictures of your mother will be in the last one. Pop it on the writing desk and we can look through it together.'

Ali found it: a scrapbook full of photographs. Most were of her mother as a young girl, and Ali realised how much she took after her, some of the pictures could have been her, except her mother's hair was longer.

'Who's this?' there was a page of pictures of her mother with another girl.

'A girl from the village. They were best friends one summer … poor girl met with an accident, your mother was beside herself for weeks.'

'Is this me?' Ali pointed to a picture of her mother with a toddler.

'It is indeed, and this one – this is my favourite.' Lady Grey pointed to a photo of a tiny Ali dancing with her mother on the garden terrace. They were both laughing; a happy day she had no memory of.

'Can I scan it? Make myself a copy?' Ali asked, fighting an urge to trace her mother's face with her finger.

'A copy? Heavens no, you can have these scrapbooks. They'll all be thrown out with our bones anyway, far better that you take them.'

'Thanks.'

'In fact, help yourself to any book that takes your eye. They're very old, but wisdom survives the generations, and it's good to read the source material where possible, don't you think?'

'I guess so.' Ali found the remark rather odd, it lacked context. Yet her aunt had turned to face her as she said it, as if to underscore its importance.

'Are you happy with your bedroom?'

'It's a bit ... well ... boring.'

'I'm sure it is,' said Lady Grey, 'it's been a while since the bedrooms were painted. 1953 or thereabouts, young Elizabeth's coronation, I think.'

'It is very dull,' said Nurse Potts. 'I took the liberty of brightening it up. I hung a picture of bluebells in there.'

'*You* put that picture in there?' Ali said, surprised.

Lady Grey appeared surprised, too; the old woman was staring at the ground as if looking for something. Ali had seen the same thing last night, how her aunt would fall silent and stare at the ground as if rummaging through a box of memories. 'You found the woodland scene, the clearing with the bluebells?'

'Yes. Sorry, was that wrong?' Potts seemed a bit flustered, and glanced briefly at Ali as if for support, then looked away. 'I can take it down.'

'No, leave it,' said Lady Grey, turning her chair with her delicate, gloved hands so she could face Potts. 'But where did you find it? I thought that painting had been thrown out years ago. My poor mother hated it.'

'It was in the attic.'

'You went up into the attic? Whatever for? What sort of business would you have to go fossicking around up there?'

'This,' said Nurse Potts, tapping the antique wheelchair. 'Lord Grey sent me up there to find the chair. Better than the one the hospital sent home with you. Heavier to push, mind. I'd be happy to swap it back.'

'This chair is splendid, thank you.' She turned back to Ali, 'I've been in this thing before. Took a spill off my pony when I was young and precocious – rather like you, in fact.'

'Never ridden a horse.'

'Good. They're like smoking, dear. Great fun, but a huge risk to life. Stick to riding that ladder over there. Much safer.'

'Cool, I will. I love this room, Lady Grey. Could I swap rooms and sleep down here?'

'You can if you stop calling me Lady Grey. You make me sound ridiculous with the inflection you put on it. It's just Aunt Martha, please.'

'Okay. Well, erm … thanks, Aunt Martha.'

'You're family, Alice. You may feel like a stranger in a strange land but—'

'Woah! You've read that book?'

'Yes. Heinlein – a bit of a rogue, an old misogamist by all accounts – but I've always enjoyed his novellas.'

'Way to go, Aunt Martha.'

'Was that approval?'

'I guess.'

'Gratefully accepted. As I say, you may feel like a stranger, and you have certainly been estranged, but you are family, Alice. Therefore treat the house as your own, and if this room speaks to you in some way that it most certainly does not speak to me, then by all means make it yours.'

'Thank you.'

'My pleasure. Now I must let Miss Potts put me through a set of hideous exercises designed to get me on my feet. To what end, I can't imagine – not the London Marathon.'

'Getting you walking, that's what for,' said Potts, 'then I won't have to push this heavy antique around.'

'Fair enough,' said Lady Grey as Potts trundled her to the door. 'I'm told we have a full day of sunshine, so be sure and get outside for part of it,' and she waved a gloved hand like a queen from the window of a royal carriage.

CHAPTER 7

DAY TWO

TRAPDOORS AND TUNNELS

———————

*'Curiouser and curiouser!' cried Alice; she was so much
surprised, that for the moment she quite forgot how to speak
good English; 'Oh dear, what nonsense I'm talking!'*

The prediction was wrong. It rained all morning. Ali spent the time in the library, flipping through the books of photos and rearranging the furniture. She pulled the writing desk into the bay window that overlooked the front drive, a view dominated by the lightening tree, its bleached form slicing through the landscape like a torn strip from a watercolour. By midday she was hungry and went to the kitchen.

There was no sign of Waxstaff, so she started making a sandwich. She found a bin of bread and looked around for a knife. A large, farm-style worktable took up the centre of the room, and in one drawer she found the breadknife. And a set of keys.

'Nice.' There were twelve in all, strung on a rusting keyring, each tagged with a paper label naming an outbuilding. Shed; stables; barn. Then she heard footsteps, dropped the keys back in the drawer and grabbed the breadknife just as Waxstaff appeared.

'Feeling peckish?' The housekeeper smiled at Ali – or tried to. Her gaunt face did the right things, the corners of her mouth pulled sideways, her eyes creased, but the way her skin stretched made her look more dead than happy.

'Yep. Thought I'd make a sandwich.'

'Ham and cheese in the fridge, tomatoes in the pantry.'

'Marmite and peanut butter?'

'That would be a joke, correct?'

'No.' Ali opened the fridge and pulled out a huge block of cheese and a bowl of tomatoes.

'Well not in this kitchen.'

'Shame. Lots of protein and B vitamins; great brain food.' Ali cut six thick slices from the crusty loaf. Waxstaff stared at the amount.

'Who else do you plan on feeding?'

'Just me. I'm hungry.'

'Clearly.' She frowned, looking from the bread to Ali. 'And do you always eat this much?'

'Depends. If I get buried in a project I forget to eat, so pig out when I surface.' Ali cut thick wedges of cheese and sliced up a tomato.

'I shall have to rethink my grocery order.'

'Cool. Add Marmite and peanut butter, would you?'

'No.'

'Any chutney?'

'Pantry.'

'Thanks.' Ali opened the pantry and she found a selection

of hand-made chutneys and pickles. She made three sandwiches and kept up the small talk. Waxstaff answered every question but gave little away.

'There, done.' She pulled up a stool and was about to sit when Waxstaff handed her a tray.

'There's a perfectly good table in the dining room.'

'I could use the company,' said Ali.

'Could you now? Well I could use a guest who cleans up their own mess.' She pointed to the aftermath of Ali's sandwich preparation. Nothing had been put away, breadcrumbs were everywhere, and the block of cheese was decorated in tomato seeds.

'My bad,' said Ali. Waxstaff grunted and left the room. Ali put down her tray and tidied up, washing the bread knife and putting it back in its drawer – where she slipped the barn key off its keyring.

The rain had stopped and the moon was a thin clipping of fingernail above the treeline. It gave a weak, diffused light, strong enough to see the ground but too weak to expose Ali if anyone was watching from the house.

She had set her mind on exploring the barn the moment she'd found the key. The rain had continued throughout the afternoon, so she'd flopped onto the library couch and taken a nap. 'Sleep credit,' her mum had called the naps they'd shared most afternoons in the golden years before school age, years when every day had seemed perfect.

Telling Ali the barn was out of bounds was a red rag to a bored bull. What might be in there didn't matter, a midnight mission and breaking the rules was the whole point. She pulled her hoodie up and grinned at the moon. No one said 'no' to Alice White.

She had asked her relatives about the barn over dinner, in her usual style – straight to the point.

'Love that old barn in the orchard. Can I look inside?' Her relatives reacted with an exchange of looks that was hard to read, but made Ali think the question had been expected.

'Afraid not,' said Lord Grey, 'bit of a safety hazard.'

'And very annoying,' added his wife. 'Some pea-brain in the council deemed it unsafe, yet we can't pull it down because it's a heritage building. Can't afford to fix it and can't knock it down! It has to sit there till it falls over. How foolish is that?'

They were lying, Ali was sure of it. So here she was, crossing the lawn on a clandestine adventure. The grass was wet from all the rain, and her canvas shoes were soaked by the time she pushed her way through the archway in the wall.

Across the orchard, the bleached timbers of the barn reflected what little moonlight there was, giving the building a faint, silvery glow.

So, Mum, did you ever come here back in the day? she wondered. Bet you did. Ali went round to the side door. It was in shadow and she had to feel for the padlock.

The barn was a good twenty yards from the house, and shielded from view by the orchard wall, so she switched on a penlight she'd found in the library desk to light up the lock.

The padlock clicked open easily and so did the door. She swung the beam of light over the bare floorboards. The barn was empty except for the sticks of furniture and packing cases stacked at one end.

'So then! What's in you lot?'

In total, there were fifteen storage boxes, four tea chests, a suitcase, and two items of furniture, both covered in dust sheets. Ali pulled the sheets away. The furniture looked antique, handcrafted from exotic woods. There was a single bed and a dresser with a full-length mirror and four drawers. The light reflecting from the mirror seemed at odds with the moonlight in the barn.

Ali looked closer. Maybe it was an age thing – did glass lose its sparkle over the years? Or maybe the reflective surface behind the glass became dull from cigar smoke and dust. She checked the drawers. Three were empty, one boasted an old hairbrush, half a dozen bangles and some hair clips. One clip fell to the ground and bounced under the bed. Ali bent to retrieve it and saw a rusty hinge set into the floorboards.

Interesting. The bed was heavy – solid wood with an iron headboard. Ali pushed, and it moved a few feet. The bed had been sitting over a trapdoor.

Better and better. Ali swung the door up and shone her penlight into the dark throat beneath. Hanging from the frame was a set of five iron steps. She felt a spike of excitement, quickly undermined by a wave of loneliness so unexpected and so intense she felt tears coming. There was nobody to share this adventure with, not right now. She gave in to the tears. It was either that or kick the barn down and get a set of bruises that would last for days. Crying was less painful, so long as nobody was around to see.

The tears didn't last long; a few minutes, enough for loneliness to climb back in its box and give curiosity centre stage. Ali lowered herself down through the trapdoor into a narrow tunnel. It was so low that if she stood on her toes she could still peer out across the barn floor, the top of her head poking up.

She bent, and began to walk in a stooped shuffle, her hair brushing against the ceiling. The tunnel was round, like a drain, and lined with red bricks. Ali kept her light on the ceiling, checking for spiders.

'Listen up. No one takes a ride on my back!' Her penlight picked out a few small cobwebs, but nothing scary. She followed the passageway. There were no features, corners or side tunnels, just the same curving red bricks lining the walls. It ended at a vertical chimney where there was another ladder, and faint silver moonlight fell from a circle of sky above.

Ali climbed the ladder. The brick chimney emerged in the far corner of the main gardens. She was in a well, an ornamental feature with no water.

'Ha! No need for keys, I've got a back door.' Ali climbed down and made her way back along the tunnel to the barn. Why would anyone build a tunnel under a barn? Under the manor house, yes; Ali could imagine that, a grand lady sneaking out for illicit affairs. But a barn? Smuggling, maybe? Didn't that happen in coastal towns like Cornwall and Devon, not here in the middle of England?

Ali clambered up into the barn, closed the trap door and pushed the bed back to hide it. Then she checked the contents of the storage boxes and cases. She started with a dusty travel case, hoisting it onto the bed and flicking open the catches.

Boring. It was full of old textbooks, a mix of history, forensic science and Chinese medicine. Plus two children's books, early editions of *The Adventures of Alice in Wonderland* and *Through the Looking Glass.* Ali had never read them. She'd seen a film of the first book with her dad when she was about ten. He'd been a bit weird about going, and was very happy to leave halfway through when Ali declared her damning opinion to the people around them. She grinned at the memory – the things she'd put her dad through.

She flicked through the first few pages *of Alice In Wonderland.* The copy had been loved to death by someone, every margin was filled with handwritten notes. There was still the stub of pencil the reader had used, sewn into a cotton sleeve in the back cover, the end frayed from chewing. The notes were easy to read, the language fresh and chatty, like someone writing to themselves in a private diary.

There was something familiar about the handwriting. Ali couldn't put a finger on it, but she'd seen something like it recently. She closed her eyes and pictured her uncle's newspaper on the breakfast table, a pad of paper next to it where he drafted answers to the clues. Maybe.

Ali settled back on the bed and tried reading the book. She lasted a few chapters before giving up. 'Annoying little shit!' Ali couldn't believe the Alice character. The girl was unbelievably irritating. Had kids really talked like that, a mix of submissive cringe and puffed up confidence? And her relentless dialogue took verbal diarrhoea to a whole new level.

'I have to punch her, I really have to punch her stupid face ...' She found an illustration of the Alice character and slapped it as if swatting a fly. 'If you don't have anything interesting to say, keep it shut!'

There was no real story to it, as far as Ali could tell. The book was more like a series of nonsense meetings and conversations stitched together. And riddles, lots of riddles, but they seemed to have no point to them; there was no pressure on the character to solve them; nothing at stake if she failed.

'What's the difference between a raven and a writing desk? Who cares? No one in the stupid book seems to, so what's the point of it?' Ali gave up, lay back on the bed and watched shards of moonlight flicker about on the far wall. The moon must have set behind the trees, its light strobing through the branches in the light wind.

CHAPTER 8

DAY TWO

MIDNIGHT DREAMING

————————

'When I used to read fairy-tales, I fancied this kind of thing
never happened, and now here I am in the middle of one!
There ought to be a book written about me.
And when I grow up, I'll write one.'

The dream didn't surprise her. One minute Ali was lying on the
old bed watching the splinters of moonlight, the next she was
lying in long grass beneath a bright summer sun. She looked
down and saw the novel still open on her lap, the margins
covered in the same handwritten notes.

'Cool dream.' Ali closed her eyes and felt the sun on her
face. She could even smell the grass and wildflowers. She sat
up slowly, careful not to jog herself awake. It had a name, this
kind of super-real dreaming … what was it? Lucid dreaming.
That was it.

Her dad had told her about it one night when she'd woken screaming from a terrifying dream. He'd talked the nightmare away by switching on her rational mind; the light of scientific reason conquering the shadows.

Ali looked around now, drinking in the details. The colours were intense, even theatrical, like a bright painting. And the setting was familiar, borrowed from the woodland painting in her bedroom, complete with silver birch trees and a carpet of bluebells.

Okay, that's interesting, she thought. I've created a mash-up dream from the painting and the Wonderland book. There was something else her dad had said about this kind of lucid dreaming, something important ...

'Newt, you must learn to find your hands, you must hold them up to your face and look at them.'

Ali lifted them now and examined them.

'If this ever happens again, if you wake up inside a bad dream and I'm not here to wake you up, you must find your hands, Newt. Remember that, okay? Lift your hands up and stare at them. It puts you in control of your dream. If you can instruct yourself to look at your hands, you can tell yourself to do anything in the dream. Got it? It means you decide what happens, good things instead of bad things. No more nightmares.'

Ali stared at her hands and laughed. Her dad was going to be pissed off when she told him about this. He'd studied altered states when he was a student, everything from meditation to astral projection; all hippy-dippy shit like tree-hugging and talking to hedgehogs.

He'd even spent nights in sleep tanks, floating in warm saltwater, trying to have a dream like this one, an intense, lucid dream. He'd never succeeded.

'Okay, Dad. This is for you.'

Ali opened the book on her lap and told herself that the stub of pencil would be there. It was, wedged in its tube of ribbon in the back cover, and she began scribbling her own notes in the few margins where there was still space to write.

'So, Dad. I'm lucid dreaming, and for some dumb reason I'm writing this all down in an imaginary dream book.'

She noted everything she could see, then remembered something else her dad had told her, about how to conjure things up, how to manifest them by imagining them in as much detail as possible.

Her mother? Hell, no. Ali squashed the idea. In the first year after her mother's death, all she ever saw when she closed her eyes was her mother's last moments, her beautiful body torn apart by the bomb.

She opened the book again and flicked through the pages till she found a picture of a white rabbit in a waistcoat. She closed her eyes and tried to picture the rabbit in full colour, a real creature with soft white fur and pink ears.

When she opened them again, there was no rabbit; instead, two young boys appeared from between the trees on the far side of the clearing. She waved to them, and after a moment of earnest discussion, the boys waved back.

'I won't bite!' Ali yelled out to them. The two boys became agitated, looked around, gestured for her to be quiet, then hurried over.

'Be so good as to not shout,' said one. He was taller than the second. They looked of similar age, not quite teenagers, twelve at most, and decked out in odd, theatrical clothing with leather tunics and bright leggings.

'Are you the best I can come up with?' said Ali.

'Pardon?' said the first boy.

'She's new here,' said the second. 'Just arrived by the look of her.'

'Yes,' said Ali, 'a few moments ago, express delivery.'

'It was an observation,' sniffed the boy, 'not a question. It is perfectly plain you are newly arrived here.'

'That so? How'd you guess?'

'Your clothes,' said the first boy.

'And your airs,' said the second. 'Your manner, generally.'

'Good to know. Speaking of manners ...' Ali got to her feet and extended a hand, 'we've not been introduced. I'm Alice White.' The boys looked at her hand but didn't take it. Instead they turned to each other and started arguing.

'She remembers her name,' said the shorter boy.

'Perhaps,' his companion replied, 'or she just made it up on the spot.'

'This is embarrassing,' Ali laughed. 'Look at you! What part of my sad imagination have you two been crawling about in?'

'I think that was rude,' said the taller boy. 'Were you being rude?'

'No, you're in my dream, so you're part of me. I can't be rude to myself, can I?' Ali began to circle them. 'But are you really the best I can dream up? Two beanpoles in stupid clothes? Why not Einstein? Or a cute pirate in boots and dreads?'

'We're not pirates.'

'Obviously. But you must be important – I must have dragged you up for a reason, you must have come from some old memory.'

'We came from the Royal Gardens,' said the tall boy. 'We know all sorts of things. We know *The Walrus and The Carpenter*. Alice taught it to us.'

'Oh bloody hell. That's it, you're from that second book. The sequel. And you were in the film, right? The two fat boys.'

'Fat?'

'Yes, with those stupid names, Tweedledum and Tweedle-dee.'

'Those are *not* our names!' The boys puffed out their chests, clenched their hands into fists and planted them on their hips. 'Alice gave us those names. But we know our real ones.'

'Yes, we remember our real names. We say them to each other every day, over and over, so we don't lose them. Ricky and Teddy, I'm Teddy.'

'And I'm Ricky.'

'Good for you. So, Alice gave you those silly names. Why?'

'To protect us,' said Ricky. 'That's what she said.'

'To protect you from what?'

'People who want us dead,' said Teddy, and his chin wobbled. Ali studied their faces. They were different, but clearly brothers. How did she dream up this much detail, and why was she making it a murder mystery?

'People want to kill you? Why?'

'We don't know, she didn't say,' sniffed Teddy. 'I don't want to talk about her anymore, she broke a promise.'

'Yes,' Ricky folded his arms, 'she promised to go back and find our real story. She never did. She forgot, like everyone else here.'

'Except us; we remember our real names. Ricky and Teddy.' The two boys turned and embraced each other. Ali laughed. They were really rather sweet. The taller boy tapped his brother on the shoulder and whispered in his ear. They nodded gravely to each other, as if sharing an insight, then raced off without another word.

'Hey, I didn't decide you could do that. Come back.' The boys ignored her, disappearing into the woods. Alice looked around for what might have driven them away. A young man in a battered hat was standing behind her, his features lost in shadow. He was wearing a long jacket of red and gold, and his head was tilted to one side as if he was lost in thought.

'Spotted,' said Ali. The young man stepped forward onto the carpet of bluebells, removed his hat and bowed.

'Holy shit!' He was drop-dead handsome. Clearly her sub-conscious had been hard at work all this time. That's more like it, she thought, brushing her hands, ready to greet him; then laughed. I made him, I don't have to impress him. He walked over and stopped in front of her, his blue eyes blazing with electric intensity. Ali realised she was lost for words and couldn't believe it. She'd never in her life been lost for words!

'Do you remember your name?' said the young man.

'Alice White.'

'I knew an Alice once.' He looked into her eyes, tilting his head further to the side as if puzzled by what he saw there. A large wasp buzzed past her face and she brushed it away.

'And you? You have a name, right?'

'Undoubtedly.'

'So what is it?'

'I can't remember. That's why you're here, is it not? To help us recover them? Until then I have a label of sorts; the gentle folk over here call me the Hatter.'

A large wasp flew at Ali's face, she slapped it away but it whipped around and stung her on the neck.

'SHIT!' The stab of pain was intense, A pinprick of fire that punched the air from her lungs and sent her sprawling forward on her hands and knees.

CHAPTER 9

DAY TWO

RAVENS AND WRITING DESKS

––––––––––

The Hatter opened his eyes and said 'Why is a raven like a
writing-desk?' Alice thought over all she could remember about
ravens and writing-desks, which wasn't much. 'I give it up,
what's the answer?' 'I haven't the slightest idea,' said the Hatter.

The next instant Ali was wide awake, her neck burning with
pain. Then a wave of nausea struck. She leant over the side of
the bed and threw up on the barn floor. She stayed that way
for a long time, sweat dripping from every pore, panting for
breath and hugging her stomach as she retched again.

She groaned when the waves of nausea started to fade.
She felt exhausted, wrung out, her throat still burning from
the hot bile. She needed water and stumbled from the bed,
stepping over the pool of vomit as she looked around for a tap.

There was a workbench along the far side with a stone
basin and one tap fixed high on the wall above. She turned it

on. The pipe rattled as a pocket of air worked its way through. Ali kept it running till the rattling stopped and the water turned clear. Then she drank till she was fit to burst.

How the frack can a dream do that? she wondered. She staggered back towards the bed, unsteady on her feet and desperate to sit down again. She touched her neck. There was a welt there, a lump the size of a marble. From what? Not the wasp in her dream, obviously. Some bug here in the barn? Had she been bitten as she lay on the bed, her sleeping mind creating a dream wasp to explain the sudden pain. But bitten by what? There were no bees or wasps at night, and a mosquito bite didn't hurt like that.

A snake? Have I been bitten by a snake? A rat?

Ali swung her penlight across the floor and under the bed. Nothing to see but her pool of vomit. Nice. Cleaning that up could wait till the morning. Right now all she needed was sleep.

She relocked the barn and made her way back to the house. The night air was like a tonic, washing her blood with every breath she took. By the time she'd put the keys back and tiptoed to her bedroom, she felt a whole lot better. Her stomach still ached, and her neck throbbed, but the waves of nausea had passed. She flopped on her bed without bothering to change and fell into a deep sleep; one without any dreams.

Four hours later, she was wide awake. It was still dark outside, but she felt alert and hungry; her stomach growling and rumbling, demanding food.

'All right. Shut up, we'll get something.' She went down to the kitchen and made three slices of toast, plastering them with butter and jam. She poured a glass of milk, drank it, poured a second, and took the milk and the toast to the library where she flopped on the couch and waved at the stuffed animals.

'My place now. Lady Grey said I could set up camp, so big smiles or I turn everyone to face the wall.' As she ate, she scanned the shelving and its collection of books. There were a lot of scientific texts, a medical journal on exotic diseases, books on codes and cryptology, dozens of history books, a whole section devoted to metaphysics, and several recipe books for cooking with mushrooms.

Ali pulled out a book about codes and puzzles: *Decoding Dodgson, the Cryptography of Wonderland.*

'That's a puzzle, right there.' Ali waved the book at the stuffed animals, 'Why give a book such a boring title if you want to sell it?' She took another bite of toast, and started flicking through the pages.

It was a discussion about the two Alice In Wonderland novels. The author was arguing that all the poems and riddles, even the character names, should be read as encrypted messages. And the margins in this book were covered in notes as well, all written in the same neat hand as the notes in the two novels.

'Who *are* you?' said Ali. Here was another puzzle itching to be solved, the identity of the obsessive note-scribbler. One chapter was dedicated to solving the writing desk riddle. *Why is a raven like a writing desk?*

'Any suggestions?' Ali raised an eyebrow to the stuffed birds and animals. One was a raven. She went over to it. The bird was huge, inside a glass bell-jar one-third the size of Ali herself.

'You were alive once – what do you think? A writing desk was alive when it was a tree. But that feels like a cheat answer. A desk has four legs and you only have two. So, maybe it's a math question, four is a multiple of two, so they both have 'two' in common. Which means the answer is two.'

Ali went back to the couch and carried on reading. At some point she must have dozed off, because she woke to bright sunlight spilling in through the library window, and the buzz of breakfast conversation drifting down the hall. She raced upstairs, washed her face, put on a long-sleeve tee and hurried to join the others. Lord and Lady Grey smiled when she entered, their delight on seeing her was instant and undisguised.

'Just the person,' said Lord Grey. 'Back me up here, Alice, and tell these good ladies why breakfast can never be breakfast without the Times crossword.' He waved her to a seat and directed his full attention on her.

Ali was impressed. In one sentence, this cheerful old man had welcomed her into the room, brought her up to speed with the conversation and invited her to participate. One sentence. She smiled back at him, sat down and plugged into her Jane Austen.

'Well, Uncle Bertie, I would venture to suggest that the mind, and not just the body, needs something of substance to chew on first thing in the morning.'

'Ha! Exactly!' Lord Grey thumped the table in delight, bouncing the toast and teacups. 'I've just spent two minutes spraying buckshot all around that idea, and you pin it between the ears with one crack. Young minds, can't beat them; have a boiled egg.'

Ali did. Two eggs, a large bowl of porridge and several rounds of toast.

'Someone's hungry,' observed Nurse Potts.

'Someone certainly is,' Ali agreed.

'It makes me a little exhausted just watching you,' said Lady

Grey. 'Never go to bed hungry, that's the rule in this house.'

'Quite right,' her husband pointed up at the ceiling, 'I keep a stash of food rations up in the room, an entire squirrel's nest of contraband.'

'Brandy is not food,' said Nurse Potts. Then she pointed at Ali. 'What's that on your neck?'

'A sting, I guess, or a bite. Hurts like crap whichever it is.'

'Alice!'

'Sorry, Aunt Martha.'

'Not bed mites, I hope?' said Lord Grey.

'That's not possible,' Waxstaff glared up the table at him, 'I change the bed linen every week and the laundry company has an excellent reputation.'

'Knew a chap plagued with bed mites. We all wanted him in our tent, every bug imaginable took a nibble at him. Rest of us slept like angels.'

'Come and see me after breakfast,' said Nurse Potts. 'Anti-histamine cream might help. Very least it'll take the swelling down.'

'Okay. Sure.'

There was a lull in the conversation as everyone focused on eating, the only sounds the scratching of knives on toast, the slow ticking of the clock on the mantle, and a squabble of birdsong from the garden.

Sunlight coloured the table with a warm mix of golds, and dust motes hung in its angled beams. It felt to Ali as if a warm and very comfortable blanket had descended on the room.

'Aunt Martha, can I ask you about my name?'

'Your name, dear?'

'Dad said it was a compromise. He and mum had different choices.'

'Sounds like a rum deal,' said her Uncle.

'Maybe not, their first choices were Storm and Berri!'

'Ha!' Lord Grey stabbed a rasher of bacon, and went on, 'I knew a chap with beriberi! Nasty business; too much port by all accounts.'

'Alice was second choice on Mum's list. Anyone with my name swinging through the family tree?'

'Yes, dear', said her aunt, 'many generations ago, when so many died as they pushed into this world, or in their cots shortly after.'

'And recently, the last few generations?'

'Not recently, no.'

Ali looked down at her toast. Lady Grey had just lied. It was clear from the brief glance she'd given her husband – a warning glance.

'I can hazard a guess,' said Lord Grey. 'Your mother was an avid reader as a child. Loved the Alice in Wonderland books. Just a guess.'

And that was the end of it. Except Lord Grey reached out and tenderly laid a hand on his wife's gloved arm.

'What are your plans today?' asked Aunt Martha, clearly changing the subject. 'It's a lovely day for a walk. Have you seen the grounds yet?'

'Some, I'll have a proper explore later. First, can I move my stuff into the library – make it my room?'

'Whatever for?' asked Waxstaff. 'Another room to clean. We don't have the staff for it.'

'The girl has hands, Miss Waxstaff. I'm sure Alice is capable of cleaning her own room.' Lady Grey smiled at Ali and gave a little nod. 'By all means make it your own, but I suggest you turn those dusty stuffed creatures to the wall, so they don't plague your dreams.'

CHAPTER 10

DAY TWO

PETER

───────────

Alice lifted up her head in some alarm. Her first thought was that she had been dreaming. 'I do hope it's my dream, and not the Red King's! I don't like belonging to another person's dream, I've a great mind to go and wake him, and see what happens!'

Ten minutes later Ali was pulling the mattress from her bed and dragging it downstairs, ignoring disapproving looks from Waxstaff. She dropped it in a pool of sunlight by the French windows, threw the duvet on top, then scattered it with red and brown cushions from the library chairs. She grinned at the result; a cross between a nest of autumn leaves and the cover of a trashy romance novel.

'Good start,' she said to the room, 'now to Feng Shui the crap out of the rest of you,' and she started dragging the furniture about till the room felt more like a studio apartment. Then she remembered the pool of vomit back in the barn.

Damn it! She'd have to clean that up. But right now the sun was calling, and she needed to get outside.

The grounds were alive with the heat of summer. Every footstep brought a new scent, a new play of light. Bees and butterflies hovered among the flowers and a line of glittering, metal-green beetles were crossing a flagstone step.

Ali let it wash over her, and suddenly, with no effort, the chattering debate that usually filled her head fell silent. There was just this, the simple delight of exploring a country garden. She crossed the main lawn, smiled at the ornamental well in the far corner, and set off down a path through the fringe of woodland that encircled the estate.

Beams of sunlight angled down through the trees, turning patches of ground into pools of green and gold. Then she saw a young man. He was lying in the shade of a cedar, his back resting on its broad trunk, and he was snoring. Ali felt a surge of irritation. She was enjoying how her mind had been cruising on autopilot. Now she would have to re-engage.

She veered off towards him, making no effort to be quiet. He looked about the same age as her, good-looking in a scrawny, no-muscle kind of way – apart from his school uniform and the snoring.

'Hey! Noise pollution!' She kicked him, more of a nudge, expecting him to leap to his feet. He didn't. He opened one eye and raised a lazy arm to block the glare of the sun.

'And hello to you, too,' he said.

'Private property,' said Ali. 'You know that, right?'

The boy didn't reply so she aimed for the bony point of his hip. And kicked a little harder.

'Ow! Is this your idea of coming on to me? Needs work.' He lifted himself onto his elbows and scanned her up and down. 'Not a local then.'

'Obviously.'

'Obvious, how?'

'Small village, you've never seen me before. Ipso facto – not local.'

'Latin now. That meant to impress?'

'Does it?'

'More than kicking me.'

Ali started walking away, her default response; trust issues a speciality. But she might need an ally here, and she definitely needed a phone.

'Got a phone on you?'

'Sure.'

'Let me use it?' Ali stretched out a hand.

'No.'

'I'll call the police.'

'What with?'

'Good point …' She bobbed her head from side to side in a mock display of deep thought. 'Could you lend me your phone, *please*.'

'Better.' He grinned at her, a natural smile with real warmth to it. 'If you tell me why you need it?'

'It's private.'

'Not when I'll be right here listening to you.' He pulled a mobile from his backpack, unlocked the screen and handed it to her.

'It's my dad. I'm just leaving a message. He won't answer.' She dialled as she talked, hoping she'd be proved wrong, that her dad would be above ground. He wasn't; the call went straight to voice message.

'Hi Dad, ignore the number, borrowed phone. They took mine – part of this bootcamp crap. Pissed that you never told me about these rellies of Mum's, they're kind of sweet. Bored out of my fracking mind but there's enough crazy shit going down to keep my brain from rotting. Visit when you surface. Don't like you much right now, but love you. Bye.'

'You always talk to your dad like that?'

'Like what?'

'Spoilt-bitch sort of thing.'

'That was the nice me. Can I google some stuff?'

'No data credit.'

'What sort of retro plan are you on?' Ali had a twenty in her pocket, she fished it out and waved it at him. 'Tomorrow, same time, okay?'

'Have you always been this rude?'

'No, takes practice.' She was still holding the twenty out. 'Are you going to take this or what?'

'Depends. Who am I doing this for? Why are you here?'

'Suspended.'

'For what?'

'Punched a dipshit in the face and got this whole boot-camp thing.'

'Keep my distance, then.' He laughed and took the twenty.

'That would be smart.'

'And why here? You know the Greys?'

'They're family. How about this: I don't report you for trespassing, and you let me use your phone for an hour every day?'

'Like a regular date?'

'Yes, my foot, your ribs. Tomorrow then. What's your name?'

'Peter. You?'

'Alice. So tomorrow, same time. You and the phone. If you can't make it, call the Greys. Do you know them?'

'Everyone does. From church.'

'You go to church?' Ali was surprised, and disappointed.

'Yep, every Sunday.' He laughed at her expression.

'And you admit to this?'

'Bless little me. Want to give me the atheist rant now or save it for later?'

'Not worth it, no logic gets through.'

'Tell me, I need the ammo.' He was still sitting on the ground, grinning up at her, she crouched back down in front of him. Deciding how far to push it.

'You wouldn't understand. Christians are simple life forms, barely evolved from protozoan bottom feeders.'

'Nice line,' he laughed, 'go on.'

'Not mine – Dad's. He's a scientist – thinks all religions are small-minded, the universe is too big to package into a mythology. He taught me to challenge everything and everyone; any idea about anything is just a model, it's not real.'

'This tree's real, if I bang my head on it the pain will be real.'

'Except it's not there, not down at the quantum level, it's just lots of little energy fields buzzing round each other.'

'Says you.'

'Says science. Every model of the world is a cardboard box we choose to live in. Science pokes holes in the box to see if there's more out there – let the light in, then maybe tear up the box completely. Religions own their own boxes, they don't want holes poked in them. Bad for business.'

'My dad said something like that once. Said smart people realise they don't know anything for certain. Think our dads might get along?' He grinned again.

'We'll never know.'

'Plus, my dad's the vicar.'

'Woah! Strike two.'

'He's okay. Just an old hippy, hugging trees and voting Green. When I was a kid I played the organ on Sundays to keep him happy and get cash. That's where I'd see the Greys. They owned half the village back in the day.'

'Happy days,' Ali got up to leave, 'so, see you tomorrow, with your phone.'

'Sure, it's a date,' he said, laughing. Ali kicked him again and set off.

CHAPTER 11

DAY TWO

THE LETTER

———————

'Beware the Jabberwock, my son!
The jaws that bite, the claws that catch!
Beware the Jubjub bird, and shun the frumious Bandersnatch!'

Ali waited for the house to go silent. Now that she was sleeping in the library, it was easy to sneak out. There was bright moonlight again, so she skirted the lawn, keeping to the shadow of the trees, and lowered herself into the well.

She made her way along the brick passageway. She'd brought a bucket full of cleaning gear and she set it down on the tunnel floor beneath the trapdoor.

It was only now that an obvious problem struck her. Crap! What an idiot. How wide would the trapdoor open upwards under the bed? Last night, she'd pushed the bed back into position over the top of it. How dumb was that! If she couldn't squeeze through, she'd have to go back and get the key.

She pushed on the trapdoor and heard it thud against the underside of the bed. It looked like the gap was wide enough, and she tested it by squeezing her head, arms and shoulders through.

'It's all about the bum,' she whispered, and decided it wasn't worth the risk. The thought of getting stuck there, half in and half out of a trapdoor in a barn nobody came to, was a recipe for an undignified end. Ali began to slide backward … and found she couldn't.

'What the frack!'

The trapdoor was resting on her back. She could edge forwards, but when she tried to shuffle backwards the trapdoor clamped down like the lip of a giant clam. She fought a wave of panic, telling herself to keep still. Then she focused on her breathing and began to crawl her way forwards, using her elbows on the floor like short legs.

Then a new problem presented itself – the trapdoor opened towards her puddle of vomit.

'Oh great!' She had no choice but to shuffle like a worm straight at it, trying as best she could to arch her chest above the congealing mess, her elbows on either side. Doing her best not to breathe in the acrid smell, she scrambled to her feet, shining her penlight over her clothes. Her jeans had escaped, but the front of her T-shirt had a long smear of vomit.

'Gross!' She carefully peeled the shirt over her head, holding it away from her face and hair. Then she dragged the bed to one side and retrieved the bucket of cleaning gear from the tunnel.

It didn't take long to scrub the floor and rinse the patch of vomit from her shirt. She pulled her shirt back on and was about to drop the bucket down into the passage when she saw something move out of the corner of her eye.

'Woah!' Ali jumped backwards. Whatever it was, it had darted between the stacks of boxes. It moved like a rat, its coat black and sleek, but it had been too big. A cat, maybe? Ali clambered onto the bed and swept her light over the boxes. Nothing.

'Hello, creepy thing. Come on out where I can see you.' She looked round the barn for something to use as a weapon. Apart from the boxes and furniture, the place was pretty bare. Then the creature started whimpering.

Ali remembered nursing a stray when she was a child. The poor animal had been in a fight and one of its ears was badly torn so it must have been in pain, but it had chosen to suffer in silence. Whatever this thing was, it was not a cat.

She crawled to the end of the bed to get a better view between two boxes ... and saw a pair of yellow eyes. She'd read about the chill of fear, how it felt like ice moving up the spine, but she'd never felt it herself. Until now. The creature was little more than a dark shape crouched in shadow; only its eyes were visible, two yellow slits staring back at her.

Ali ran through her options for getting out. She could jump into the tunnel and run to the well. But if that thing jumped down after her? No thanks.

She shone her penlight at the nearest window. If she ran full speed, it would take her two or three seconds, a few more to break the glass and climb out. If the creature's teeth were as big as its eyes, it could do a lot of damage in that time. And she had nothing to beat it off with.

Or maybe she did. The bed had an iron frame with vertical bars in the headboard. If they were screwed into the base of the frame, they could be unscrewed. Ali tried each bar till she found one that turned. She unscrewed it till it came free.

'Show time,' she said, switching her penlight back on

and directing it at the boxes. The rat thing wasn't in the gap anymore. She climbed down and went over to the boxes, gave one a kick and stepped back. Nothing. She kicked again and got a glimpse of the creature as it darted behind a packing case.

'What the hell *are* you?' Not a cat; the body was too long and too low to the ground. A stoat? She lifted the iron bar and kicked over the packing case.

There it was, still half in shadow: it had pointed ears and a long snout, and there was something clamped in its jaws – a sheet of paper. Ali hadn't packed away her mess from the night before and the various books and paperwork were still lying around. The creature gave a shrill squeak and crouched, as if preparing to pounce.

Ali waved her iron bar. The creature yelped, dropped the sheet of paper, and jumped onto the dressing table.

'Shit!' Ali lifted the bar again, ready to defend herself, but the creature was gone; only the sheet of paper remained, falling slowly to the floor.

'Yeah, piss off why don't you!' Ali screamed. She felt the blood pumping in her temples, her heart racing from the rush of adrenalin. 'And don't come back! I'll squish your ugly face if I see it again.' She picked up the sheet of paper, which was punctured with small teeth marks. A little forensic science was called for; the spacing of the teeth might tell her something about the creature.

She started to leave, and realised she couldn't. The bed was on top of the trapdoor. She'd been able to push it up from below to get into the barn, but there was no way she could lift the trapdoor to get out, not if she was under the bed herself. And if she pulled the bed out of the way first, it would leave the trapdoor in plain sight to anyone passing the barn window in the morning.

There had to be a smarter way to do this. What if she moved everything, like props on a film set, moved them a few feet to the right? She could put one of the storage trunks over the trap door instead of the bed. She emptied the trunk, stuffing its books under the bed, then dragged it till it sat directly over the trapdoor. The handle was on the far side, visible to anyone who came inside and took a really close look, but only if they peered right over the trunk.

Ali felt pretty good about the result. Anyone looking through the window would never spot the change. She tried lifting the trapdoor, it was heavy, but the trunk tilted up and tilted down and stayed in place, so long as she didn't open the trapdoor more than halfway. Plenty of room to squeeze in and out.

When she got back to the library, she was too wired to sleep. 'Hot milk, I need hot milk.' She went to the kitchen and began poking around for a saucepan. Then Waxstaff appeared in the doorway.

'Looking for something?

'Milk saucepan,' said Ali. 'Can't sleep.'

'Bad dreams?' Something about the way Waxstaff looked at her, her head to the side, made Ali feel uneasy.

'No. House specialty, is it? Ghosts and bad dreams part of the package?'

'It is for your aunt – she's always sleepwalking,' said Waxstaff.

'That right? Good to know. I just fancied a hot milk.'

'After the amount of food you put away at dinner?'

'I know! Where do I put it, right?' She grabbed a carton of milk from the fridge and carried on looking for the saucepan.

'Under the bench, third cupboard. Need help?'

'No, all good.'

'Clean it when you're done,' said Waxstaff. 'The pans are ancient and milk sets like concrete if you don't rinse them.' And she left the kitchen.

Ali poured the milk and set it on the stove, then took the sheet of paper from her pocket and studied the teeth marks. They were small, and there were a lot of them. What creature had that many teeth? The sheet of paper itself was a short, hand-written letter. Ali leaned back against the kitchen bench and began read.

Dearest Alice, my great-grandniece to be,

I pray these books survive undisturbed until your arrival so many years from now. I will explain all when we meet, for meet we must. I entrust my safety to you. Everything you need to know is hidden in these books, penned as childish tales of distraction. The books hold the key to finding me. Forgive their cryptic conceits; I have to protect access to this peculiar world from dark hearts who are set on destroying it.

Dear child, please find me. More is at stake than my survival or I would not send this bottle across the tide of years to your future shore.

With hope and affection,
your great-aunt, Alice

Ali stared at the letter, read it through again, and began to shake. Part of her, the rational scientist, was sneering with disbelief; a far deeper part was being torn and shredded.

'This must be a fracking joke!' she whispered as her legs gave way and she sagged to the floor, her back sliding down the cupboard. The conversation with Peter came flooding back, her lecture about models of reality, about being brave and poking holes in what we think we know. In that moment, as the milk boiled over on the stove above, Ali knew with complete conviction that her life would never be the same again.

CHAPTER 12

DAY THREE

THE POSSIBILITY OF MADNESS

———————

*'When I was your age,' remarked the Queen, 'sometimes
I believed as many as six impossible things before breakfast.'*

Ali lay in the library, staring at the ceiling. Sleep was impossible. She had spent the past hour cleaning burnt milk from the kitchen stove, scrubbing with her hands while her mind paddled frantically, treading water like a drowning swimmer, her feet scrambling for solid ground.

She turned her gaze to the side, to the bluebell painting she'd brought down from her bedroom. It was the meadow from her lucid dream, or rather, her dream had featured this picture: the same pathway wound past the same silver birch trees with the same carpet of bluebells.

Had the rat creature been a lucid dream too? Had she fallen asleep in the barn after cleaning up the vomit? She looked at the note on the pillow beside her. Could she have written it to herself … in her sleep? She'd heard about people doing that, writing in their sleep and then wondering who'd done it when they woke up.

That would fit, going mad and making everything up. At least it was a rational explanation. Years ago, before her mum had died, the kid next door had an imaginary friend, a talking hedgehog called Beetroot. Ali had been four at the time, but now, whenever she remembered the kid from next door, she always saw Beetroot playing beside him. Her memories had filled in the imaginary hedgehog.

Her dad had tried to explain it; how anyone can retreat from the world to avoid a trauma that's too hard to bear, how they create a tapestry of cause and effect where every thread is woven into their delusion to keep it self-consistent. Ali rolled onto her side and watched the bluebell woods flickering in the candlelight, then she fell into a dreamless sleep.

She woke to brilliant sunshine, it was a thin slice, bright as a blade of gold, cutting through a gap between the curtains. Ali sat up and realised she felt good.

'Thank you, room,' she mumbled. That was the best night's sleep she'd had for ages. For months. Then she began scratching. 'Crap!' Ali leapt out of bed. Bed bugs! She'd been bitten by them once in a hotel bed. It was a long time ago, but the memory of the itching stayed with her. She pulled up her T-shirt. There were no bites on her body, just on her wrists. Ahh … mosquito bites. She'd ask her aunt for repellent.

Ali opened the curtains and squinted against the glare, letting the warmth bathe her eyelids and wash away the madness of the night before. Then she picked up the note again.

'Okay, someone's messing with my head. Has to be.'

Ten minutes later, she was soaking in a hot bath, the water a little too hot, just the way she liked it. She lay still, letting the heat work its magic, and thought about the note and the rat creature. The idea that it had been a delusion wasn't helpful. She couldn't test that; her answers would be part of the same delusion. Better to treat the event as real, investigate it like a science experiment, and then share everything with her dad when he showed up.

First, she would look for the rat creature, take some video with Peter's phone and post it online. Some expert would know what it was, or what it was supposed to be; life could be cruel and threw up mutations all the time.

As for the note? The logical explanation was a prank – someone messing with her head. But why? Who stood to gain? The idea was full of holes. Whoever wrote it knew she would go to the barn, knew she would read the Alice books. Which meant it was a set-up. But at least it made more sense than getting a note from a missing aunt called Alice who was stuck in a parallel world with two books written about her. An aunt who could defy all the laws of space-time by leaving a note to a niece who wouldn't be born for another hundred years.

She opened her eyes. Yes, definitely a prank, she decided. So today's mission was to track down the person behind it – and the reason for it – starting with the handwriting.

'Ah! Good! Here she is,' said Lord Grey when Ali walked in for breakfast fifteen minutes later. It looked like the others had almost finished.

'Sorry I'm a bit late. Nodded off in a hot bath.'

'Good for you! Awake now, I hope, because I have a clue here that sounds like complete gobbledegook.'

'Fire away,' said Ali. 'I'll load up with coffee.'

'Two words, twelve letters and then three, starting with S and C.'

'Please solve it, dear,' said Lady Grey, 'he's been impossible over this one.'

'*To be or not to be, just open the box,*' Lord Grey read the clue, 'first twelve-letter word is 'Shakespeare's' obviously, but what the deuce is the second?'

Ali grinned at him. 'It's got nothing to do with Shakespeare.'

'Nonsense. Has to be, letters starting with S – fits like a glove.'

'It might fit, but so does the right answer, which is Schrödinger's Cat.'

'What?'

'It's an old idea in science. There's a cat in a box. It might be dead, or it might be alive, the only way of finding out is to open the box. Until you do, it's both dead and alive at the same time, at least in theory.'

'Never heard of it, but it fits perfectly. I'll be damned!'

'Thank goodness,' said his wife, and she gestured to the window. 'Look at that sunshine. We can't spend a minute longer inside today, it would be criminal.'

'Suits me,' said her husband, 'a deckchair in the shade.'

'And you, Ali? You still look a bit pale. You should get some sun.'

'I will. I'll explore the grounds; a day of bugs and botany.'

'Days of Bugs and Botany,' repeated her uncle.

'And, speaking of bugs,' Ali looked down at the red dots of inflammation on her wrists, 'do you have some mosquito repellent?'

'I don't believe so.' Her aunt turned to Nurse Potts. 'Do you have any?'

'Might have, I'll look when I go up for your meds.'

'Days of Bugs and Botany,' repeated her uncle, 'sounds like a book by that Durrell fellow. Bit of a dull book, has to be said.'

'Excuse me, Bertie!' Lady Grey put down her cup and gave her husband a stern look. 'I knew every plant on these grounds when I was a child. I pressed more flowers than I had books to bury them in.'

'Bark rubbing,' said her husband. 'That was my thing, at Kew Gardens. I've done a few bark rubbings in that place, I can tell you. Happy days.'

'Nice. Have you finished with the paper, uncle?'

Ali congratulated herself as she left the dining room clutching the Times. Her uncle had jotted his crossword notes all over one page, a good sample of his handwriting.

She would need to find something of Waxstaff's, maybe an old grocery list, and Potts always scribbled in a medical diary when she measured Lady Grey's blood pressure. And Lady Grey herself kept a diary by her bed. Easy.

Now to get the books and journals from the barn and start comparing the handwriting in those. Pressing flowers was a great cover for taking multiple trips across the lawn and no one would see her climbing in and out of the well as it was hidden behind a dense thicket of rhododendrons.

'Let the adventures begin!' she said, dropping the Times on the desk in the library and grabbing her college backpack. At the very least she had something to exercise her brain – a mystery to unravel.

Ten minutes later, she was halfway across the lawn with her backpack in one hand and her uncle's walking stick in the other – just in case the rat creature was lurking in the underground passage.

It wasn't. The tunnel was empty, and Ali spent the morning

squirrelling the collection of books over to the library. Nine trips in all. There was plenty of room on the bookshelves, space vacated by two stuffed animals that now sat facing her from the back corners of the desk: a dormouse and a white rat.

'Okay team,' she said to her stuffed audience, 'time to solve some riddles. But first – lunch!'

CHAPTER 13

DAY THREE

IDENTITY REVEALED

'Fan her head!' the Red Queen interrupted, 'she'll be feverish after so much thinking.' So they set to work and fanned her with bunches of leaves.

Ali went to the kitchen, loaded a tray with banana sandwiches and juice, and carried it back to the library. Brain fuel, her dad called it, but all food was brain fuel to him. When she was about eight, Ali had made him a worm sandwich. He'd taken a bite before noticing, then looked up, smiled, and carried on chewing with his mouth open so she could see the chomped-up worm. Then he'd swallowed. 'It tastes of dirt, Newt, I don't recommend it.'

Ali put the tray on the desk, wished her dad was here to share it with her, and for the next two hours sat reading and eating. The first thing she noticed was that all the books fell into two groups, based on era.

The books in the larger grouping had all been published in the second half of the nineteenth century; the second and smaller group from about thirty years ago. Ali started with the two Wonderland novels, reading them aloud to the stuffed dormouse and rat. The lengthy notes in the margins of both books covered six topics. Only six. Ali grabbed a blank notepad from her suitcase, and listed the topics.

1. *Cold cases*
2. *Mushrooms*
3. *Safe passage*
4. *Roses*
5. *Crows and Ravens*
6. *Riddles*

The reader seemed convinced that the characters in both novels were coded descriptions of real people. Every time a new character appeared, the reader listed names of potential people who'd gone missing.

'Conspiracy theory on steroids,' Ali said to the dormouse. She studied the handwriting. It was neat, all in pencil, and nothing like the writing on the freaky, tooth-punctured note. And nothing like her uncle's writing either.

She carried on reading, came to the end of the book, turned the last page, and froze. What the …?

The blank end sheet was covered *in her own writing* – the notes she'd written in her dream while two odd boys had chatted away at her.

How was that possible? Unless she'd written them in the barn, sitting on the bed in a cone of madness, weaving a neat little thread to fit her delusion. How pathetic was that? The tears came, silently at first, building slowly.

'Whatever's the matter?' Her uncle was standing in the doorway, his face a picture of concern. 'Sorry, I didn't mean to intrude, just popped by to see if you've had lunch. Want me to disappear?'

'Yes … I mean yes, I've had some lunch, thanks. And no, don't disappear.'

'Want to talk about it? Not that there's any need. Stuck in this house with a couple of old farts is enough to make anyone burst into tears.'

'I think I'm going mad.'

'Well of course you are. Madness is the only sane response to this life … not sure who said that. Not me, of course – far too smart a remark for yours truly.'

'I think you're pretty smart, Uncle Bertie.'

'Except with the Times crossword, right?'

'Right,' Ali forced a laugh. She wasn't sure where to take the conversation from here. 'And yes, I just meant I'm going mad with boredom. Never been more than a day without a screen of some kind.'

'Yes, I've been reading about that. A new addiction by all accounts, every kind of distraction right there at your fingertips. That how it goes?'

'Pretty much.'

'And now it's back to the basics of old-fashioned page-turning.' He pointed to the Wonderland novels on the desk beside her. 'I thought Martha had cleared these out years ago.'

'Were they yours?'

'Mine, lord no. They were your dear mother's.'

'Mum's?' Ali stared at him, her self-pity evaporating like ice in a hot bath.

'Yes. Talking of addictions, this was her tipple of choice for a while. All she read for weeks on end when she was about your age.'

'Oh my god, she might be the mystery scribbler!'

'Not following.'

'Someone wrote notes on every page. Look.' She handed one of the books to him.

He flipped through a few pages. 'Might be her. She sent us a few postcards over the years. Have a squizz through Martha's scrapbooks – might find a match.'

He left the room and Ali pounced on the scrapbooks. There were five postcards from her mother.

The writing matched!

'Bloody hell!'

Ali had almost nothing of her mother's. There was the silver pendant, a few books, a collection of old CDs Ali couldn't play, and a favourite duffle coat. Her mum hadn't been a hoarder and had thrown out the detritus of her student years when she'd moved in with Ali's dad.

Now here were two books filled with her notes, books from some long-ago summer spent right here in this house. For the next hour, Ali read the notes again, every note on every page of both books. They were an unexpected window into her mother's early life – a slightly disturbing window.

Ali closed her eyes and pictured her mum sitting in the library, sitting at the same desk, writing these notes in the two books, and Ali made a decision. She would suspend her disbelief; she would go on the same mental journey as her mother; she would pick up threads of her investigation and run with it.

'Let's do this', Ali said to her small stuffed audience, and she pulled down her aunt's scrapbooks and flipped through them, looking for every photo of her mum. There were fourteen. Ali placed them between the pages of the novels, pressing them like a collection of precious flowers.

'There. You and me, Mum. Our books now, and talking to you is a bit less crazy than talking to a stuffed dormouse, right?' A movement out in the garden caught her eye. She looked up and saw Waxstaff heading off down the drive. The housekeeper seemed to be in a hurry.

What was she scurrying out for, Ali wondered. Groceries? Opening the library window, she climbed out and started to follow.

'Off for a stroll?'

Ali turned. Lady Grey was sitting on the terrace a few yards away.

'Yep, more of a jog,' Ali began sprinting on the spot to emphasise the point. 'I've been reading for hours. Got to burn off some energy.'

'Good. However I suggest you burn it off in the other direction, and not down the driveway in pursuit of Miss Waxstaff.'

'Oh, did she go this way? I didn't notice.'

'Of course you did. I won't have you relieving your boredom by spying on her tryst. Everyone is entitled to a little privacy.'

'A tryst! You mean, like in … tryst?'

'Like in your beloved Jane Austen, yes. An assignation.'

'Waxstaff!' Ali stared down the driveway in disbelief.

'Don't sound so horrified. There's someone for everyone, or so they say. Leave her be and jog through the orchard instead.'

'Sure. Okay.' Now Ali really was intrigued. What sort of person would date a walking skeleton like Waxstaff? She waved to her aunt and set off towards the orchard. Once through the brick archway she put on a burst of speed, raced for the fringe of woodland that circled the estate, then followed the path through the trees until she was ten metres from the gates. The perimeter wall was twice her height. Ali found a decent tree to climb, pulled herself up and scanned the street beyond. No sign of Waxstaff. But a black sedan was parked further down the road past the gates to the drive.

'Tryst wagon!' Ali climbed down, carried on down the path, crossed the drive and chose another tree to climb. Halfway up, she heard Waxstaff's voice.

'Not good enough!' The housekeeper sounded angry.

Ali kept climbing and peered over the wall. The sedan had tinted windows. Waxstaff was leaning in on the passenger side and slapped the roof with the flat of her hand. 'I never agreed to this! You can't spring it on me.' She slapped the roof a third time, straightened up, and marched back in through the gates.

CHAPTER 14

DAY THREE

HUDSON

———————

*'This young lady wants to know your history,' said the Griffin.
'I'll tell it her,' said the Mock Turtle in a deep, hollow tone,
'sit down and don't speak a word till I've finished.'*

'Nothing romantic about that,' thought Ali as she watched Waxstaff march back to the house, 'something else going on there, that's for sure.'

She didn't follow Waxstaff back up the drive, she kept to the path that ran alongside the boundary wall. What had the housekeeper meant? *You can't spring these things on me.* What things? And that last remark: *I've worked too hard for this to fall apart.* What was Waxstaff up to? Was she planning some elaborate scam to rip off Ali's relatives?

Maybe the person in the car was working for her; that was quite an earful she'd given them. And you don't thump an expensive car like that unless you're in charge. Who the hell was this woman?

The path through the trees wandered a little, but generally followed the same circle as the boundary wall, and Ali soon found herself back at the orchard. Feeling thirsty from her walk, she made her way to the kitchen, drank a glass of water, poured another, and took it to the library.

Aunt Martha was there. Alone. She was in her antique wheelchair in front of the woodland painting. She turned and smiled as her niece came in, a wistful smile that Ali couldn't quite measure.

'Did you have a nice run, dear?'

'Yep, I found the path that winds through the trees inside the wall.'

'It's pretty, isn't it? I helped my father plant it. Or plan it, I should say. We had a gardener back then who did the real work. I was quite smitten with him. I used to take long walks in the hope he'd stop for a chat. How foolish – I would scarcely have been in my teens.'

'There you are!' Nurse Potts bustled in. 'I left you in the shade. Who moved you around?'

'I'm not a piece of furniture to be arranged, Nurse Potts. I can wheel myself about if I so choose. And you're to blame anyway. You brought this picture down from the attic. I wanted a few minutes alone with it, to get reacquainted.'

'That right?'

'It meant a great deal to me at one time, my mother hated the thing and always threatened to be rid of it. It was quite a surprise seeing it resurface after all these years.'

'I can take it back up if it's causing bother.'

'On the contrary, I'm delighted to see it again. When Ali returns to London we shall put it in the main room where it used to hang.' She smiled at Ali. 'Until then, it remains in here with my niece.'

'Thanks,' said Ali.

'You're welcome, and you need a splash of colour with all these stuffed creatures in here. They were my father's collection. I never warmed to them.' She gestured with a gloved hand to the nurse. 'Come along, Nurse Potts, you may rearrange me back to wherever.'

'I liked it when I saw it up in the attic,' the nurse said, nodding at the picture as she turned the wheelchair to the door. 'Not so sure now. There's something a little bit not-right about it.'

'Yes,' said Lady Grey as Potts trundled her from the room, 'you put it very well. My mother held to the same opinion.'

When they were gone, Ali went over to the picture. Potts was right, there was something disturbing about it. She remembered her mother taking her to see a Van Gogh exhibition. This picture had the same kind of intensity, as if painted in a frenzy; the artist desperate to capture a fading memory. Ali had begged her mother to buy a print for her bedroom wall. They'd bought a postcard which had lived on their fridge for months. Ali went to the desk where she'd left the two novels, bulging now from the photographs pressed between their pages.

'Okay, Mum – let's do this.' She opened her notebook and scanned the list of items her mother had fixated on, starting with 'Cold cases.'

'So, you think Wonderland was a real place. Aunt Alice stumbled through, and then went zipping back and forth trying to figure out the names of people who got stuck over there? And the riddles are clues to their identities?' Ali looked up at the shelves. 'Were you stuck in here while it was pissing with rain outside, bored out of your mind, and flicking through all these books?'

She pulled down a history book at random, a collection of biographies of missing people. 'What did you find? What got you hooked?' She flicked through the book, then another; nothing stood out. She opened a third – and *Bingo!* The margins were crammed with notes. Not her mother's; the style was more eloquent, and far more elaborate. Great-aunt Alice?

Ali unfolded the note she'd found in the barn. The handwriting matched, neat and precise, the ink fading in places, the edges of some letters blooming in spidery threads.

'Holy crap.' Ali began flicking through more history books, stopping to read the text wherever a note was scribbled beside it. Then she found one written by her mother. It was underlined, as if she'd been angry with Aunt Alice.

Where are they, these files you keep talking about – your investigations? Did you hide them? Take them through? I only found your page on the Hudsons, that's all.

'What page?' Ali held up the book and shook it. A single page of yellowed paper fell out, the handwriting neat and elegant.

The melancholy pair, the Walrus and the Carpenter, for that I shall name them, are British, that much is clear from their accents alone. But I believe I have come upon their true history, though my reasoning is tenuous at best. Based on the few confused memories they still possess, I sought to explore files lodged at the National Geographic Society. It led me to read their earlier journals, all housed there, though for reasons of both age and gender it took a great

*deal of subterfuge to access them. I had but twenty minutes
in a library cupboard with only a candle to read by. Yet I am
convinced they are two of the missing crew of Henry Hudson,
and given their emotional attachment, each to the other,
perhaps one is Hudson himself, and the other his unfortunate
son. Given the nature and circumstances of their great
misfortune, I believe they managed to subsist entirely on
a diet of raw oysters before stumbling through and losing
themselves and their memories in that place of hopeless
enchantment.*

Ali sat and read the note a second time. Is this what had
got her mother hooked? Had someone created a game for her,
a home-made parlour game to while away a rainy weekend?
No, that didn't fit. It was in the same handwriting as the note
the rat-creature had dropped. And that had been addressed
to her!

'Enough!' Ali folded both notes into her journal and checked
the clock on the mantel. Time to meet Peter and use his phone
– if he kept his word and bothered to show.

She walked the driveway again. Copper beech trees lined
either side like giant umbrellas, reducing the sunlight to
muted browns and purples. It was like walking through a sepia
photograph from the days of her missing great-aunt.

Before the gates, she stepped into the necklace of
woodland that fringed the estate, and followed the path till
she came to the spot where she'd met Peter the day before.
He wasn't there. Damn it! Ali sat down and waited. It went
against her instincts to wait as she felt it sent the wrong
message, made her look needy. But she was; she needed his
phone!

She sat with her back to a tree. The day was still hot, even in the shade, and she fought an urge to doze off. Right away, she knew it was just an ordinary dream, nothing like the lucid dream of the day before. She was dressed like the pictures of Alice in the books. Blue dress and white apron.

'No way!' She stared down at the hideous dress, then looked around for someone to be angry with. And saw her science teacher! Mr Kepler was a giant caterpillar addressing a bunch of daisies on the subject of gravity wells.

'Everything, in its own way, is a gravity well,' he was saying, 'the coalition and compression of matter is an expression of gravity.' He beamed at the daisies who were paying him no attention whatsoever. The flowers all had Waxstaff's face, and Ali began stamping on as many as she could.

'And you accuse me of snoring,' said a voice above her. She opened her eyes to see Peter grinning down at her.

'Bring your phone?'

'Heard you before I saw you. Thought only blokes snored.'

'Still open doors for us, too?'

'Yep,' he sat down in front of her and pulled his phone out. 'Bought the data and charged the battery. Good to go.'

'Thanks,' she took the phone.'

'But there's a time limit. Not on the phone … me. Skipped out early and need to get back for the bell. Got a detention.'

'Vicar's boy goes rogue, that'll make the village paper.'

'Not in this village,' Peter laughed, 'too much real scandal. So what do you want to search?'

'A guy called Hudson.'

'The dead actor? Fancy him?'

'Yeah, sure.' Ali typed in the full name, Henry Hudson. And there he was, page after page, multiple sites. 'So, he was famous,' she said, scrolling for key points, 'some kind of explorer back when it was cool to go to the States.'

'Except it was called the Americas back when poor old Henry Hudson was doing his thing.'

'You've heard of him? I'm in danger of being impressed.'

'Hudson Bay, Hudson River. I think he was the bloke who got all obsessed with finding a route through to Asia.'

'Yep, that's him. Loads on him here.' Ali scrolled down, looking for how he died and where he was buried. That would spoil the parlour game. You can't be missing if you're dead and buried.

'Who's Jack?' asked Peter. 'Boyfriend?' he pointed to the pendant Ali was fidgeting with.

'No. Mum's. An old flame of hers.' She didn't elaborate; didn't tell Peter how her mum always kissed the pendant when she put it on; how she wore it when she went on her UN field trips. Until the last one.

Ali pushed the memory away, carried on scrolling – and found what she was looking for.

Henry Hudson left England in April 1610 on his last voyage. He entered what became Hudson Bay and got trapped in ice and had to spend the winter there. Mutineers put Hudson and his son in a small boat and set them adrift. They were never seen again.

'Holy crap!'

'What?'

'He was never found, his crew got pissed off and put him in a lifeboat with his son. Sailed off and left them to rot.'

'Charming. So what's your interest?'

'There's a note about him in the library, like a short story.'

'A house with its own library? That's cool,' he started to get up. 'Anyway, I should get going, don't want to double down on my detention.'

'Two minutes, nearly done.' Ali did a quick search for any reference to an Aunt Alice in the Grey family. There was nothing. As far as any digital data bases were concerned, no such person had ever existed in the area.

'Got to go,' said Peter, holding his hand out for the phone.

'Tomorrow?' Ali asked.

'Sure. More history?'

'Multiverse theory.'

'You're shitting me.'

'No, I'll tell you about it next time. I'm doing it in science.'

'We just cut up dead frogs.'

'Nice. Just bring the phone, okay?' Ali got up and finger-waved over her shoulder as she walked off down the path.

Back in the library she found the one-page article on Hudson and stared at it. There were three explanations she could think of. One, it was part of a rainy-day parlour game someone in her family had made up generations ago. Two, it had been created for her benefit, a puzzle designed to pull her into some kind of scam to rob her relatives. Or three, she'd lost her mind and everything was part of an elaborate delusion she was constructing.

Ali chose another history book, and took it out to a shady spot on the lawn. The text was dry and factual, and so boring that she struggled to focus. Her mind kept drifting back to Waxstaff and that meeting out on the street; and where did Potts fit in? Were they a tag team, ripping off vulnerable old folk?

CHAPTER 15

DAY THREE

GLASS EYES

———————

'Who am I then? Tell me that first, and if I like being that person then I'll come up; if not, I'll stay down here till I'm somebody else.'

That evening, the conversation over dinner was forced and dull. Everyone seemed tired from the heat of the day. Ali asked if there'd been word from her dad. There hadn't.

Her uncle excused himself from the table early, complaining of indigestion.

'That's because you didn't take a walk today,' Aunt Martha said, waving a finger at him. 'You should walk to the village at the very least. Go and find someone to have one of your famous altercations with.'

'Will do, my dear. Will do. Tomorrow. Right now, a little brandy will do the trick. Always does.' His wife let it go, it was too hot even for their playful banter, and before long the meal was over.

Ali went back to the library and lay on her bed staring at the ceiling. The day had been a rollercoaster, especially after discovering the notes in the novels were her mum's. And they were her mum's, she was sure of it. No one would go to that much trouble to forge her handwriting. Or maybe she just wanted to believe that, wanted it so badly it was clouding her judgement.

As she lay staring at the ceiling, memories of happy times with her mother began peeking up at her, reaching up through cracks in the concrete floor she'd buried them under. She let them come, and lay watching them without judgement and without tears.

Tap, tap, tap.

Ali sat up. She was on the bed, still dressed, the reading lamp on the desk still lighting the room. She looked at the clock on the mantel. Ten past midnight.

Tap, tap, tap.

The drapes were open and Peter's face was pressed to the glass.

'Shit!' Ali jumped up and let him in. 'What the hell are you doing?'

'Not sleeping, obviously.'

'Well, go and not-sleep in your own house. This is all kinds of wrong. How long were you out there perving on me?'

'Pervs don't tap on the glass. We need to talk.'

'Tomorrow.'

'Can't wait that long. Some weird guy came to the school and I got a heap of shit thrown at me.'

'Tough. Not a reason to come midnight creeping!'

'They came because you called your dad on my phone.'

'What? Why?'

'His number must be on some secure database.'

'He's a scientist, not a secret agent. I call him all the time.'

'On your phone. They must have your number in their system. Mine set the lights flashing.' He paused. 'Are you going to let me in?'

Ali stepped aside, Peter climbed in and flopped down in one of the comfy leather chairs; he patted the arms, 'This is nice.'

'So, what happened?'

'Some MI6 type wanted to know why I lent you my phone … how we met … what's the relationship. All kinds of crap like that. So what's going on? Are you really here just for punching some dick in the face?'

'No, I'm a secret spy, youngest ever, I borrow traceable phones because I'm the best. What else did they want to know?'

'How long I'd been sneaking about the manor, had I met you before, did I know people in London, was my dad still an active member of the Green Party? Who wants to know that stuff unless there's something more going on that you're not telling me?'

'There's lots I'm not telling you because I don't understand any of it yet.'

'Okay. Got any food?'

'Always.' Ali went to the desk and pulled out a packet of biscuits.

'Great, thanks.' He was three biscuits in before he realised Ali had her hand out for one herself.

'Sorry, distracted. So what aren't you telling me?'

'Have you seen the two weird-looking women who work here?'

'Not sure.'

'If you'd seen them you'd be sure. They're straight out of a cartoon. There's a nurse, she's huge, like she pushes weights.

And a housekeeper, Waxstaff, thin as a stick. She's unhealthy looking, like she's anorexic, except she isn't – she eats as much as everyone at dinner. Even me.' Ali took another biscuit.

'I think I've seen the thin one, didn't realised she worked here. But she's in the village quite a bit. Hard to miss. What about them?'

'Not sure, they might be working on some scam to rip the Greys off.'

'How?'

'Don't know, just a feeling.'

'A scam wouldn't trigger a government heavy to come and lean on me.'

'I know, but my dad does heavyweight research for the government. Maybe they keep tabs on his phone in case some industrial spy comes sniffing around.'

'Great, so now I'm in a file somewhere.'

'We're all on a million files, Peter, we're all customers to somebody.' Ali took another biscuit and grinned. 'Kind of cute that you risked coming out here to tell me this. Tomorrow would have been fine.'

'About that. Better make it lunchtime tomorrow – twelve thirty? I can't skip classes with all this going on.'

'Okay. Same place?'

'Yeah.' He took another biscuit and headed for the window, then turned and grinned. 'Midnight meetings … a little bit cool and romantic, right?'

'No, not even a little bit. Night.'

'Night.' Peter left, taking the rest of the biscuits with him. Ali closed the drapes behind him, thought about changing into her pjs, but the biscuits had set her stomach off and she needed some serious midnight feasting.

She was halfway down the hall when she heard a low buzz of conversation coming from the kitchen. The door was closed, but a slice of light spilled from the gap at the bottom. Ali tiptoed forward and bent over, her eye to the keyhole.

Waxstaff stood at the sideboard chopping mushrooms. Potts was helping a third woman who sat at the table, her back to the door. She wore a headscarf wrapped round her head like a turban; the kind Ali had seen in cartoons where genies lived in magic lanterns. It was dark red and sparkled with sequins.

The woman seemed to have a problem with her spine, a deformity that made her hunch over. Hunchback? Ali knew the term, though it didn't sound very PC and she made a mental note to google it when she got Peter's phone.

The back of the woman's neck was exposed. Potts was rubbing ointment onto a large boil that was weeping blood. They were talking in hushed voices, so Ali turned her head and put her ear to the keyhole.

'... not worth the risk, not at this time of night.' It was Potts talking. 'Makes no sense if you want my opinion.'

'We don't.' Waxstaff's voice.

'If you must lecture someone, lecture the moon.' A third voice, unfamiliar. 'It has to be full – a few hours either side and the potency drops.' Ali wanted to hear more, but also wanted to see the stranger's face, so she put her eye back to the keyhole – and bumped the door handle with her nose. Everyone in the kitchen swivelled to look at the door. The stranger had two glass eyes.

'Shit!' Ali jumped back from the door. The blind woman had looked directly at her! As if the door wasn't there! As if she could see perfectly with glass eyes.

For a second, Ali didn't move, surprise freezing her brain.

Then adrenalin kicked in and she scrambled back to the library. She threw herself into her bed and lay waiting for the blind stranger to come down the hallway, waiting like a terrified child, the covers pulled over her head against a nightmare.

Nobody came. The next thing Ali knew, bright sunshine was flooding the room – she'd forgotten to close the curtains. She reached down and scratched new and very itchy bites on both ankles – Peter hadn't closed the window either. Then she remembered the stranger, and jumped out of bed.

Had that even happened? Or had she fallen asleep the moment Peter left? She stretched, went over to the stuffed dormouse on the desk and tapped one of its glass eyes.

'I think you snuck into my dreams last night. You were a weird old woman with glass eyes and a boil on your neck.' Then she wrinkled her nose, it hurt. She put a hand up and touched the side. Ow, tender! And she remembered the knock from the door handle. So, not a dream.

At breakfast, she waited for Waxstaff or Potts to raise the incident. They didn't. Which Ali found odd. Why wouldn't they use it to score points against her, accuse her of eavesdropping? Did they want to keep the visitor a secret?

'Who was that blind zombie last night?'

The two women glanced at each other. Nurse Potts reached for the teapot, realised her cup was already full, and looked at Waxstaff again, as if expecting her to take the lead.

'Woman?' asked Lord Grey.

'Yes, Uncle Bertie, there was a blind woman in the kitchen last night.'

'We had a visitor?' asked Martha. Ali watched their

reactions. Her aunt and uncle were genuinely surprised.

'We did,' Ali replied for them. 'I went to get a bite from the kitchen and Nurse Potts was patching her up.'

'It was a lady from the village,' said Miss Waxstaff.

'A blind woman, on the grounds?' Lord Grey seemed confused. 'In the night? What on earth for?'

'Mushrooms,' said Potts, 'she was picking them. You know, that Mrs King woman.'

'Mrs King who helps at the church?'

'Yes.'

'Why would she pick mushrooms at night?'

'My point exactly,' said Potts. 'Said as much to her last night. Not sure I like the look of her. Bit of a crackpot.'

'Not at all,' said Waxstaff, 'quite the contrary, she's very knowledgeable. Last night was a waning moon, and as I understand it from Mrs King, that's the best time to pick medicinal mushrooms.'

'Like I said,' snorted Potts. 'Crackpot quackery.'

'Try saying that fast three times,' laughed Lord Grey. And he did, making a complete mess of it.

'Delightful,' said Waxstaff, and she stared pointedly at the crumbs of toast his lordship had sprayed down the front of his shirt. 'The short of it is, Mrs King stumbled while she was out there, and took a small cut to her neck. I woke Nurse Potts who made a poultice and bandaged her up.'

'And drove her to hospital, I trust?' said Lord Grey.

'Offered and rejected. She insisted on walking home.'

'She's blind,' said Ali.

'Indeed she is,' Waxstaff threw Ali a withering look, 'and she likes to walk without assistance, as do many blind folk. Shall we lock them all up?'

'Knew a blind chap once,' said Lord Grey. 'Terrific fellow,

could burp piano sonatas from memory – Erik Satie mostly – and pitch perfect.'

'Thank you, darling,' said his wife, 'it's very taxing how some memories we retain while others get stripped away.' She wiped her mouth with a serviette and pushed her wheelchair back from the table.

'Take me out into the sunshine, would you, Miss Potts? And please follow up on Mrs King, check she's all right.'

'Yes,' echoed her husband, 'and tell her she can pick mushrooms anytime. Big garden like this, it's only proper we share its bounty where we can.'

'And Alice?' Aunt Martha turned to face her niece. 'Please don't refer to Mrs King in such derogatory terms. The woman has been a pillar of the community for many years, she is the first to help others and I hold her in very high regard.'

'Quite so,' agreed her husband, 'she's the very best kind of zombie.'

'Bertie! That is not helpful.'

Ali smothered a laugh, and started to help Miss Waxstaff clear the table. The woman protested but Ali ignored her and carried a tray of dishes back to the kitchen. The bench was still covered in chopped mushrooms.

'What will you do with these?' she asked as she stacked the dishwasher.

'Casserole,' said Waxstaff. 'Mushroom casserole.'

'Great, I love mushrooms. So did my mum, apparently.'

'Is that right?'

'Well, I guess she did. She wrote about them – research stuff. She got a bit obsessed by the looks of it. There must be a dozen books in the library on their medical properties, all with Mum's writing in the margins.'

She put the last plate in the dishwasher and straightened

up – and was shocked by Waxstaff's expression. The woman was standing very still, listening intently and smiling at her. The effect was deeply unsettling, as if a skull was grinning at her.

'How interesting.' Waxstaff narrowed her eyes, yet continued to smile; the effect was even more disturbing. 'And what do you make of them?'

'The books on mushrooms?'

'Yes.'

'Not sure yet, I've only flicked through them. Mostly to read Mum's notes,' she paused. 'Potts was pretty dismissive.'

'Hardly surprising,' said Waxstaff, 'most people don't like what they don't understand. The medical profession are no exception.'

'And what do you think?'

'About mushrooms or Potts?'

'Mushrooms.'

'I find them beneficial. I have a stomach condition and they seem to help.'

'What, like constipation?'

'Why do you insist on being rude?'

'It was just a question.'

'No, you're not unpleasant by accident, you delight in it. Deep down, under all those layers of attitude, I think you're rather a cruel person.'

For a moment Ali was stunned. She'd been accused of all kinds of things over the years. But never that.

'And you're a bit thin-skinned.'

'Yes I am, literally. Part of the same illness as the stomach condition. This skin and muscle wasting is due to an illness I had when I was young. The doctors were useless, but Mrs King has helped me with her mushrooms.' She paused, as if she'd said too much and wanted to end the conversation. 'Last night she was picking here at my invitation. She has a very good eye for them.'

'Figure of speech?'

'No, I think she sees far better that we do, just a little differently. Now, if you'll excuse me, I have a lot to do.'

Ali wanted to ask what Waxstaff meant by that last remark. She'd had the same feeling, that Mrs King had looked directly at her through the keyhole last night, but Waxstaff had turned away, making it clear the conversation was over.

CHAPTER 16

DAY FOUR

A STONE FROG

———————

*'Let's pretend there's a way of getting through into it,
somehow; let's pretend the glass has gone all soft like gauze.'
And certainly the glass was beginning to melt away like
a bright silvery mist.*

Ali headed outside wondering what that little exchange
was all about. Odd that Waxstaff was into mushrooms too,
like the King woman. Like her mum? Every time mushrooms
appeared in one of the Wonderland novels, her mother had
marked it, treating every reference like a riddle. In one margin
she'd written:

Is this how to get out safely? Are mushrooms the answer?

Get out safely ... get out of what? she pondered. She
did a full tour of the garden, walking the driveway and the

perimeter pathway through the woods. It was a decent walk. She felt refreshed, ready for another session with the books.

Back in the library she scanned the shelves. Then she climbed the ladder and scanned them again in a series of graceful fly-bys. There were six books on mushrooms. One was a botanical guide with descriptions of every fungi known in Europe; one covered their medicinal properties; one the place of fungi in folklore; two were cookbooks on how to pick and cook different varieties; and the sixth was written in Mandarin with beautiful ink drawings showing how to dry and preserve them.

Ali took all six to the desk and flicked through them, pausing to read every annotation from great-aunt Alice and the notes from her mother. Both focused on the medicinal properties. Even the notes in the cookery books were about which methods of cooking would preserve the health benefits of the mushrooms.

'So, Mum … what's with the fixation? Were you one of those kids who got sick all the time, is that it?'

Ali put the books back. She couldn't decide what to read next, so started gliding back and forth on the ladder, picking out books at random. She turned each one upside down and gave it a shake, hoping another hidden note would fall out like the one about Hudson and his son.

And one did. A hand-drawn map floated like a leaf to the carpet. It came from a book that seemed out of place in the collection: a short history of London, written for tourists in 1851 at the time of the Great Exhibition.

Ali couldn't make any sense of it at first. It was a hand-drawn map of the city centre. She didn't know London that well, but enough to know some of the buildings had been drawn in the wrong place. Plus there was a wall around the outside, a complete ring labelled 'Old Roman Wall.' Ali remembered her mother once taking her to see the small section that was still standing.

'What are you?' Ali stared at the map. It looked familiar, not because of the London landmarks, but because of its shape. Twelve buildings inside a circle.

Duh! Ali almost smacked her head. It was here! It was a map of the estate! But why? Why go to the trouble? The house was drawn as Saint Paul's Cathedral, the barn was the Tower of London; and the stable, sheds and other outbuildings were drawn as smaller city landmarks. Each building was neatly labelled with its London name, written in her great-aunt's careful, elegant handwriting.

'Okay, Mum …' Ali lay on the bed and closed her eyes against the sunshine, 'why did great-aunt Alice draw a map of the grounds and go to all this trouble to disguise it as somewhere else? Simple. It's a treasure map.'

Her mother had made plenty of simple treasure maps for Ali when she was younger, maps to show where a present was hidden. And that's what this was, Ali was sure of it. The mysterious great-aunt Alice had buried something valuable in the grounds, then drawn the map to make sure she could find it again. A stranger flipping through the book would see it as a map of London scribbled by a tourist. It was a treasure map – hidden in plain sight.

'Coffee. Need coffee.' It was only mid-morning, but already Ali felt drowsy from the heat. She went to the kitchen and was filling the kettle when Waxstaff came in from the garden with basket of carrots.

'Coffee! At your age?'

'Sure,' Ali shrugged the question away, 'why not?'

'It's very a powerful stimulant, that's why not.'

'Exactly, I need a quick punch in the brain, sun's making me sleepy.'

'Then take a nap.' Waxstaff tipped the carrots onto the kitchen table. 'But first, come with me,' she directed, heading back out into the garden.

'I'm fine thanks,' Ali called out, 'just need my coffee.'

'It wasn't a suggestion,' Waxstaff called back. Ali bit her tongue, prepped the coffee, then followed the housekeeper outside.

'Is it important?' she said.

'Depends on what you value.' Waxstaff was heading to the herb garden. It was impressive. Twenty raised beds with flagstone pathways between them, the whole area fenced off against rabbits. Ali had walked past it a dozen times but never ventured inside. She followed Waxstaff in through a small picket gate.

'Who looks after this?'

'I do,' said Waxstaff, 'under your aunt's watchful eye. When she was young she helped plan it.' The housekeeper stopped and pointed to the beds on her left, 'everything on this side is for cooking, flavours for stews and so forth. And over here on this side, these are all medicinal.'

Ali wondered where this was going. 'Good to know,' she said, 'and the point is?'

'The other day you said science didn't need a point. Knowledge for the sake of knowledge, you said.'

'Yeah, sometimes, and sometimes it's got a target in its sights. We were just talking about coffee – you said it was a powerful stimulant, then you march me out here. So you have a point to make. What is it?'

'It's these. It's the herbs.' Waxstaff pointed to a bed in the far corner. 'Over there are varieties that calm and sooth, like

St John's Wort, and chamomile. In the next bed are ones that do the opposite, they're powerful stimulants.'

'Like coffee.'

'Exactly. And a great deal stronger in some cases.'

'Good, I'll know where to come. Right now, coffee will do fine.' Ali walked back to the kitchen. What was that lecture about? Not coffee, that was for sure. Then she stopped. Bloody hell! Waxstaff had just threatened her! The woman had powerful herbs for making all kinds of drugs. For making … poison? Ali shuddered, suddenly feeling cold despite the sun, and hurried to the kitchen.

At least the coffee was ready. She pushed the plunger down, filled a large mug and took it outside. A giant cedar stood in one corner of the main lawn, its flat branches reaching out like fans to shade the grass below. Ali sat between two massive roots. They curved up beside her, polished by time and the feet of children, generations of ambitious tree climbers. Her own mother among them, probably.

'Okay Mum, time to play pirates.' Ali opened her notebook and unfolded the map. If great-aunt Alice had buried something in the grounds, there had to be an X to mark the spot.

There wasn't, but there was a frog. Or what looked like a frog. It was drawn near the east wall of the barn, and it was the only detail that wasn't a building.

'Got to be it. Let's go see.' Ali drained her coffee, balanced the mug on one of the armchair roots, and set off for the orchard. The area was so neglected and overgrown that a systematic search was impossible. There were too many fallen branches and tangled thickets of blackberry. She spent half an hour pacing the spaces in between, swiping the long grass with a stick, but found nothing, and was ready to give up when her toe struck something hard.

'Ouch!' Half buried in the long grass was a statue of a frog. Ali cleared the ground around it, tearing the grass up in handfuls. It looked old, carved from a soft stone, the edges worn away, the corners chipped.

'Well, look at you.' She tried lifting it, but the frog wouldn't budge. She tried getting her fingers under it, and couldn't. The statue wasn't free-standing, it had a carved base.

'Later, froggy,' she waved a finger at the carving, 'you, me and a spade.' Right now it was too hot to do anything but take a nap. She headed back to the shade of the cedar tree and settled down between the huge, polished roots.

The summer heat was lifting scent from everything, the intensity and mix of smells so strong that it reminded Ali of her dream in the bluebell clearing. Was that normal? To remember the smell of a dream? She closed her eyes, trying to recall more details, and a wave of melancholy washed over her. Her memory of the dream had all but gone. She could still feel the reality of the dream, the impact of it, but not the details.

And she wanted it again. The dream. Could something about this place, the house and grounds, make people have the kind of lucid dreaming her dad had told her about?

Is that it, Mum? Did you get super-real dreams here too? Is that what got you into all this? You told me about places that became famous for weird stuff happening, places like Stonehenge and Glastonbury. Is this one of those?

Her father had dismissed the idea as pre-scientific thinking. He thought places became notorious because of some incident like a battle, and folklore would hand the stories down, embellish them, giving places a significance they didn't have.

But what if he was wrong, what if places of power were real. Ali kept her eyes shut, picturing her dad sitting under the tree beside her, listening patiently to her thoughts.

What if great-aunt Alice was a sensitive type who read the Wonderland books and then dreamed about them? Maybe her lucid dreams were so real that she became obsessed with 'saving' the people she met in her dreams, the ones she'd been reading about. Back then, back in her day, what would they do? Maybe lock her up, get her certified, a skeleton in the family cupboard that no one talks about. Then years later, Mum finds the books and all the crazy notes, and she starts dreaming too!

Ali got up and headed back towards the house. It wasn't much of a theory, but at least it was one she could test. After her lunchtime meeting with Peter, she would try to reproduce the events that led to her first dream. She would lie on the old bed in the barn, read the Wonderland book, and try to nod off.

CHAPTER 17

DAY FOUR

MULTIVERSE

———————

So she sat on, with closed eyes, and half believed
herself in Wonderland, though she knew she had but
to open them again, and all would change to dull reality.

'Alice! Fancy a biscuit?' Ali looked up. Lord Grey was waving
to her from the terrace. A beaker of iced tea and a plate of
biscuits sat on the patio table.

'Here you go,' her uncle poured her a drink as she sat down.
'Martha's in her room having physio from Potts. I hate seeing
her go through it, it's nothing short of bullying, with all those
pins clamping her pelvis together, but she's a stoic thing;
waves it off, of course, but it gives her a lot of gyp.'

'How did she fall?'

'Sleepwalking.'

'Seriously?'

'Yes. Waxstaff found her, she'd walked off the patio. Soft

landing on the grass but fell badly, poor old soul. Aging bones and all that.'

'Does she sleepwalk a lot?' Ali took a sip of the tea; it was delicious. She'd never had iced tea before.

'As a wee nipper she did. The family started locking her room at night after they found her wandering about in the barn. She was sitting on a horse blanket, fast asleep, eyes tight shut, talking gibberish. Grew out of it in time. Then a few months ago she started doing it again. Woke me up most times, so I was able to guide her back to bed. But then … the patio! She'd made it all the way downstairs, thank god, safe as you like, as if part of her was awake and knew what she was doing. Same on the patio, one foot to the left and she would have been safely on the steps.'

'Do you think she was going to the barn?'

'Who knows? Not going anywhere for a while now, that much is for sure.' He drained his glass, gestured for Ali to do the same, and refilled them.

'Thanks. This is really good. How did you find Nurse Potts? An agency?'

'Believe so, yes. Waxstaff arranged it, bless her.'

'That right?' Ali sat back and sipped her tea. Waxstaff found Aunt Martha when she fell, and Waxstaff hired Potts. It sounded more and more like they were a pair of scam artists working a number on the old couple.

'Heard the one about the burglar who thinks he's a moth?'

'Yes, uncle, you told me yesterday.'

'I did?'

'Yes,' she said, helping herself to a biscuit, 'the burglar broke in to see his doctor one night because the doctor left his light on.'

'Damn. Okay, then. Three men go into a tuck shop …'

They sat together for a while, sipping tea and telling jokes neither could remember properly. Ali finally got a punchline right, and looked up for the applause, but her uncle had fallen asleep, a half-eaten gingernut clasped in one hand.

Ali headed inside, to the library and her mother's books. It was only 11.30, an hour before her meeting with Peter. She settled on the bed and read the first Wonderland novel again. Nothing about the story was compelling. According to her mother, that was the point, the story was only wrapping paper. One of her notes summed it up:

Forget the story. This is a guidebook! A set of rules for getting over there and back again safely. Nothing matters except figuring out these rules.

Not only had her mother been convinced Wonderland was real, she also thought the books held the secret for getting there safely. Which meant crossing over was risky.

Ali rolled onto her back and stared at the ceiling. She wanted so much to play along with her mother's obsession.

Peter was already waiting at the clearing when Ali arrived. He was in his school uniform and sitting against tree.

'Someone's eager,' said Ali.

'Yeah, had to beat the lunch bell. Too many eyes when that goes off, harder to slip away.'

'More dark suits hassling you?'

'No, but they're still in the village. Taken rooms at the pub. Looks like they're going to keep you safe from strange folk like me. Whatever work your dad's doing, he's valuable to someone.'

'Maybe.' Ali sat opposite him. 'Do they have a car with black-tinted windows?'

'Yep, why?'

'Our housekeeper was talking to them yesterday, sounded pissed off. I think she's plotting to scam my folks.'

'You reckon?'

'Just a feeling.'

'Classic.' He shook his head at her.

'What?'

'You. Do you always do this, invite drama into your life?'

'No. The opposite.'

'Not from where I sit.' Peter paused, as if trying to decide how far to push this. 'My dad's a bit of a psychologist. He's pretty good, has to be; plenty of lost souls end up crying on his shoulder. So he's good at figuring people out. He had me pinned once. He said I had a Jesus complex.'

'Ha! Like that fits!'

'No, he was right – sort of. Except in my case it was a Batman complex. I made this den up in the bell tower when I was about twelve.

'A Batcave in a bell tower?' Ali chuckled. 'That's a bit cute. Mostly sad.'

'Totally.' Peter laughed and shook his head, 'I'd sit for hours looking down at the village. They were my flock, waiting to be saved from super villains.'

'This is going somewhere?'

'Dad's good at reading people, that's all.'

'And?'

'He said some folk make everything into a drama. They need high energy noise around them, the more the better. They can focus on that instead of their real problems.'

'The man's a genius.' Ali tried to sound dismissive. She'd behaved like that as a kid, creating dramas that would bring her dad running. It was just attention-seeking, nothing else.

'Just an observation,' Peter handed her his phone. 'Here you go. Multiverse theory, wasn't it?'

'Yep.' She started thumbing in her first question.

'Figures. You act like you're from another planet.'

'Funny ... now let me do this. Ten minutes, all right?'

'If the data lasts that long ... and no texting your dad again!' He pulled his sketchpad from his pack and left Ali to her searching. He started drawing her, too engrossed in her research to notice.

'Damn!' A message popped up: Out of data. She glared at the phone, then tossed it back to Peter. 'I'd just got started.'

Peter checked the search history. 'You've been online for fifteen minutes.'

'I gave you a twenty!'

'I was racing Sonic way past midnight.'

'With my data!'

'My phone, so, what's all this for? School assignment?'

'No, this is about my mum. I found some stuff she wrote when she was my age. She was into the idea of other worlds.'

'Me too. Love science fiction.'

'Except multiverse theory isn't science fiction, it's an idea in fundamental physics; helps make the maths work, helps explain the missing dark matter.'

'Been there, read the books. It's all wardrobes and science fiction.'

'Everything's science fiction until it isn't. Space travel, black holes, laser beams, quantum computers.'

'That's shit logic. If all those old books became reality we'd all have flying cars and sexy robot servants by now.'

'Sexy robot servants?' Ali raised an eyebrow.

'You know what I mean.'

'No, and I'm not sure I want to.'

'Fair enough.' Peter closed his sketchpad. 'All I'm saying is that just because we can dream something up doesn't mean it gets created one day.'

'Because that would be God's job, right?'

'Exactly.' He laughed and closed his eyes, his brow creasing. 'So tell me if I've got this … scientists sit around doing maths to explain how the universe works, but then when the maths don't add up, they come up with another way for the universe to work, right?'

'Sort of.'

'So it's not real – it's just nerds pushing numbers round till they look nice.'

'Until they work, yes. Then everyone tries to pull it apart. Shake the hell out of the maths till it stops falling over. Like building a bridge out of matchsticks – there's a thousand ways to do it, but they all fall down when you shake the table. Then one day someone comes up with a solution, and the bridge stays up.'

'That's a crappy analogy.'

'A model with just one universe doesn't survive. But if you add in lots more universes – bingo! – the bridge stays up.'

'So, where are they?'

'Right here.' She waved at the woods. 'They're taking up the same space'.

'If they were here, I'd see them.'

'No you wouldn't. Our senses evolved for us to survive in this universe, to see and hear this one, not those others.'

'Is this seriously what geeks like your dad do? They get taxpayer money to come up with stupid ideas?'

'Nice job, huh? And I just scrolled a blog that says quantum fluctuations cause small bubble universes to pop into existence.'

'Too much.' Peter got up and stretched. 'That does my head in, I have enough trouble understanding *this* world, don't need more of them popping up.'

'Science is cool like that.' Ali pointed to Peter's sketchpad. 'Can I see?'

'I guess.' Peter handed it to her. Ali was impressed; he could really draw. He'd sketched her staring at the phone, her face a mask of concentration. She flipped the pages, looking at his other sketches, and laughed. It was all monsters, spaceships and leather clad girls with big guns and big breasts.

'Seriously?'

'Fantasy art, what can I say!'

'How can that girl even fire a gun with those things in the way?'

'Not the point.' Peter grabbed the pad back, 'I'll need more data if you want to use my phone again tomorrow.'

'I'll get some cash out.' Ali got up slowly; it was still hot and she didn't feel like going anywhere. 'Is there a cash machine in the village?'

'I thought you were grounded.'

'I am. But the place falls quiet after lunch. I reckon I could jog to the village and back before anyone notices. I've been going for long walks round the estate anyway and no one grills me when I get back.'

'Okay, it's your life. There's an ATM in the main street.'

'Great – and coffee?'

'A teashop, but it does coffee.'

'Good.' She paused. 'And I need another favour. I need you to come back tonight, about midnight if you can?'

'For what?' His face split into a huge grin. 'More biscuits?'

'I've found a treasure map.'

'You're kidding me!'

'Nope, for real. Someone buried something under a statue. But it's too heavy to move on my own.'

Peter punched the air. 'Yes! No one's asked me to be their muscle before. See, knew I was a superhero. Let's go shift it now.'

'No. It's in the orchard – too open. Potts or Waxstaff might come by. After dark's safer. Know where the orchard is?'

'Sure, every inch of the place – you don't grow up a kid in this village without jumping these walls and scouting the place.'

'Good, and bring a torch. I'm off for a siesta and some lucid dreaming.'

'Lucid what?'

'Tell you later, it's a bit weird.'

'There's a surprise.' Peter hoisted his backpack and headed off.

CHAPTER 18

DAY FOUR

MUSHROOM QUICHE

—————

*The shop seemed to be full of all manner of curious things,
but when she looked hard at any shelf, that shelf was always
quite empty.*

Ali made her way to the back of the main lawn, skirted the rhododendron bushes and climbed into the well. When she pushed up into the barn she could still smell disinfectant from her clean up. She adjusted the bed and the boxes till everything was how she remembered it from her first visit – except for the bright sunshine, but there was nothing she could do about that.

'Okay, let's do this.' She'd brought the novel, and lay back on the bed and started to read. Nothing happened. Damn! Ali felt a surge of disappointment and regretted drinking all the coffee earlier. 'I'm not giving up,' she announced to the barn, 'we'll do this tonight!'

Ali climbed from the well, and set off back to the house. As she crossed the lawn she saw her relatives finishing lunch on the patio. It was like watching a silent movie, her uncle making expansive gestures; her aunt shaking her head and laughing. Then, quite suddenly, Ali was overcome with a wave of sadness.

Frack! Where the hell had that come from? There was nothing sad about the scene, quite the opposite. She was watching a couple in love; still in love and laughing together after a long life of ups and downs. What was sad about that?

Realisation arrived like a hammer blow. The sadness wasn't for her. It was for her dad. He would never know this. He would never spend a lifetime with the woman he fell in love with. He would never grow old with her and share a lifetime of memories like the Greys, not even a lunch on a sunlit patio.

Ali ducked back into the trees and headed for the main gate. She needed a distraction from this, from smacking herself in the face with emotions she'd managed to stuff into good strong boxes years ago. Cash and coffee. If she was going to break the rules and duck out for some cash, now was a good time, while everyone took their after lunch nap.

There were no pavements on the street outside, but no traffic either, so Ali jogged down the centre of the road.

Five minutes later she was standing across from the village green. Hardly anyone was about. A church marked the centre, its walls flanked by scaffolding on two sides. Peter's church? The centre of the village was tiny: a cluster of shops, a few dozen cottages.

The ATM was set into the front wall of a bakery. She crossed to it, inserted her card, keyed in her request and watched the money spit out.

'Now, coffee!' The teashop was two stores along, and there was a sign in the window: 'Free Wi-Fi.' Not much use to her without her phone, but it might have a computer for older customers, like an internet café from the dark ages.

Ali went in. It was grotesquely pretty inside, everything pink and frilly, from the tablecloths to the net curtains.

Ali felt like she'd walked into a packet of mashmallows. But there was a computer. It looked as old as the net curtains and sat on a table in the far corner. The were no other customers and no one behind the polished counter, but Ali could hear dishes being stacked in a back kitchen.

'Hello,' she called. No response. There was a handbell on the counter, and a label taped beside it that read 'Ring Me.' Ali did.

'Coming!' A small woman bustled from the back room. It was Glass Eyes, the stranger from the other night. She saw Ali and smiled, her whole face lighting up, except for the glass eyes.

'Hello, you're the young lady staying up at the Greys?'

'Yes, that's me.' Ali tried not to stare, but it was hard, the woman was still wearing her bright red turban, the sequins sparkling as she moved. 'And you're Mrs King. You were gathering mushrooms the other night.'

'I was. What can I do for you? A pot of tea?'

'Coffee please, black. And can I go online with your computer?'

'It's a bit slow. You'll need to be patient.'

'Slow is fine. How much?'

'Free to customers.' The woman seemed to be looking straight at her, right into her eyes, it was freaky.

'Great. Make the coffee a double espresso, and maybe I'll have a biscuit.'

'Tea it is.'

'You don't have coffee?'

'Yes, but not for you. Keep it for when you need a big punch of adrenaline, that would be my advice.' Mrs King cocked her head, as if expecting a response. Ali didn't know what to say. Two women in as many hours giving her a hard time over coffee! How was that possible?

'Have you been talking to the housekeeper about me?'

'Yes dear, we're short of gossip in the village. Take a seat and fire up the computer; there's no password. I'll bring your tea and a slice of quiche.'

'I didn't ask for quiche.'

'No, but you need quiche. Asking and needing are very different. So quiche you shall have. I won't be a moment,' and with that she turned and bustled back out to the kitchen.

'Okay,' Ali whispered, 'that was weird.' She sat down at the computer and switched it on. Mrs King hadn't been exaggerating when she said it was slow; it was a pedal car on the information superhighway. Ali kept her search simple, looking for any references to a missing relative called Alice. There was nothing.

'Here we are.' Mrs King returned with a pot of tea and a slice of mushroom quiche. Both were delicious. Ali felt a warm glow spreading through her stomach. The cramps that had persisted since her lucid dream began to ease, melting like ice in the sun.

'Another slice?'

'Sure, love one. How much?'

'Free to you, since the mushrooms are from the manor house. So what are you looking up on the internet?'

'Homework assignment. Science.'

'What has this missing Alice person got to do with science?'

'Sorry?' Ali stared at the woman's glass eyes and felt the room begin to swim. 'How did you know that?'

'I was reading the screen, dear.' Mrs. King laughed and tapped one eye with a fingernail.

Tink, tink.

'Not my original colour and a little too big. I had a pair that were just the right size, but they rolled in the sockets, I seemed to be forever fascinated with my toes!'

'So what are they – camera gear? Some kind of cyber-tech?'

'Can you buy such things?'

'I don't think so, not yet.'

'Let me know when they are. Meanwhile I'm as blind as a bat, which is to say, not blind at all. I see perfectly well with my ears so long as I keep clicking. It's the bouncing that does it, all those sound waves pinging around the room.'

'Like sonar?'

'So I'm told. I click with my tongue and see the waves as they bounce off the walls and the furniture. No good outside, hopeless in fact.'

'You can't read a glass screen, even with sonar.'

'Correct. I was listening, bless the National Health Service, they pay for text recognition for the blind. Text-to-voice. You can even choose the voice! I have a bored young man with a speech impediment. But we get by.'

'You were eavesdropping?' Ali laughed. 'Do you have another monitor out the back?'

'I do. I have to keep entertained somehow. Have you tried the church records for your missing aunt?'

'Didn't think of that.'

'Births, marriages and deaths were all recorded in Parish registers. Come along, I have a key.' Without another word,

Mrs King opened the front door and left the café. Ali scrambled up and followed.

Following a blind woman who moved at speed and with no hesitation was unnerving. Ali's instinct was to help, to open doors or guide her by the elbow, but she could hardly keep up.

'Falling down, is it?' Ali asked as they went down the side of the church through a tunnel of scaffolding.

'Just the steeple. Getting old like me. Can't ring the bell till it's fixed. Hasn't been rung in years – there's a collection if you want to donate.'

'Not my thing.'

'What isn't? Charity, or renovation?'

'Churches.'

'Really? I rather like them.' She stopped at a side door and led Ali into a small vestry. 'I do the flowers every Sunday.'

'You can see flowers with your clicky-tongue sonar thing?'

'No, too soft and springy, no good for sound bouncing.' Mrs King held her hands out and wiggled her fingers like a magician. 'May I touch your face?'

'No.' Ali's refusal was like a slap. Given without thinking. She started to apologise, but Mrs King just laughed.

'Not offended. Who wants a creepy old woman feeling your face.'

'That's not what I meant.'

'Yes you did, and quite right too. I was rude to ask. The clicking gives me spaces and the big forms, but no detail. The fingers do that. Reach those down, would you?' She pointed to a set of books in the corner of the vestry. They were heavy. Ali set them on a table beneath the room's only window.

'They go back over three hundred years. But it's a small village, so most years there's only a page or two of entries – except for the war years of course.'

Ali leafed through the ledgers till she found the entries for the 1800s, then started finger scrolling down the lines of neat writing.

And there she was, Alice Caroll Grey, her existence revealed in a line of blue ink. There was a second reference … she was baptised the following year, but no marriage had been recorded. And no death. Ali thanked Mrs King and excused herself; she needed to get back. Needed to process this.

'Got to run. Thanks for the quiche.'

'You're welcome. Plenty more if you pop by again.'

'Okay, thanks.' Ali set off at a gentle pace, her mind whirling. There really had been a Great-aunt Alice. Born right here in this village. But there was no record of her death. Why had her relatives lied to her? Was it a guilty family secret? Had she been locked away in an institution and died there, a delusional girl dreaming of another world? Had she been killed and buried on the grounds, accused of being a witch and murdered by a fanatical priest?

Maybe Peter was right after all. She was manufacturing the whole thing. Stitching a drama together for the sheer noise of it, a distraction to keep her from doing the one thing she had been sent here to do – a spot of quiet introspection.

CHAPTER 19

DAY FOUR

A WHITE RABBIT

'How am I to get in?' asked Alice again. 'Are you to get in at all?'
said the Footman, 'that's the first question, you know.'

Ali went straight to the well and through to the barn. She had to try and have that dream again. There was plenty of time before dinner to have a siesta, and the jog had made her sleepy. So had the tea and the slice of quiche. And thanks to the weird Mrs King there was no coffee pumping through her system. The desire to wake up inside a lucid dream again had really got its claws in her. Was this what addiction felt like?

'Research,' she whispered to herself, 'that's all it is'. She grabbed the novel that she'd left on the dressing table and settled down on the bed.

One minute she was trying to focus on the book, the next she was in the bluebell meadow. The beauty of it was overwhelming. Ali always scoffed when friends posted about love;

about the intensity of their emotions when they were with someone special. Yet right now, waking up in this familiar dream, she felt it herself; she was where she longed to be.

'This is so awesome.' Ali remembered her dad's instruction about taking control of the dream by finding her hands. She lifted them up to her face and wiggled her fingers. Yes!

'Houston, we have control of the mission!' She dropped her hands and looked round at all the detail.

'The same place. Definitely the same place.' It was the meadow from her first lucid dream. There was the same warm sunlight angling down through the same stand of birch trees, the same carpet of bluebells. Everything exactly the same … until a large white rabbit stepped out from behind a tree.

'Shit!' Ali took a step back. 'Where did you spring from?'

'I might ask the same of you,' said the rabbit. Ali took another step back, then burst into laughter and applauded.

'Brilliant, you even talk! Of course you do. I've pulled you straight from the book. So where's the waistcoat?'

'No time for pleasantries,' said the rabbit in a high-pitched, slightly nasal voice, 'we need to leave right away.'

'All wrong,' said Ali, more to herself than to the rabbit.

'No, we quite definitely need to leave.'

'I mean *you* are all wrong. You have no waistcoat or pocket watch.'

'I stand chastised,' said the rabbit, 'I didn't know there was a dress code.' He looked at Ali's jeans, 'What are those absurd britches?'

Ali didn't reply, but began circling the rabbit as if judging a sculpture in a college art class. 'You're so well done; the detail's incredible.'

'Meaning?'

'Your fur. It's so realistic. I can see every hair …' She leaned in. 'You've even got bits of grass stuck in it. Why would I bother to add extra details, got to be a reason. Something to discuss in my paper.'

'Paper?'

'Science paper.'

'I'm sure this is making perfect sense to you,' said the rabbit. 'Shall I wait a short distance away while you finish your discourse?'

'Nope. So the question is: how can a figment of my imagination change its appearance? Maybe you're a blend of memories, I remember holding a rabbit at a petting zoo once.'

'Please, in your own time. It's not as if we're in dreadful danger or anything. Except that we are.'

'And if dreams are a projection of the subconscious – then how sad am I? Instead of conjuring up the hot guy in the hat, what do I dream up? A rabbit.'

'Reassuring to know I'm not your first choice of companion.'

'Where is he?'

'Who?'

'The man in the hat. The man I saw in my last dream.'

'Dream?'

'Yes.'

'Understandable, I'm told we all think that when we first arrive. Not that I can remember, but the Queen's scholars all agree upon it.'

'Not interested. Where's the hat man?'

'He waited for a while. A week or so, we all took turns. But not just us, others too. Word has spread. Which is why we have to go, right now.'

'A week or so?

'Correct.'

'Hah! Fancy that. I'm adding time dilation and relativity into the mix, Dad would be impressed. Okay, so how do I get back to the barn if I need to?'

'You can't. No one can get back, not safely anyway. Not without doing yourself a lot of damage.'

'Why?'

'We don't know. The scholars have been working on it for years. We were hoping you might know. Which is why the Queen wanted to see you the moment you came back. Now, if you'll follow me, she doesn't like to be kept waiting.'

'Tough!' Ali closed her eyes and wished herself awake. When she opened them again, the rabbit was still there.

'Okay, rabbit. Three options as I see it. One, this is a lucid dream, which is my best guess right now. Two, I'm losing it, and this is a delusion. Or three, this is real and I've stepped through into another bubble of space-time ...' She paused and snorted. 'Hah! Can you believe I even said that?

'Hard to say, since I understood nothing of that, except the part about you being mad. Based on my observations thus far, I think you have a point.'

'So, following good scientific process, I will wake myself up, proving that this is a lucid dream. Then, when I'm safely back in the barn, I'll try and go back to sleep, and dream all this up again, including you.'

'But you can't!' The rabbit shook its head and sighed. 'You're stuck here with the rest of us.'

'You reckon?' Ali grabbed the skin on one wrist and pinched.

'If you are quite done, please follow me.' The rabbit set off across the meadow.

Ali pinched herself again, as hard as she could. 'Ow! That hurt!' Nothing. Then she slapped her face. 'Shit, ouch!'

'For decency's sake, please stop.' The rabbit's agitation was growing.

'Shock or pain, which is it?' Ali slapped her face again.

'If it was that easy we would all be slapping ourselves silly to get out. Now come quickly, before any of the banished find you.'

Banished? That didn't sound good. Ali gave herself a massive slap to her face. It stung like crazy and made her eyes water. But rabbit and woodland were still there.

'Stupid, stupid child. Why not run full tilt into a tree and break your nose?'

'Yes ... yes, you're right!' Ali looked at the silver birch. If adrenalin was the key, then face-planting a tree should hurt enough.

'No! Please, no!' The rabbit took a step towards her. 'I was merely making a point, not a suggestion – big difference young lady.' Ali could feel herself starting to panic. If this wasn't a dream, if this was a real place, could she become trapped here like Hudson and the others?

'Sorry rabbit,' Ali lined herself up with the tree, 'in science, sometimes you have to conduct experiments on yourself.'

'Running into a tree is not an experiment, it's stupidity!'

'It can be both,' Ali ran at the tree. The impact sent her reeling backwards, and the next moment she was lying in the barn – a red-hot pain blazing through her forehead.

'Idiot,' she groaned.

CHAPTER 20

DAY FOUR

WHITE LIES

———————

*In another moment down went Alice, never once
considering how in the world she was to get out again.*

A trickle of blood started down the bridge of her nose; then
a wave of nausea overwhelmed her, followed by a searing
cramp, deep in her stomach. For a long while she couldn't
move. Eventually she forced herself to roll over onto her side,
curling up in a ball and hugging her knees. She fought the
urge to vomit till the pressure rose like a volcano – unstop-
pable – and she crawled to the stone sink and gave in. Wave
after wave of retching reduced her to a shaking mess and
she struggled to keep her grip on the edge of the sink. When
it was finally over, she collapsed to her knees, her stomach
bruised, her throat raw.

How long had it been? It was still light outside, but the
golden light of late afternoon. Ali slapped water on her face,

took a drink straight from the tap and staggered to the old mirror. She had a cut over one eye, blood had dried in tracks across her cheek, and her skin was the colour of chalk.

How was she going to explain this? One look and her aunt would call for a doctor. She'd be ordered to bed with Potts looking after her! Frack that. This was too important, whatever 'this' was. She needed time to make sense of everything; to write it up in her journal. Analyse it. But first, a bath!

Ali cleaned the barn as best she could, made it back to the house without bumping into anyone, and spent the next hour soaking in a hot bath. It helped to sooth the stomach cramps, but did nothing for her face. She wrapped herself in a towel, wiped steam from the bathroom mirror, and stared at the damage.

'Bloody hell, you look like a zombie!' Ali never wore make-up. She kept one stick of foundation to cover the occasional pimple, but she'd never tried using it on her whole face. It took a while to get it right, to get a little colour back without her face looking like a plate of dried porridge. There was no way to hide the cut, and she thought about skipping dinner, but that would only draw more attention to being sick. Better to shrug it off with a white lie.

'How did you get that gash?' Aunt Martha noticed the cut as soon as Ali joined them for dinner. 'It looks dreadful!'

A lifetime of confrontations at school had taught Ali that a lie worked best if it was just a few degrees from the truth.

'I had a fight with a tree. The tree won.' At the end of the table Waxstaff had stopped eating and was studying Ali intently. It was unnerving; the woman had her head cocked to one side again, and she was looking very smug.

'Canny buggers, trees,' Lord Grey said, pointing a fork at Ali. 'Never known a tree that wasn't out to get you.'

'Don't be silly, Bertie dear,' said his wife.

'I take offence.'

'Good.'

'I've had two clashes with trees,' he said, still waving his fork. 'Never came off on the winning side. No bounce in them.'

'On both occasions, you were thrown at the trees by that lunatic gypsy cob you insisted, against all advice, to keep in the stables.'

'Ah yes, Balzac. Now that was a horse.' Lord Grey nodded vigorously. 'Get some dinner inside you, my dear. Best cure for bruises is a full stomach.'

'Sure.' As Ali eyed the food she felt the nausea returning. She poured a glass of milk and spooned some dessert into a bowl: fruit and yogurt.

'Is that it?' snorted Potts. 'Must have been a good smack to the head to lose your appetite!'

'I must remember to thank the tree,' said Waxstaff. 'The grocery bill has taken a hammering.'

'So, this tree you fought,' Aunt Martha said, smiling at Ali, 'tell me about it.'

'Tripped on a fallen branch and faceplanted a pinus radiata.'

'Ha!' Lord Grey gave her a nod of approval. 'Know your enemy, excellent. Pinus radiata. Sounds like the devil tree itself.'

'It's a simple pine tree, Bertie. Ali was just being specific.' Martha gave her niece a huge smile. 'I used to know all the trees here. We should head down the driveway one evening and you can reacquaint me. How many would you know?'

'Quite a few. Dad made walks into a botanical quiz.' Ali drained her glass of milk, it was soothing on her raw throat. She poured a second.

'And you're still taking a close interest,' chuckled Lord Grey, pointing his fork at Ali's forehead.

'I'll steer clear of them from now on, I promise.'

'Very wise,' said Aunt Martha. 'So, enough of trees, tell me all about time.'

'Time? Sure, what about it?'

'I tried to follow your teacher's logic the other night, but I was left floundering.'

'Not surprising, my dear.' Lord Grey patted his wife's arm through its lace glove. 'The fellow was speaking complete tosh. All we need to know about time is that it's a fickle devil. It starts out slow when you're a child, positively drags along in your teens, then the damn thing breaks into a gallop and the years blink past. Finally, you get to our age and it slows back to a snail's pace. Am I right, Ali?'

'You are, Uncle Bertie. Time is relative to the observer.'

'Ridiculous,' sighed Nurse Potts, 'a minute is a minute whichever way you look at it.'

'And I'm sure your world is flat too,' said Ali, 'whichever way you look at it.'

'And what is that supposed to mean?'

'Please,' Lady Grey said, holding up a hand, 'no squabbling at my table. One thing I do know about time is that, while behaviour may have moved on in other houses, here in the manor I uphold the courtesies of a more elegant age.'

'Bravo!' Her husband tapped the table in gentle applause. 'Very well put.'

'Like the Mad Hatter's tea party,' said Ali, glancing round to check for any reaction. Only Waxstaff seemed to go on high alert. That was interesting.

'Sorry, dear,' said her aunt, 'you've lost me.'

'The Mad Hatter's tea party – in the Wonderland book

– I was reading that chapter today. Time stopped on teatime. But only in the meadow where they had the tea party.'

'If you say so,' said Lord Grey. 'Blowed if I can remember. Must be fifty years since I read that book.'

'The Hatter upset Old Father Time,' said Waxstaff, 'so Time punished him by stopping at teatime. Isn't that right Miss Alice?'

'Yes.' Ali was impressed, but tried not to show it. 'The scene's almost a metaphor for the edge of a gravity well, a place where time slows right down at the event horizon. Dodgson was a bit of a maths geek.'

'Dodgson?' asked Lord Grey. 'Who's that?'

'The writer,' said Ali.

'Ha! There you're wrong,' said Nurse Potts, delighted at catching Ali out. 'Everybody knows it was written by Lewis Carroll.'

Ali glanced up at the giant woman. 'Carroll was his pen name.'

'Is that right?' Potts glared back, her neck glowing red.

'Yes, Dodgson was into maths and metaphysics; he talks a lot about time.'

'That Red Queen character,' said her aunt, 'had to run really fast just to stand still.'

'Which makes no sense,' said Ali.

'It's not supposed to,' said Lord Grey. 'Surely that's the point. The whole thing's a lot of harmless nonsense.'

'I mean, it makes no sense that Dodgson is describing how gravity affects time. He wrote the book before Einstein was born, before anyone talked about gravity wells or relativity.'

'Yes ... well ...' Her uncle scratched at his beard. 'Put like that – bit of a puzzle.'

'Unless he was describing something he'd seen with his own eyes.'

'Like the Chinese,' said Lord Grey.

'Here we go,' said his wife, shaking her head, 'have you been following us at all?'

'Absolutely I have. Gunpowder, printing, telescopes.' He emphasised each example by tapping the table with the base of his fork. 'Clever chaps the Chinese, knew a heap of stuff long before we did.'

'And?'

'People stumble across things long before they get written up by scientific types. This Dodgson fellow probably had a weekend in the backwaters of Devon, somewhere so boring that time stood still; two days felt like a week. You don't need Einstein to explain things when you've got Devon.'

Back in the library, after supper, Ali stretched out on the bed and rubbed her stomach. The milk had soothed her throat, but her stomach still ached from the vomiting. And the bruise above her eye was starting to throb. She closed her eyes and did her best to recall the dream. Some of the details were fading, but most of it was still there.

'I talked to a rabbit!' She laughed, then clutched her stomach. Mustn't laugh, it hurt! She stared at the ceiling. 'How messed up is that?'

Dream rabbit or real rabbit? She wanted so much to believe her mum's notes, to believe that her aunt was missing in a parallel bubble of space-time.

And whether it be a dream world or a real place, she knew she had to go back. Without the cramps and the nausea. Which meant she had to discover the second thing her mum banged on about in her notes – the secret to safe passage. Was that the treasure her Great Aunt Alice had buried under the concrete frog?

CHAPTER 21

DAY FIVE

MUSHROOMS

———————

*'I could tell you my adventures from this morning,' said Alice a
little timidly, 'but it's no use going back to yesterday because
I was a different person then.'*

Midnight. Ali wanted to keep her meeting with Peter, but it
was hard climbing out of the window. Moving hurt. Breathing
hurt. Everything hurt. Peter was already in the orchard when
she arrived. He had a spade with him.

'What's that for?'

'You said it was a treasure hunt. I'm not digging with my
bare hands.'

'We just have to move a small statue.'

'If it was small, you wouldn't need my help. So part of it
must be buried.'

Ali didn't argue. Instead she started looking for the circle
of paving stones. It was a while before moonrise so she used

her penlight, walking back and forth, sweeping the ground with the narrow beam. 'Ah, there!'

She knelt down beside the stone frog and played her light around the base. Peter was right. The carving was just the top of a much larger block half-buried in the ground. Peter set to work with the spade and dug a shallow trench around the statue.

'Should be enough.' Peter dropped the spade and straightened up. 'What's under it – any bets?'

'No idea.'

'My guess? A love letter and cheap jewellery.' He put a foot on the statue and pushed. It took a few goes, with Ali joining in, until the frog toppled over.

A tin! The statue had been sitting on a second layer of paving stones, but there was a gap in them, right under the frog. In the gap was a small tin. Ali bent and picked it up, it was old and rusty but intact.

'Junk jewellery, I'll put money on it,' said Peter.

'How d'you figure that?'

'Some woman had a secret lover who went off to war. They had this little ceremony … buried a love token …'

'That is so …'

'Romantic?'

'… dumb.' Ali pulled on the lid. It broke right off, the rusty hinges tearing like paper. Inside was a folded note.

'Told you,' Peter laughed. 'A love letter.' Ali unfolded it carefully and shone her penlight over it. It was stained with rust and difficult to read, but there was writing on it. And what looked like a drawing.

'We need to clean it,' said Ali, 'without damaging it.'

'How?'

'Not sure, but some nerd online will. We'll have to buy stuff.'

'Like what?' Peter put the spade under the frog and tried to lever it back upright.

'Like basic kitchen stuff.' Ali bent and helped him push. 'Things like baking soda and lemon juice.'

'Baking soda and lemon juice?'

'Just for example.'

'Pretty specific examples.' They made one last effort and got the frog on its feet again. Ali sat down, her whole body shaking from the work. She felt like throwing up again.

'I played science games when I was a kid.' Ali folded the note and put it back in the rusty tin. 'Dad would leave secret messages lying around, notes written with invisible ink, made from stuff like lemon juice.'

'Lucky you.' Peter picked up the spade and began filling in the trench. 'All I got were piano lessons and sermons about STDs.' The moon was rising, brushing the orchard with white light. Peter glanced up, saw her face, and stopped digging.

'Holy crap, you look like shit.'

Next morning, Ali woke to birdsong and sunlight. She stretched her arms and sat up. She still felt bruised in the stomach, but pretty good. The clock on the mantel said it was an hour until breakfast, enough time to gather her thoughts and decide on her next move.

'Got to figure this out, Mum.' She'd stumbled on something far bigger than a family secret. Something her dad would give his scientific teeth for.

'Coffee! I need coffee!' There had to be some in the kitchen somewhere. Her uncle drank it every morning, so Waxstaff can't have ditched it.

Ali pulled on yesterday's T-shirt, and stopped. Woah! It stank. Whatever had made her sick had made her stink as well. She wrapped herself in a towel and went upstairs for another bath. She ran it hot, and kept on topping it up as she lay there, her muscles relaxing, her mind drifting.

'I have to be careful,' Ali muttered to herself three times; like a mantra, like a parent reminding a child to be on their best behaviour. Everything had been turned on its head. Two days ago she was scared of being bored here, now she was scared of being sent away. One wrong step and the secrets of this house could be taken away from her; like a birthday present she would never get to open.

She dried and put on fresh clothes, picked up the second of the Wonderland novels and went to the kitchen. Waxstaff was preparing breakfast. And coffee.

'Coffee! Yes! Can I have a mug?'

'And good morning to you,' said Waxstaff.

'Sorry, good morning, Miss Waxstaff. Could I help myself to a mug of your wonderful morning coffee? Please?'

'So it's Jane Austen again, is it? I'm not your mother, poison yourself with as much as you like. Can't really stop you, can I?'

'Gracious no, but all advice most terribly welcome.'

'Don't be irritating. You sound exactly like that other Alice girl.'

'What?'

'In your book.' Waxstaff pointed to Ali's novel. 'She talks gibberish.'

'Maybe all kids spoke like that back then.'

'Jump into one of those time holes you were on about, and see.'

'Gravity wells, not time holes. And you can't travel through them, they just bend space-time. In theory, anyway.'

Ali poured a coffee and took it to the patio. The tiles had soaked up the early sun. They were warm under her bare feet.

She settled into a wicker chair and started reading again – mostly her mother's notes.

There were dozens of references to 'safe passage.' One included a sketch of a figure sitting in the lotus position in front of a large mirror. Above it was the word 'IN'. Next to it was a sketch of a mushroom and the word 'OUT,' followed by a row of question marks.

Was that it? Sit in front of a mirror and go into some hippy trance to enter the other universe, then eat a few mushrooms to come back safely? Is that what weird scene with the Caterpillar is all about? The fictional Alice eats mushrooms to change size which lets her enter a beautiful garden. Is that what Dodgson is saying with the metaphor? Mushrooms open doors into enchanted worlds?

'All right, Mum, our aunt collected books on medicinal fungi, and that glass-eyed woman was wandering about collecting mushrooms under a full moon.'

Ali tried to recall what she'd seen. Her view through the keyhole had been limited, but while Potts had been taking care of Mrs King's injury, Waxstaff had been chopping mushrooms on the bench. Were all three women in on the secret? Was there a big stash of mushrooms somewhere?

Ali put the book down and went back to the kitchen for a refill. Waxstaff was heading down the hallway with a tray to set breakfast in the dining room.

'Okay, let's do this,' said Ali, putting her mug on the table. Waxstaff would be gone for a few minutes. Time for a quick nosey. She checked every cupboard. No sign of mushrooms. She opened the small pantry. No mushrooms. She went to close the pantry door and stopped.

'Interesting.'

There was a curved scratch on the floor of the pantry, a

perfect half circle starting in one back corner. A door? Was the whole back wall of the cupboard a door? She grabbed the iron bracket of one shelf and pulled. The wall, complete with its shelves and jars, swung open. Behind was a second pantry.

'Mushroom city!' Ali scanned the small room. Mushrooms were hanging in bundles like dried flowers and pickled in glass jars. Enough mushrooms to feed an army. Or to protect them.

'And she needs to get out of that chair.' Potts' voice.

Crap! Ali stepped out into the main pantry and pulled the secret door closed behind her.

'She can be the judge of that.' Waxstaff's voice. The women were coming down the hall. Ali scanned the shelves for a food alibi, some snack she could pretend to be looking for, and grabbed a jar just as Waxstaff stepped in to the kitchen.

'What are you doing in my pantry?' asked Waxstaff

'Hungry. Thought I'd make a sandwich.'

'With those?' Potts frowned at the jar Ali was holding.

'Yes,' Ali held it up. Raw fish stared back at her, their grey bodies pressed against the glass like a bunch of fingers. 'Pickled herring. Yum.'

'Breakfast is almost ready.' Waxstaff folded her arms, watching as Ali went on with her pantomime – unscrewing the jar and trying hard not to flinch from the disgusting smell.

'Just needed a little something,' she tried to breathe through her mouth as she sliced the grey bodies and lay them to rest like cadavers on a slice of bread.

'Must be a family thing,' said Waxstaff. 'The only person who eats those revolting things is his Lordship. Defies logic. Nothing but oil and salt.'

'Each to their own,' Ali said, covering the fish with a second slice of bread. 'Same with mushrooms, I guess.' She glanced up as she said it.

'Mushrooms?' said Waxstaff. 'How are fish like mushrooms?'

'Sounds like a riddle,' Ali cut the sandwich and put it on a plate, 'how are fish like mushrooms? Bit like the raven and writing desk. Mushrooms are like pickled fish because some people can't stand them and others love them.'

'And you?'

'Mushrooms? Love them. Any left?' Ali locked eyes with the housekeeper, holding her gaze; a direct challenge.

'Left?'

'From the other night. You were chopping them up, the ones the blind woman collected. Any left?'

'Plenty, they're for a casserole' – Waxstaff pointed to the oven – 'if you have an appetite left.' She gestured to the sandwich.

'I'm surprised you can eat anything at all,' said Potts. 'You should be in bed with an aspirin. You look as grey as the herring. Do you have a fever?'

'Upset tummy that's all. I threw up last night.'

'Threw up?' said Potts. 'Not pregnant are you?'

'What?!'

'Throwing up, and now this …' she pointed at the sandwich, 'food cravings.'

'No!' Ali took her sandwich and marched out of the kitchen. In the library she put it on the desk and stared at it.

'What the hell do I do with you now? Not eat you, that's for shit sure.' Instead, she climbed through the window and gave the sandwich a decent burial out of sight of the house.

CHAPTER 22

DAY FIVE

OBSESSION

She sat on, with closed eyes, and half believed herself
in Wonderland, though she knew she had but to open
them again, and all would change to dull reality.

'I like the make-up. Very fetching.' Lord Grey noticed the thick layer of foundation the moment Ali walked in. After burying the fish she'd gone up to the bathroom to bury her white face as well, with more foundation. If Potts had noticed, then Aunt Martha would too.

'Fetching?'

'Yes, you know,' he waved the air as if the gesture explained everything.

'Not really.' Ali sat down and poured a glass of orange juice. 'But since I'm good at crosswords I can work it out. I think you mean it as a compliment.'

'Absolutely I do.'

Aunt Martha shook her head and smiled at her niece. Ali grinned back, two women on the same page.

'Thank you, Uncle Bertie, I know it can mean retrieving, like a dog fetching a stick. But how does it describe girls? Fetching compliments, perhaps? Or maybe fetching a good price at market?'

'Hardly.'

'Oh!' Ali put on a crushed expression. 'You mean you don't think I'd fetch a good price?'

'No, no! Quite the reverse. You would – a king's ransom.'

'She's teasing you, Bertie,' said Lady Grey. 'Alice knows perfectly well what the expression means. She simply wonders why you would choose to use it, with all its gender baggage.' She grinned up at Ali. 'Am I right?'

'Completely right. The compliment was grading me like a commodity.'

'Really?' Lord Grey beamed round the table. 'So it was an elegant insult?'

'Yes.'

'Bully for me! Thought it was a dying art, but seems I can still touch the odd nerve.' He gave Ali a wink and they settled down to breakfast and the crossword. Fifteen minutes later Lord Grey slapped the table; they'd completed it together in under fifteen minutes.

'That must be some kind of record,' he said. 'Haven't even started my toast and marmalade.'

Aunt Martha made a show of applause by tapping one finger on the table. Then she frowned at Ali. 'What's wrong with your neck?'

'My neck?'

'It's white. I noticed as you leant forward. Are you wearing make-up?'

'Just a little foundation.'

'Whatever for? I thought you despised all that nonsense.'

'Like you, my dear,' her husband said, patting her slender, gloved arm, 'no need for a paint job. Au naturel at its best.'

'Pickled herrings,' said Potts.

'Where?' asked Lord Grey.

'The white face. Your niece helped herself to a pickled herring sandwich, and last night she threw up.' Potts shook her head. 'You don't have to be a nurse to know what that means.'

'Thanks for sharing,' snapped Ali. She went to launch a counterattack, then stopped when she saw the look on her aunt's face.

'I'm not pregnant, Aunt Martha. I just got sick yesterday.'

'Vomiting?' whispered her Aunt.

'Yes.'

'And stomach cramps?' Aunt Martha's eyes locked onto Ali's, demanding her to be honest.

'Yes,' was all Ali could think to say.

'Stop it, child, please stop it.'

'Stop it? Stop what? I don't understand.'

'Don't insult me, you understand perfectly well, and I implore you to stop. Whatever you think is happening, whatever odd satisfaction these experiments are bringing. I ask you to stop before they take a terrible toll on all of us.'

Ali cut free of her aunt's gaze and looked around at the others. Her uncle and Potts looked confused. Waxstaff was watching with a cold intensity.

'Are we talking boys?' asked Lord Grey.

'No!' Ali and her aunt replied in chorus.

'Look, Aunty, can we talk about this later – privately?'

'Yes, I think we should.'

'I don't understand,' said Lord Grey. 'All this fuss over pickled herring?'

Everyone fell silent and Ali focused on her breakfast. What did her aunt mean by that little outburst? Did she know about the dreams?

'This evening,' said Lady Grey, as if tracking Ali's thoughts, 'we'll sit together and have a little heart to heart. Until then, please do as I ask.'

Ali didn't. As soon as breakfast was over she went to the barn and lay on the bed. She knew this whole thing was becoming an obsession, but she had to know for sure, was Wonderland real or a vivid type of dream.

She lay still for almost an hour. Nothing happened. The barn was too hot and too bright. She was ready to give up when she heard footsteps outside.

'Shit!' she scanned the room. Everything looked normal, so long as no one searched the boxes or noticed how everything had been moved about six feet. She grabbed her book and rolled under the bed as a key turned in the lock.

'Spooks me out.' It was Potts' voice.

'Ha! Big thing like you.' Waxstaff's voice. Ali heard her own breath and pressed her mouth into the crook of her arm, the fabric of her shirt muffling her breathing.

'Why in here, of all places?' Potts again.

'She didn't say, but she was very precise. And what Lady Grey wants, Lady Grey gets. And it has to be tonight, midnight precisely.'

'Why midnight?'

'Who knows? A sense of melodrama perhaps.'

Ali heard them approach the bed. She was concealed by the dust sheet which hung to the ground, but what if they had come to clean? What if they lifted the sheet?

'And why tonight?'

'She didn't tell me.'

'Guesses?'

'I never guess, Potts. I plan. Guessing is for idiots and gamblers.'

'All right, I'll wheel her in like you say, then bugger off. Has she invited the niece along?'

'No!' Waxstaff almost barked her reply.

'Just asking – keep your wig on! She's a spoilt little bitch, that one, quoting her science at me. Like to take her across my knee and teach her some manners.'

'Just carry on biting your tongue. We have bigger fish to fry. Can I leave you to set the chairs up in here for this evening?'

'I'll do it before my brandy.'

'Best you do,' said Waxstaff. Then the women left the barn and locked the door. Ali crawled out and crossed over to the window.

'I'll figure you out,' she whispered as she watched them set off across the orchard. 'Whatever scam you're up to, I'll figure it out.'

Half an hour later Ali was lying in the shade of the giant cedar, watching the house. She needed both women to be out at the same time. The moment came soon enough. Waxstaff emerged to pick vegetables from the garden just as Potts set off down the driveway pushing Lady Grey in her wheelchair.

'Perfect!' Ali went back inside through the library window, scooted to the kitchen, found the large ring of keys, and raced up the stairs. Whatever the two women were up to, there had to be clues lying about in their personal stuff.

Both doors were locked, no surprise there. One by one she tried the keys. None of them worked. Frack! She would have to climb in through their windows like a real spy. The next room was a bathroom with large windows. Ali opened one and peered out along the wall. Strands of ivy were everywhere, the tendrils creeping over each other, thick as ropes. Below the window a line of bricks stuck out slightly, an ornamental feature that circled the house creating a narrow ledge about two inches deep.

Ali looked down and immediately pulled her head in. Potts and Lady Grey had reached the end of the driveway and would turn back soon.

Later, Ali promised herself. And anyway, it was almost time for her next meeting with Peter.

CHAPTER 23

DAY FIVE

SECOND OPINION

——————

The Red Queen shook her head, 'You may call it nonsense,
but I've heard nonsense, compared with which THAT would
be as sensible as a dictionary!'

Peter wasn't there. Ali waited half an hour and was getting set to leave when he came sprinting down the path.

'You're late.'

'Nice to see you too.' He pulled a plastic bag from his pack. 'Baking soda, for cleaning your map. Pour heaps on the paper, completely cover it, and leave it for a few hours.'

'Thanks,' Ali reached out to take it. Peter pulled it back.

'You'll include me, right?' He was panting, still catching his breath. 'I mean, you'll keep me in the loop when you've cleaned it.'

'Maybe.'

'I'm serious.' He swung the plastic bag into her hands,

dropped his pack and slumped down on the grass. 'Only fair. You've pulled me into this – whatever this is – so we should figure it out together, starting now. Sit down.'

'Please.'

'Sit down, please. And no face punching.' They sat and looked at each other for a moment, both waiting. Ali tried to figure him out, or at least how she felt about him. She wanted to trust him, and he'd been okay so far, but everyone had an angle. What was his?

'What?' Peter shook his head and grinned at her.

'Nothing. Not used to sharing, that's all. Trust issues.'

'Sad life, got to dive in sometimes. Like me, getting myself involved with a complete stranger who's causing me and my dad a load of grief.'

'Your dad?'

'Those two suits that came to school? They also came to my house. They were at the kitchen table giving my dad the third degree.'

'Why?'

'My phone's in his name coz the church has a discount scheme – ten percent off all kinds of stuff.'

'You're scamming the church?'

'Dad gets a shit salary, so we save where we can. There, one secret revealed. Taking a risk trusting you with that one.'

'Sure,' Ali laughed. Maybe he was okay. Maybe.

'The suits were grilling him about my search history; my interest in the multiverse. Which means they're not just tracking my calls, they've fully hacked my phone. Is that even legal?'

'Doubt it. Hope your dad told them to piss off?'

'He lectured them on privacy and Big Brother and asked for some ID. They wouldn't give any, so he called the cops and they buggered off. He wants to know what I'm mixed up in, who I lent the phone to.'

'And you told him what?'

'Nothing to tell. You like science and punching people.'

'That's pretty much me.'

'Is your dad working on this multiverse research?'

'Not directly. He's into gravity waves.'

'So who are those guys?' Peter stretched and lay back. He folded one arm behind his head as a pillow, enough that he could watch Ali over the bridge of his nose. 'What's really going on here? Has to be big to get government agency types all worked up.'

'Can't tell you because I don't know. Not yet,' Ali paused, unsure how much to say, 'I have an idea but it's too mad to share, you'd treat me like I'm an escapee from some asylum.'

'Like I don't already?'

'Thanks.'

'You're not Little Miss Normal. So what have you got to lose?'

'Self-respect. Even I think my theory is completely nuts. And it's not just that, and it's not just a trust issue ... I don't want the idea shot down in flames.'

'But that's your famous scientific process, isn't it?'

'Yes, when it's ready. This one's only half-baked.'

'Try me.'

'Okay.' She sat forward and hugged her knees. 'You really want me to pull you into my madness?'

'Yes.' He paused. 'So long as I can be honest with you – tell you exactly what I think of it.'

'All right.' Ali put her face onto her knees for a moment, unsure how best to explain it, how to package it. There wasn't a best way. 'I think there's a bubble of space-time bumping up against ours, right here in the old barn. That's where it touches our universe – there's a door.'

'A door?'

'Yes, sort of. A point of transition where they touch each other.'

'Oka-a-ay,' Peter studied her face for long time. 'You're not taking the piss out of me, are you?'

'No.'

'What's it look like, this door?'

'You can't see it. It's a location I think.'

'If you can't see it, how d'you know it's there?'

'By accident. I fell asleep and woke up on the other side.'

Peter studied her face a moment longer, then dropped his head back onto the grass and stared up at the canopy of leaves.

'I said you wouldn't believe me.' Ali sighed, angry with herself.

Peter stood up, looking disappointed. 'So you don't want to tell me what's really going on?'

'I just did.'

'Okay, message received.' He picked up his bag and started walking off. 'I'll keep out of your way.'

'This is exactly why I didn't tell you – because I know it sounds so fracking stupid. I didn't want you to walk out on me.'

'Want to know what I think?' Peter stopped and turned back to her. 'Like, do you *really* want to know? Because I can give you both barrels.'

'Yes. But first I have to tell you the rest of it. Then you can rip into me, honest feedback, no holding back.'

'Okay, but total honesty, all right? No bullshit.'

'No bullshit. Just truth.' She patted the grass beside her. Peter dropped his bag and sat down, closer this time, right in front on her, his legs crossed, his hands in his lap, his eyes fixed on hers.

'I'll know if you're lying.'

'Good. The first time I went through, I thought it was a dream. I met a bunch of weird characters. They were from a book I'd been reading just before I fell asleep, so they had to be in a dream, right?'

'No argument from me.'

'When I woke up, I was sick as a dog, vomiting my guts out.'

'You looked like total shit the next day, I remember. Just like last night … so you did it again, right, whatever it was?'

'Yes …' She paused, trying to gauge Peter's reaction, but he had his poker face on. 'I had found a bunch of notes written by a relative, and I think she used to go back and forth without getting sick. She found a secret recipe, some antidote or drug she could take.'

'Still listening.'

'Believe me so far?'

'You're not lying.'

'Same difference.'

'No it's not. So give me the rest.'

'My relative – an old aunt from way back – thought people got trapped over there. They stumble though and slowly lose their memories of this life. She was helping them.'

'Like the Hudson bloke?'

'Yes, she was finding out who they really are. And then something went wrong; she got scared. She went through one last time and never came back. But first she hid the secret for going there and back. I think it's the note we dug up last night.' She stopped and looked at him.

'All done?'

'Done.' Ali sat back. Peter's poker face was gone. Now he

looked worried, like he was figuring out how to break bad news. 'Let me say it for you,' said Ali, 'you think I've gone nuts.'

'No, not nuts. I know you're super smart and a science nerd. Which means you're hard-out rational, so I'm going to throw rational back at you. And then you can tell me I'm wrong.'

Ali didn't reply, she just nodded, and realised she was scared. Not because she didn't trust him. But because she did. Peter stared down at the ground for a moment, as if debating exactly how honest he should be.

'Here's what I see, just the facts. I see a very cool, very smart person with some big anger management thing going on. She's been given home detention, or whatever it's called. And I see two staff who've been hired to keep an eye on her, one of them is a nurse to make sure she stays safe. Maybe she even gives her meds for the anger thing, sedatives. And that's all it takes to explain everything you just told me. I don't think you're lying. I think you're trying to make sense of what's happening to you. You don't need fancy doors into other worlds to explain hallucinations and feeling like shit and vomiting. But you'll need to tell them so they can figure your meds out, stop the side effects.'

'Good.' Ali nodded slowly. She was impressed. That was very clinical and very brutal. 'Very logical ... except it doesn't explain the guys in suits.'

'Yes it does, but don't make me go there.'

'Go there. Honest feedback, we said.'

'Okay, but you can't punch me in the face for this.'

'No promises.'

'It's ugly.'

'Just frackin' tell me!' Ali almost kicked him, then laughed. 'And remember ... I'm dangerous, I have anger issues and I'm on drugs.'

'Well … you're the daughter of an important government science guy, so it makes sense that there are people keeping you safe; people keeping tabs on strangers like me who bump into you while you're in recovery.'

'Recovery!'

'Just a word. But yes. I think this story you hang on to about your dad being down in some top-secret underground research lab having no contact with the outside world is part of some protective delusion thing.'

'Okay, you can stop there.'

'No. You wanted honest feedback and I'm giving it. Nowhere can be that isolated, not with modern tech. Which means it's a story you've made up to keep yourself happy because the truth is too painful.'

'Frack you.' Ali swallowed and tried to hold his gaze.

'You said you wanted both barrels – you want me to hold back now? Want me to lie to you like everyone else seems to be doing?'

'No.'

'Okay, here it is. Dad's a busy man, too busy for his little girl.' Peter kept his eyes glued to hers. 'You talk about him like he's some kind of best mate.'

'He is.'

'Feels like wishful thinking to me, part of a nice little delusion.' He stopped and looked away, sensing he'd gone a step too far. 'Tell me I'm wrong, Ali, tell me that doesn't fit the facts a lot better than your fantasy story.'

'Wish I could,' she said, her voice almost a whisper.

'Sorry, that all came out too harsh.'

'No. It came out honest. If I was you, I'd think the same. Except for all the notes and maps and my missing aunt. I didn't write those. She was investigating this long before I was born.'

'All families have a crazy in their cupboard. One summer your aunt gets bored and turns a kids' book into a game, complete with missing people and treasure maps.'

'You're good at this.' Ali let out a long breath and didn't try to argue. Peter's version made more sense than talking rabbits.

'No face punch?'

'No.' She managed a laugh. But it was hollow. If this was all in her head, if it was one big complicated delusion she was constructing, how would she know? How could she step outside the delusion, detach herself and see it for what it was? 'Thanks.' She reached forward and gave him an awkward sitting hug.

'I think your family's doing their best trying to keep you safe.'

'From?'

'From yourself.'

CHAPTER 24

DAY FIVE

TREASURE TROVE

———————

Alice explained that she had lost her way.
'I don't know what you mean by your way,' said the Queen:
'all the ways about here belong to me.'

Back in the library, Ali started cleaning the second map and tried not to dwell on Peter's opinion. Which was impossible. He had nailed it; packaged up the delusion scenario perfectly; wrapped it in string and put a bow on it. Except that he was wrong, it was that simple, and she would prove it – to him and to herself. And to her dad when he showed up.

She spread the stained note out on the desk and poured the contents of the plastic bag over it, a small mountain of baking soda.

'Now – sleep!' She pulled the heavy drapes against the sunshine and dropped on the bed. She was exhausted, and needed to bank some sleep if she was going to stay up half the night spying on Waxstaff in the barn.

Ali slept the whole afternoon. She couldn't believe it! She stretched out, testing her body. Her stomach still hurt from all the vomiting, but her muscles didn't ache and the sweaty fever had gone. Good sleep! The drapes were pulled against the sun, but over at the desk a thin slice leaked through, falling in a tight beam across the small mountain of baking soda. She went over and tapped the powder off the note.

'Well look at you,' she said, taking the note over to the window and pulling open the drapes, 'good old kitchen science does it again.'

The brown stains had gone. There were still smudges, but the clean-up had been successful. The note was another sketch map of London landmarks. Whatever had been hidden was lying under a building depicted as Westminster Abbey. The abbey had a horse drawn at one corner.

'Crap!' This was an outbuilding that no longer existed. A set of stables had stood near the brick wall bordering the orchard. Now the area was a sprawling patch of nettles and wild grasses.

Ali looked more closely at the map. Something was wrong, it was getting lighter, even the sketches were beginning to fade.

'Crap, I overdid it!' She raced to the kitchen and turned on the tap, soaking the map to stop the chemical reaction. It didn't work. Two minutes later she was staring at a small handful of paper soup.

'Okay, so we do it the hard way.'

Ali collected a spade from the potting shed and set to work. An hour later she gave up, there were no signs of a stable floor beneath the weeds and nettles, no paving stones or wooden piles.

'What are you doing,' Waxstaff was ten yards away and closing.

'A project.' Ali had prepped an explanation. 'There used to be a building here.'

'So I understand.' She looked down at the spade, and back up at Ali's sweating face. 'And you plan to rebuild it, do you?'

'No.' Ali silently applauded the woman's response. Good one, Waxstaff. 'Just curious though – this spot's been left all in nettles, so I wanted to know why; now I do. Ground's too hard. It's a crappy area for growing anything.'

'On the contrary, it's the perfect soil for a wilderness garden. Which is why it was established as such twenty years ago by Lady Grey. There's a thriving ecology of native plants in here. Except where a brainless vandal has smashed holes in it.'

'Oh!' Ali looked around, seeing the ground with fresh eyes. 'I'm an idiot!'

'We agree on something,' said Waxstaff. 'I suggest you put it back as best you can before your aunt sees it.' She turned to leave, saying, 'Dinner's in forty minutes – it's mushroom casserole. I imagine you'll have a good appetite after all this.'

Cleaning up the damage left Ali with no time for a bath before dinner. She scrubbed her face and hands, changed her top and checked her face. Some of her colour had returned – more pale, less zombie – and she decided to leave it. No foundation.

Dinner followed its usual pattern: a general catch-up on the day's events, then a slow descent into what Lady Grey called 'barrack humour', as her husband recounted an adventure he'd had in the Sudan as a young officer.

'Bertie, must I remind you that you're the only male at the table. You seem to forget your audience.'

'Not at all my dear. To edit myself because of the gender of the audience would be unthinkable; our niece would certainly take me to task. Right, Alice?'

'Don't answer that,' said Lady Grey. 'He's setting some sort of trap. He's still smarting from the other day when he called you fetching.'

'All right, my dear. Understood. No more barrack tales at the dinner table; they join the ranks of the unspoken, along with politics and religion; and death, of course. Especially tonight.'

'Tonight?' Ali looked up. Her uncle looked like a deer in the headlights and turned to his wife for help.

'He means there should be no chitchat about death while you're here," Lady Grey explained. 'At our age, it becomes something of an obsession, after all. It is the elephant in the room.'

'In the waiting room,' laughed Lord Grey.

'Don't avoid it on my account,' said Ali.

'Then avoid it on mine,' grumbled Potts. 'Far nicer things to talk about.'

'I agree.' Waxstaff looked up from her meal and grinned at Ali. 'What about gardening? Everybody loves a spot of gardening.'

'Or cricket,' said Lord Grey.

'Then we're back to death,' said Potts, 'stupid game bores me to death.'

'Well said.' Aunt Martha laughed and tapped the table. 'Then death it is. Tell me, Alice, how does your generation view the topic?'

'Depends. Death of the planet is the big one, we all talk about that. Mass extinction by neglect. Suicide's a problem too. Lot of chatrooms on that, some kids get obsessed about it, like suicide's a romantic thing.'

'And what's your view?'

'Mine? My view on death?'

'Yes. Do you think we might have a spirit,' Aunt Martha tapped her husband's glass of whisky, 'and I don't mean this tipple, but some essence of ourselves that lives on after the body fails?'

'Mine's failed already,' joked her husband, lifting his glass and toasting Ali across the table, 'and you don't have to answer since it's clear my wife and I are on the brink of finding out very soon. If I go first, I shall manifest the case for the affirmative by waving all the curtains and rattling my chains.'

'I'm sure you will, my dear. But I would still like to know what our great-niece thinks about such matters.' And with that, she put down her knife and fork, folded her hands in her lap and smiled. Simple gestures, yet they commanded attention; nothing left but the question, which hung above the table and wasn't going away.

Ali returned the smile. How did her aunt do this? A frail old woman taking total control of a room, it was impressive. And a little scary.

'What do I think about death and ghosts and souls?'

'Precisely.'

'I think … it would be nice to imagine Mum was still alive in some way.'

'Yes,' Lady Grey nodded, 'that would be nice, wouldn't it?'

'And I think that if I wanted it enough, I could force myself to imagine it. So I get why people want churches and nice stories to make them feel okay about all that. But it would be in my head. Wanting something doesn't make it real. So I'll stick with science, and right now, there's no evidence for it.'

'But science has to remain open-minded, yes?'

'Sure, that's the whole point of science. Everything's a theory, everything has to be challenged.'

'Well put!' Lady Grey beamed at the others. 'Everything has to be challenged.' Ali helped herself to more casserole and wondered where her aunt was going with all this. She was making a point. But what point?

'And you, Alice.' Her aunt picked up her knife and fork. 'You challenge, correct? You approach everything with a robust confrontation of the facts.'

'I try to,' Ali said, suddenly aware that everyone round the table was on high alert. Was Peter right? Was this all about her? About her mother's death.

I think your family's doing their best to keep you safe from yourself. Is that what this dinner was all about – a therapy session? Trauma counselling?

'This is boring,' said Lord Grey, 'and not the least bit funny. I want funny with my meal, thank you very much,' and he started telling a joke which ran out of steam as he searched the ceiling for the punchline.

The conversation slowed further as they started on the cheese and biscuits.

'No more blue cheese, Bertie – you know what it does to your sleep.'

'I do not; always too busy snoring.' He winked across the table at Ali who grinned back. Martha smiled too and shook her head.

'Excuse him, dear, he so loves an audience. But it brings out the worst in him and he rather over-performs.'

'Yes, but I see his purpose in it,' said Ali, borrowing from her aunt's stately phrasing and enjoying it. The more controlled and ladylike she behaved, the more it seemed to piss off Potts and Waxstaff.

'And what might that be? I've lived with his nonsense all these years and fail to see any purpose in it whatsoever. Poppycock is what it is.'

'He's jabbing our dinner guests.' Ali smiled down the table at Potts and Waxstaff.

'Jabbing?' Potts didn't seem to understand the term.

'Yes, jabbing, you know: elbowing, jab-jab, needle-needle.'

'Ahhh, yes! Could well be needling,' said Lord Grey, 'yes, it forces everyone at the table to engage. Is that what I'm doing, Alice?'

'I believe it is, Uncle Bertie.' Alice looked directly at Miss Potts, challenging her to respond.

She did. 'Lord Grey, my apologies, but if the price of sitting here for dinner is to be your sparring partner, I would rather take my meals in the kitchen.'

'Ha! There you go ... finally! Nurse Potts engages in the gentle arts. You see, Martha, Ali has the measure of me. I am merely sparring.'

'You have certainly been intolerably rude at this table over the years in the name of entertainment.'

'Thank you my dear.'

'It was not a compliment.'

'It most certainly was,' Lord Grey stabbed a wedge of blue cheese with a fork and waved it around like a prop. 'The world's a stage, etcetera, and the dinner table plays its many parts.'

'Not our table. And cheese is taken with the knife. Must you lose your manners with your marbles?'

'I believe I must.' With a theatrical flourish, Lord Grey popped the wedge of cheese in his mouth.

'That cheese will keep you awake all night,' said Lady Grey.

'What of it? If I must stay up tonight, I might as well do it properly, with port and cheese.' His remark was met with complete silence. It was a moment before Lord Grey realised his mistake. Ali looked around the table. The easy, relaxed atmosphere had completely evaporated. So something else *was* going on. Peter was wrong; all the talk about death wasn't for her. This was about the barn. This was about her aunt's plans for that night.

Ali wanted to slap the table in triumph. It was time to shake the tree. 'Why must you stay up tonight, Uncle Bertie?' Ali made the question sound offhand and innocent. Lord Grey didn't reply, merely glanced at his wife for support.

'Let me guess ...' Ali pushed on, 'it's some full moon thing ... like witches dancing among the trees ... can I come?'

'Of course you can,' her uncle said, looking relieved, 'and bring the ketchup. We haven't used real blood for years.'

Ali was watching Aunt Martha. The woman seemed to be winding up like a spring, on the verge of bursting into tears.

'Sorry, Uncle, you can fetch your own ketchup. Witches are no longer in the service of wizards – we're independent professionals,' Ali said, beaming a big, innocent smile at Waxstaff and Potts, 'aren't we, ladies?'

'I am,' said Potts. 'Exactly what you're capable of is a mystery, aside from getting into fights and putting on airs with all your Jane Austen talk.'

'I'm sure you're right, Miss Potts,' replied Ali. 'But then I'm not exactly sure what your professional qualifications are.'

'That's enough.' Lady Grey almost barked at her.

'Just putting it out there, Aunt Martha. You've opened your house to these two *professionals*,' Ali managed to make the term sound like an insult, 'and I'm sure you got all the right references. Can't be too careful these days.'

'Alice!' Lady Grey's rebuke was almost an explosion.

'Just saying.'

'Everyone will remember their manners at my table.'

'Sorry.'

'No, you are not! That much is plain. It's hardly surprising you get thrown out of one school after another if this is how you conduct yourself.'

'I was—'

'Enough! You are here because you are family, and because life caused you a grievous injury, one that has affected you very deeply. That is the way of life, and you must deal with it! None of us is without scars, but they are not an excuse for poor behaviour. In your case it should be the reverse. It should be a reason for exemplary behaviour. You are all that is left of your dear mother; her one legacy on this wretched planet. Never say you are sorry unless you mean it, and always make that apology to her – to the memory of your sweet mother!'

Ali sat in shocked silence; all bravado gone. She couldn't think what to say or do. She waited for the red cloud of rage to come to her rescue, to take control and cut an escape path. It didn't. Instead she felt tears welling up. She blinked to push them back and saw Potts gloating at her.

'Excuse me.' Ali got up from the table and tried not to run from the room. She made it to the library and collapsed on the bed. The tears came, but no rage. This was a new place. This was shock.

CHAPTER 25

DAY FIVE

A BARN DANCE

———————

*'You ought to be ashamed of yourself,' said Alice, 'a girl like
you to go on crying in this way! Stop this moment, I tell you!'*

The tears streamed for ten minutes or more; silent tears.
Ali lay very still, her mind spinning with long-forgotten
memories of her mother. Happy moments and sad ones, flash-
backs to tantrums and fights, to the screaming and swearing
she'd inflicted on her father.

She lay like a statue, staring up at the ceiling, watching
the tapestry of memories freewheeling behind her eyes. And
then, all of a sudden, it felt as if they belonged to someone
else; to a small child she had known long ago.

'What the hell was that about?' Ali sat up and wondered
what to do next? Her aunt had made it very clear she wanted
a chat with Ali later. And Ali wanted it too, a chance to be
alone with Aunt Martha - no Potts - a chance to ask her aunt

a thousand questions. So she changed into her pyjamas and went to find her. Lady Grey was in the drawing room. She was alone, clearly waiting for Ali. She'd parked herself by the open window and was looking out at the night sky.

'Come and sit with me.' She didn't turn, but simply gestured with a frail hand to the space beside her.

Ali shuffled a chair across and sat down. 'Sorry I walked out on dinner.'

'Everyone understood. I meant every word, but every word was meant for the best.'

'I can be a real bitch,' said Ali.

'Yes, you can, and it's nothing to be proud of.'

'I know.'

'No, I don't think you do. You wear it like a badge of honour, when there is nothing the least bit honourable about it.'

Ali didn't know how to respond. She'd come to make peace and was getting both barrels again. 'I'm trying. You're seeing a pretty good version of me, you know.'

'That's depressing to hear. You need to find a different modus operandi. Experiment a little.'

'I've started counting to ten when Potts says something stupid.'

'So does she, when you say something spiteful. Using your intelligence to belittle those less gifted is bullying – plain and simple.' Aunt Martha reached out and took one of Ali's hands, holding it lightly. 'This is the curse of relatives: they can't be discarded like troublesome friends, you must work with them and you must allow them to work with you. That's the way of it.'

Ali didn't reply, she just nodded. Every instinct was telling her to argue, to pull her hand away and start pacing the room, to tell her aunt precisely what she thought of her psychobabble counselling. But she couldn't, for it was true. All of it. The frail old woman had nailed her with a big soft nail.

'So, tell me about your nausea and stomach cramps.'

'I'm not pregnant.'

'Good to hear. I didn't for a moment think you were. So tell me – what's making you sick, it's important.'

'I broke your rules. I went in the barn.' Ali felt her aunt's hand tighten a little around hers.

'Did you indeed. How very disappointing.'

'And I think I know why you keep it locked up.'

'I doubt that, but go on.'

'I fell asleep on the old bed and had a weird dream, beautiful but a bit creepy. When I woke up I started puking my guts out like I'd been poisoned.'

'You may well have been.' Lady Grey let go of Ali's hand and pushed on the rim of one wheel, turning her chair to face her niece. 'I told you a white lie about the barn. The building isn't in danger of falling down any time soon. But I believe there's something toxic in there. Which is why a car is on its way right now to take you to the local clinic for a check-up.'

'What? Why? No, I'm fine.'

'I hope you are, but what would your father say if I don't have you checked out. Miss Waxstaff has arranged everything.'

'Seriously? Waxstaff. Why not Potts, she's the nurse?'

'Potts is new, Waxstaff has been with us for years and knows the village. She's arranged for the local doctor to open his surgery for us, he can give you a proper check-up and send blood samples away.'

'Oh this just gets better. Blood now!'

'Are you afraid of needles?'

'No.'

'Are you afraid of knowledge?'

'What? No, of course not. The opposite.'

Her aunt was still lying, Ali was sure of it, but she was lying to protect her, steering her away from taking more dream trips. Which meant her aunt knew what they did, knew about the stomach cramps and nausea. About the skin going zombie white.

'You're right. I'll get checked out. Were chemicals stored in the barn?'

'Weedkiller, once upon a time.'

'Or it might have been food poisoning ...'

'Please don't raise that with Miss Waxstaff, she will take offence.'

There was a knock at the door and Nurse Potts came in with two mugs of hot chocolate. 'The car's five minutes away. Plenty of time for a hot drink, keep you going as it were.'

'Thank you,' said Lady Grey, taking the mug and cradling it carefully. She waited till Potts had left, then smiled at Ali. 'Hot chocolate needs a bedtime story,' she said. 'Indulge an old woman and tell me about this dream of yours.'

'It's hard to remember the details, they're fading.'

'Try, nevertheless.' They turned back to face the night sky, and Ali began. She recounted it slowly, what she could remember of it. The two boys, the Hatter and the large talking rabbit. When she was done, Ali turned and studied her aunt. She looked serene and happy, and silent tears were rolling down her cheeks.

CHAPTER 26

DAY FIVE

BLOOD AND BULLSHIT

───────

'There's nothing like eating hay when you're faint,'
remarked the King.
'Throwing cold water over you would be better,' Alice suggested.
'I didn't say there was nothing better,' the King replied.
'I said there was nothing like it.'

It was the same car. The expensive black sedan that had been parked in the street the other day when Waxstaff had gone for her meeting. A tall, solidly built man was at the wheel, Waxstaff in the front seat beside him, and Lord Grey in the back with Ali. 'Nice car,' he said, 'bit fancy for a taxi.'

'It's not a taxi,' said Waxstaff without turning round. 'A colleague from the village has kindly lent us their car – their driver too, Mr Philips.' The man dipped his head slightly, but said nothing.

'Very decent of you,' said Lord Grey, 'much obliged.'

'Bit of an overkill,' said Ali. 'I could have walked if the clinic's in the village – ten minutes, max.'

'For you, yes. The car is for Lord Grey, he insisted on chaperoning you.'

'Indeed I did. Don't want you coming back with a kidney missing.'

'Thanks, Uncle Bertie,' Ali leaned in and cuddled his arm for the remainder of the drive. They parked up and climbed out, except for the driver who reclined his seat and settled back to wait.

The reception area was dark. Waxstaff led them round the building to a staff entrance where a baby-faced doctor was waiting for them.

'You're a bit young,' Ali said as he ushered them inside.

'Lucky genes,' he laughed. 'My mum looks like a teenager. Name doesn't help either – Doctor Cherabics – you can imagine what my friends do with that.'

'Cherub?'

'Exactly. Come through and sit down.' He led them to the waiting room and asked Waxstaff and Lord Grey to make themselves comfortable. The door to his consulting room was open and he gestured for Ali to go in. There was a desk with a computer, two comfortable chairs, and a wall of certificates.

'Who made this appointment?' asked Ali as she sat down.

'I'm sorry, I don't follow?' the young doctor fired up his computer.

'Where I live, it takes days to see a doctor. You've pulled out all the stops, even opened out of hours.'

'Ah, I see your point.' He grinned at her. 'Village politics make things a little more casual. Lady Grey phoned me earlier this evening.'

'Good.'

'Good?'

'Yes.' Ali relaxed a little, unfolding her arms, trying her best to follow Aunt Martha's advice to be less confrontational. It didn't come easily. 'I just wanted to be sure Lady Grey arranged this, not someone else.'

'All I have is a formal request from your guardians asking me to examine you for any sign of poisoning.'

'Fair enough. Let's get on with it.' Ali spent the next ten minutes answering questions about her medical history and getting checked out.

'Verdict?' she asked.

'Not sure. I'll need blood for some tests.'

'And if I refuse?'

'Up to you. It's not essential, but it will fast-track getting to the bottom of it. You look anaemic. But iron deficiency should make you lethargic, hence my confusion as you look the opposite; you look like you've got energy to burn.'

'Okay, stab away. Who do you send the results to?'

'Your guardians.'

'No one else?'

'Else? Like who? Is there something I need to know?' Doctor Cherabics started prepping two syringes. 'You seem a little jumpy about this.'

'Trust issues.'

'Ha! That's refreshing. You're the generation who gives their data away without reading the small print.' He put a cuff around her arm and Ali pumped her fist to inflate the veins.

'Thanks.' The doctor tapped the enlarged veins. 'You've done this before.'

'Many times. Mum and I both gave blood for a while. We've got a rare blood type, so Mum thought it was important. I stopped when ... we moved house.'

'So, the trust issues?'

'I'm happy to share the results with my aunt, but not the woman in your waiting room. Don't want her playing courier either, she's not family.'

'Understood.' He swabbed her arm and drew off the first sample. 'What if I bring the results myself? Hand them directly to you and your aunt.'

'Great,' she said as she watched him filling the second syringe. He had good, steady hands and found the vein each time. No stabbing around like one school nurse she'd had to suffer. Ali liked watching people who were good at their jobs; she liked the reassurance it gave, how the machinery of civilisation was powered by millions of people, each good at their little bit.

'It will give me an excuse to check on your aunt. I've not seen her since her fall. Old folk can be stubborn about coming here; they think I'm plotting to find something wrong and send them on a one-way trip to hospital.' He handed Ali a swab and told her to put pressure on the small puncture marks.

'She was sleep-walking when it happened,' said Ali, 'did you know?'

'I did. Painkillers and sedatives are a hard mix to get right.' He labelled the two samples and put them in a small fridge beside his desk.

'So what will you ask the lab to test for?'

'I'm sorry?'

'Blood tests are specific. Got to know what you're looking for. Right?'

'Correct.'

'So what are you looking for?'

'You seem to know a lot about all this?'

'Dad's a scientist. He designs experiments. So, just curious, did my aunt suggest poison? From pesticides perhaps?

'No. Did you come into contact with any?'

'Don't think so. Just wondered if my aunt had suggested it. You know what I think you should look for?'

'Tell me.'

'Food poisoning.' She put her finger to her lips, gestured to the door and lowered her voice to a whisper. 'The woman out there is their housekeeper.'

'Your point being?' He had been typing notes into the computer, but now turned to her, a frown creasing his brow.

'She's in charge of the kitchen, she buys all the groceries, cooks the meals, she's got a massive herb garden, and grows all the veggies. I don't know how the money thing works, maybe she's got access to their accounts to settle all the house bills. Whatever ... all I know is she has sole charge of a sweet old couple.'

'That's a bit confronting.' He scratched his head, his frown deepening. 'How seriously should I take this? I mean, I can't go to the police asking them to look into it, not based on a worry from a patient. That would be really odd.'

'Not if you find something in my blood ...'

'Any hint of poison in your system and the lab will contact the police anyway.'

'Good to know.'

'But I will make sure the tests cover that. And I'll also take some of your aunt's blood when I make that visit. But to be honest, I think you can rest easy on that score. Accidental poisoning is a big part of being a village GP: kids who eat things they shouldn't, farmers handling chemicals, council staff with weedkillers. I see at least one case a week. But I'm not seeing it here, not at first glance. But I will get them to test for the basics.'

'Okay, thanks.'

They went out and joined the others in the waiting room. Lord Grey got straight to his feet, his face a picture of concern. 'All good, I hope?'

'I'm fine, Uncle Bertie.' Ali gave him a hug. 'Nothing to lose sleep over. The doctor's taken some blood and sent it off for testing, but I feel great.'

'So you're not … I mean, what Potts was on about … not that it would matter, we have your back, you know that, I just …'

'No, uncle, no incubation taking place on your watch.' They followed the doctor back through the building and out to the waiting car.

'The tests may take a day or two,' said the doctor as Ali helped her uncle into the back seat. 'I'll bring the results to the house.'

'No need,' said Waxstaff. 'Call me, I can pick them up.'

The young doctor caught Ali's eye and gave her smallest of nods. He would definitely be bringing the results over himself.

CHAPTER 27

DAY SIX

DISAPPEARANCE

———————

*Alice began to remember that she was a pawn,
and that it would soon be time for her to move.*

The waning moon was on the far side of the manor house, leaving the main lawn in shadow. Ali ran barefoot, the damp grass chill beneath her feet. It heightened her sense of doing something illicit, making the adventure seem less real, as if she were acting out a scene in a college play.

When they'd arrived home from the clinic, she had excused herself and gone straight to the library. Her uncle promised to give the good news to Aunt Martha. Good news? Had he really thought she might be pregnant?

Then, as soon as the house had fallen silent, she'd climbed from the library window and sprinted to the well. It was dark in the underground passage, but Ali kept her penlight switched off. If the others were already in the barn, they might see the light leaking up through gaps in the trapdoor.

She reached the iron steps and listened. Nothing. No voices, no footfalls, no scraping of chairs. She pushed the trapdoor up and wedged the corner of her notebook into the gap. It gave her a thin, worm's-eye view of the barn.

There was very little moonlight, but enough for Ali to see what Potts had set up. Three cane chairs from the patio were arranged in a half circle around a low picnic table.

'Ready when you are,' Ali whispered, and she settled down to wait. She must have dozed off, because she didn't hear the barn door open, only the voices of Waxstaff and Lord Grey and the sound of a match being struck. She got to her feet and peered out through the gap.

'In the chair please, Bertie,' Lady Grey held a hand out to her husband as Waxstaff lit three candles and set them on the picnic table.

'Must we really do this? Waste of a decent night's kip.'

'So you keep saying. Stop being so very selfish; you know how much this means to me. So be quiet and indulge me.'

'Always, my dear. But I won't pretend to be a believer.' He bent and helped his wife into one of the patio chairs. Then he and Waxstaff sat on either side.

'Hands please,' said Waxstaff in a low voice.

Ali groaned silently. Not a stupid séance. Was this how Waxstaff worked the scam? Preying on the fears of the elderly; proof of life after death, still time to unburden their wealth? Was this why her aunt had got so bloody weird at dinner – hyped up for this? Pathetic!

'Slow, deep breaths,' said Waxstaff. Then Ali heard … snoring? Her uncle's head was on his chest and he was snoring like a bulldozer. Ali almost burst into laughter and had to bite her lower lip to stop herself.

'Oh dear,' sighed Lady Grey. 'I don't think Bertie is fully engaged with the proceedings.' For the next few minutes they sat like that, their eyes closed, the sound of their breathing lost beneath the rumble of Lord Grey's snoring.

'Alice,' said Aunt Martha.

FRACK! Ali pulled herself back from the narrow opening. Had she been seen?

'My dear, dear child,' said Lady Grey in a soft coaxing voice, 'my dear lost Alice. Come back to us, dear … come back and rest.' Ali leant forward again, eyes to the gap. Was her aunt talking to the missing great-aunt Alice? Had to be!

'When I was born, you were a shadow from the past, a tale of such terrible sorrow. But I know you were a strong and fearless girl, beset by trials we cannot understand. Your mother told us of your wild ideas, of your fierce independence. Be fearless now. Let go of that enchanted place within the glass. Come home to us. Come home and rest.'

Within the glass? Did she believe her relative's spirit was trapped in the old mirror? Ali had heard old superstitions about mirrors, how they could steal a soul; how mirrors were removed from the rooms of the dying, and how breaking one was bad luck because bad spirits could be released into your life.

Was that why her aunt kept the dresser in the barn? Was the mirror too dangerous to keep in the main house, and yet too precious to be destroyed?

Then, quite suddenly, Aunt Martha was gone. One moment she was sitting in the wicker chair, the next – the chair was empty. Ali stared, forcing herself not to blink. Was this a trick? How? The candle flames had flickered, she was sure of it. They had angled towards the empty chair as if pulled by a breeze, pulled in by the sudden vacuum.

Her uncle was still fast asleep, snoring as loudly as ever, and Waxstaff ... bloody hell! Waxstaff was crying. She was looking at the vacant chair, tears on her cheeks. She didn't look surprised, just hopelessly sad, like a small child lost beyond consolation.

What had just happened? Her aunt had gone – but where? And while her head screamed the question, Ali's heart already knew the answer. Aunt Martha was in the bluebell woods.

Then, just as suddenly, she was back. The candle flames flickered briefly ... and there she was, her face white as a sheet, her eyes open and sparkling. Then she doubled over and began to vomit.

'What the devil?' Lord Grey jumped up and lifted his wife's hand, patting it softly as another bout of retching kept her bent forward. 'What happened?'

'I'm not sure,' said Waxstaff, standing abruptly and wiping her cheeks with the back of a sleeve. 'I'll get Potts.'

'Come on, my dear.' Lord Grey stooped and stroked his wife's hair. 'Let's get you to bed. That's quite enough hocus-pocus for one night.'

'I had my dream,' croaked Aunt Martha, her voice barely a whisper, 'my old dream. It was so beautiful.'

'That's lovely, my dear. You can tell me all about it later.'

'I was in the painting, Bertie. I was back in the painting.'

Ali woke to sunlight and confusion. At first she couldn't place where she was, then memories of the night's weirdness returned, images snapping into place like pieces of a jigsaw.

'Aunt Martha!'

Ali sprang out of bed, pulled on yesterday's clothes, and hurried to the dining room. There was no one there. The table was set for one, a note folded on her plate.

Tuck in, Ali, we're having breakfast in bed this morning.
Martha had a restless night and she's a bit out of sorts.
We'll catch up on the crossword later.

Bear hugs,
Uncle Bertie

Ali sat and stared at the food. She badly wanted time alone with her aunt; time to ask about last night, without letting on she'd been spying on them. She started to eat and found she was hungry. Four rounds of toast, three boiled eggs and a pot of tea later, she was knocking gently on her aunt's bedroom door.

'Go bottle yourself, Waxstaff!' Lord Grey yelled out, angry as hell.

'It's me, Uncle Bertie.'

'Ah! Hold on a jiffy.' The door opened and her uncle beckoned her in. 'Sorry about that. A bit miffed with Waxstaff right this minute. I think she poisoned your aunt last night.'

'Seriously?' Ali kept her voice low as she stepped inside.

'Not on purpose, just piss poor cooking. The old girl was sick as a dog last night, still pretty rough this morning. How about you?'

'Me? Fine, and we all ate the same food. What about you?'

'Fit as a fiddle.'

'Is that you, Alice?'

'Sure is, Aunty,' The curtains were drawn against the sun and Ali couldn't see her aunt's face till she sat beside her on the edge of the bed. Her skin was as white as the pillow.

'Heard you're feeling a bit shite.'

'Shite? Delightful. Yes, I feel shite. Just a tummy bug.'

'Tosh,' said her husband. 'Food poisoning, courtesy of Waxstaff.'

'It's nothing of the kind. Now go and have your morning stroll and don't do anything silly.'

'On the contrary, I insist on being silly; it's mandatory at my age.' Lord Grey bent and kissed his wife. 'Don't stay too long, there's a girl.'

'I won't. Promise.'

'Now then,' said Aunt Martha when the door closed behind her husband, 'tell me – what are your plans?'

'My plans? Big question. First a general science degree, then maybe I'll major in cosmology.'

'Good? Now answer the question.'

'My plans for today? Research, I think.'

'Good to hear.' Lady Grey pushed herself up a little. 'That teacher of yours promised to keep you occupied with assignments.'

'I'm researching something else … a mystery right here, in this house.'

'Let me guess. Why did a perfectly sensible girl like me marry a ridiculous man like Bertie? A mystery indeed, what was I thinking?'

'I'm sure he was a complete babe, blue cheese and all.' Ali grinned, got up from the edge of the bed, pulled a small stool over and sat down facing her aunt.

'He was,' Aunt Martha chuckled, 'and still is, the silly old bugger.'

'So, no mystery there. But I've been flicking through all the books in your library and I've come across a real brain teaser.'

'The only mystery there is why anyone in my family would gather such a hodgepodge collection.'

'Hodgepodge?'

'Yes,' she sighed, and shook her head. 'I think the generations come from different continents. Hodgepodge is a marvellous word to describe the apparently random and eclectic.'

'Cute! Good to know.'

'The collection in the library has no coherence, and holds no interest for your uncle or myself.' She pointed to a book-shelf on the opposite wall. 'It's poetry for me and novels for Bertie. And we're both addicted to salacious biographies of our peers, all of whom we've survived. It's immensely satisfying to outlive your tormentors.'

'Well, I want you to last a bit longer, Aunty. So get better.'

'A tummy bug, nothing more. I'll be right as rain in no time.'

'Good.' Ali poured a glass of water and wondered how she could turn the conversation to last night. 'So, tummy cramps and vomiting? Sounds a bit like what I had.'

'No dear,' she said, taking the water and holding Ali's gaze, 'it sounds exactly like your symptoms.'

'So what are you saying?' Ali felt her aunt's hand tighten beneath her own. 'Did you fall asleep in the barn and have the dream?'

Her aunt let out a tiny whimper, 'Sorry, dear, another tummy cramp. Give me a moment.' She took a deep breath, composing herself.

'If you did, I hope it was as beautiful as mine,' said Ali. 'The bluebell woods from the painting – I could smell the grass and feel the sun on my face.'

'It was.'

'It was?'

'Yes, my dear. It was the same dream.' Lady Grey put her arms down and pushed on the mattress, lifting her body to ease the stress on her back. 'I expect you imprinted it in my mind when you told me about it yesterday. When will the clinic have the results of your blood tests?'

'Not sure. The doc said he'd bring them over himself. You should let him take some of yours.'

'He can try! The last person to search for one of my veins endured a tirade of insults from Bertie.' She sighed and waved at her breakfast tray. 'Take this to the kitchen, my dear. I need to sleep. And tell Bertie, I managed to eat something.'

'Lie for you, Aunty?'

'Of course! He'll be worrying.'

'Okay,' Ali took a slice of toast from the tray and stole a bite as she headed for the door. 'There goes the evidence.'

'Alice?'

'Yes?'

'I would dream about the bluebell woods when I was young.' She eased herself down the bed, pulling the covers up to her chin. 'Every night, for months on end. Then, quite suddenly, they stopped.'

'Why?'

'I think I discovered boys …' She grinned at Ali and gave a little wink.

'Aunty!'

'Much more fun than bluebells.'

'Way too much sharing! So, who painted the picture?'

'I did.'

'For real?'

'For real. I missed seeing those woods, so I painted them. Please close the door behind you. We'll talk more about it later, just the two of us.'

CHAPTER 28

DAY SIX

SERENITY

———————

'What does it matter where my body happens to be?'
he said, 'my mind goes on working all the same.'

Ali took the tray to the kitchen. Her head felt like a clothes dryer, a mess of facts tumbling end over end. She needed to slow it down; she needed … a bath. Her best thinking always came while soaking in a hot bath.

'Memories of my womb', according to her mum. 'Nine months sloshing about must leave a mark.' Ali went upstairs, filled the tub and climbed in.

Questions bubbled up, dozens of questions. She watched them, but didn't engage. They rose up, hung in her mind for a moment, then drifted away. It was calming, as if she was floating in the eye of her own mental storm. She waited for the serenity to pass, for her brain to kick in with its endless parade of questions.

Instead, a single thought hovered there, waiting for Ali to register it: *The place is real – you have to go back.* She waited for it to drift away like the others. It didn't; it hung there, and everything else in her head became background noise.

The place is real – you have to go back.

Ali tried to find words for what she was feeling. It was hard because it was unfamiliar, this sense of calm certainty. Then a single word sprang into her head: *Aligned.* That was it. She felt aligned, as if she were facing her true north for the first time, and she knew it without debating the 'rightness' of the direction.

Was this how geese felt when the compulsion to migrate came over them? They didn't argue the science of it. They just responded. They knew when it was time to go. Ali climbed out of the bath and scrubbed herself dry. Then a memory came slamming back; a memory of the two young boys. Ricky and Ted.

'*We don't talk to her anymore, she promised to find our real stories but she never did.*' Ali wrapped herself in a towel and raced down to the library. She took the chewed letter from her journal and read it again.

Dearest Alice, my great-grandniece to be,

I pray these books survive undisturbed until your arrival so many years from now. I will explain all when we meet, for meet we must. I entrust my safety to you. Everything you need to know is hidden in these books, penned as childish tales of distraction. The books hold the key to finding me. Forgive their cryptic conceits; I have to protect access to this peculiar world from dark hearts who are set on destroying it.

Dear child, please find me. More is at stake than my survival or I would not send this bottle across the tide of years to your future shore.

With hope and affection,
your great-aunt, Alice

As Ali read the note, the same sense of alignment swept over her again. This note wasn't part of some Victorian parlour game. It was real. Despite all the logic of time and ageing, her great-aunt was still alive in a parallel bubble of space time, like the two forlorn boys. She was really trapped in Wonderland.

Ali folded the note. An aunt she had never known was in desperate need of her help. It was an odd feeling – to be needed. A new feeling. Here was someone reaching out for her help across an impossible span of years. How it was possible didn't matter. Not right now. If she remained observant and treated everything as a field experiment, the science behind all this would reveal itself. What mattered, right now, was to step into the current of this compulsion; step in and let it carry her forward.

Ali lay down on the bed and stared out at the sunshine.

'Okay, Aunt Alice, I'm coming to find you.' She announced it aloud, like it was a promise, a commitment. But first she had to solve the whole nausea and vomiting problem. Had her great-aunt discovered an antidote? Is that what she'd gone to great lengths to hide – a secret recipe for travelling through safely?

Where did that leave the mushrooms? Were they just one ingredient of the recipe? Perhaps that was why Waxstaff had a secret stash of them. And why she spent so much time in the herb garden – maybe she was growing the other ingredients. So what next?

Two things, Ali decided. First, find the foundations of the old stables and dig up whatever was buried there. Second, search Waxstaff's bedroom.

Ali spent the next hour looking through scrapbooks for photos of the demolished stables. If she found three pictures from three different angles, she could triangulate their exact position.

In one book she found a series of photos taken of a man walking dogs on the main lawn. Three of the pictures had the stables in the background.

Ali took them outside, lined them up with mature trees that were bigger now but easy to identify, and worked out where the stables had stood. It was a dozen paces from where she'd been digging yesterday, not in amongst the wild grasses, but close by – right in Waxstaff's herb garden! And Waxstaff was there now, snipping herbs and dropping them into a basket.

'Need a hand?' Ali called out as she strolled over.

'No thank you, nearly done.'

'What are you picking?'

'Verbena and dill,' said the housekeeper, 'and a little parsley.'

'Sounds delicious. Well no, that's dumb. I have no idea to be honest, you could have said clover and mint and I'd have nodded wisely.'

'Honesty for a change, that's almost attractive.' Waxstaff handed the basket to Ali. 'Would you take them to the kitchen for me, please? I have an appointment.'

'A date?'

'That was a joke, correct?' Waxstaff cocked her head to one side and stared at Ali without a trace of a smile.

'Tough call. If I agree, you'll be offended; if I don't, you'll think I'm stupid.'

'I'm already convinced you're stupid.'

'Good to know.'

'I have to settle the accounts. The butcher is married and the grocer is an elderly spinster. So no, Miss Alice; no dates. Not for me.'

'Play it safe, do you? Not a risk taker?'

'I was, once upon a time.' Waxstaff paused, and looked almost wistful, then her face tightened again. 'Now I work hard to eliminate risks.'

'And I embrace them.'

'Which is why you were tested for blood poisoning and I wasn't.'

'You have blood?'

'Very amusing. I'll stop by the clinic and see if your results are back.'

'No!' Ali almost barked the response. 'Sorry, I mean there's no need, the doctor promised to bring them over.'

'Is that so? How interesting. Why on earth would he do that I wonder?'

'He wants an excuse to check on Aunt Martha.'

Ali set off for the kitchen, and wondered why her last remark had unsettled Waxstaff. Was she responsible for Lady Grey skipping her check-ups at the clinic? She had to get into Waxstaff's room. Was she working alone, or was she connected to the suits who had given Peter the third degree? Perhaps they were working together for some government agency that investigated weird stuff; a watch group keeping tabs on the gateway.

No, Ali didn't think so. If the government knew about it, the grounds would be under wraps and swarming with white coats. England's very own Area 52.

CHAPTER 29

DAY SIX

CROQUET

––––––––––

*Alice replied: 'I hardly know. At least I know who I was when
I got up this morning, but I think I must have been changed
several times since then.'*

Ali set the basket of herbs on the kitchen table and headed
for the stairs. The door to her aunt's bedroom stood open and
Ali glanced in as she tiptoed past. Potts and Lord Grey were
on either side of the bed. The nurse was giving Aunt Martha
some gentle physio, and Ali's uncle was reading to her in his
deep, theatrical voice:

'With infinite complacency, men went to and fro over this
globe about their little affairs, serene in their assurance of
their empire over matter.'

Ali grinned as she crept past. She knew the book – *War of
the Worlds*. So her aunt really did like sci-fi.

Up on the next floor she checked the bedroom doors again.

They were still locked. She went into the bathroom, opened the window and looked out. She was only two stories up, but the height made her head spin. 'Don't look down, stupid.' Ali kept her eyes fixed on the next window and climbed out. The ledge was a design feature, a narrow protrusion of bricks that made a shadow line around the face of the house. It was the width of a fist, hardly a ledge at all, but there was ivy everywhere with strands as thick as rope. Handholds.

Ali moved slowly, testing every step, and was almost to the first bedroom window when she heard her uncle's voice.

'I'll set up the croquet. Give Ali a game, what do you think?' It was coming from an open window directly below her. Ali couldn't make out her aunt's reply, it was too low and weak.

'Ha! Well she can try,' laughed Lord Grey. 'Twenty quid says I thrash her.' Ali cursed under her breath. Her uncle might step onto the lawn at any moment. The next window was only a few feet away. Ali decided to push ahead and take a quick peek through the glass.

'What the hell!' Ali stared, confused. Apart from one narrow bed, the room was set up like an office. There was a desk, printer, filing cabinets and a laptop. But Ali hardly registered them. Her eyes were glued to the far wall. It was covered in photographs. Of her.

Documents were pinned up beside them: scanned pages from her notebook, printed and enlarged; a scan of the note from Aunt Alice. Plus a large print of the first map she'd found.

But not the second. Despite her shock, Ali noted this fact, and checked the wall again to be sure. No copy of the second map. Then she had to grab on tight to the ivy as her legs began to shake, her body bracing against the fog of anger rising inside her. Not now! She forced herself to slow her breathing.

'Alice, you out here?' Her uncle stepped into the sunshine

below. Ali froze, hugging the ivy wall, praying her uncle didn't glance up. He didn't. He walked off around the corner of the house, calling her name.

Think! Who did the room belong to? Potts or Waxstaff? She peered in again. There were no clothes on the bed, no personal effects. It could be either.

'Oh, there you are.' Lord Grey found her in the kitchen drinking a glass of milk. Ali did her best to look composed, to hide how breathless she was, how much her hands were trembling.

'Been looking for you everywhere. Fancy a game of croquet?'

'Don't know the rules.'

'Excellent, more chance for me then. It's all set out on the front lawn.'

'Why not?' Ali followed her uncle outside. 'How's Aunt Martha doing?'

'A little better. Waxstaff gave her some mushroom soup – very medicinal by all accounts.' The hoops had been set out on the side lawn. Her uncle handed her a mallet.

'Now, the basics: you whack your balls through each hoop while stopping me from getting mine through.' Ali tried to focus as he explained the rest of the game, but her mind was still staring into that bedroom office.

Was Peter right after all? Were Waxstaff and Potts here to keep her safe, the unstable child of a valuable scientist? It would explain everything in the room; they would be keeping tabs on her. Keeping her safe. Everything else, the idea of another world, was part of her own carefully constructed delusion.

'... so that's the rules, not much to it, think of it as snooker on grass – those hoops are the pockets. Make sense?'

'Think so. You go first.' Ali watched and copied as they took turns, her mind still churning.

If Peter was wrong, if Wonderland was a bubble of space-time stuck like a limpet on the skin of their universe, then what she saw in that room made a completely different kind of sense. Potts or Waxstaff knew about it and they were watching Ali like she was a lab rat. So had she been set up from the beginning, engineered into doing this? And who else was involved? Surely not her aunt and uncle?

'So, Uncle Bertie, what did you want to tell me?'

'Tell you?'

'You wanted to say something upstairs, but not in front of Aunty.'

'Ah, yes, a tad embarrassing really. Owe you an explanation of sorts. About the barn and a family skeleton.'

'I'm all ears.'

'That story we told you about the barn being unsafe. Load of codswallop; it's the family closet where we keep our skeleton. No one opens it, and no one talks about it; house rules.'

'Why?'

'Superstition. It's a kind of family ghost story. The first day you were here you asked if there had been an Alice in the family. There was, a few generations back. Before our time, but according to the story, the poor girl went missing one day, right in front of her mother's eyes. The woman saw her daughter waving to her from a mirror – can you believe that? A mirror! One minute her child was there, the next she was gone. Just her reflection. Then that was gone too.'

'Spooky.' Ali tried to keep the interest out of her voice. She lined up her next ball and smacked it through the hoop.

'Nice shot – you *have* played this before!' Lord Grey

scratched his beard, made a big show of setting up his shot, and messed it up completely. 'Damn it!'

'You don't believe that story, right?'

'Lord no. Romantic garbage. Girl probably ran off with some undesirable. Would have led to no end of trouble. Anyway, the family kept adding to the story over the years, like a piece of folklore. Her poor mother was convinced some kind of devilry was behind it. She became a spiritualist and spent a fortune on quackery. She truly believed her daughter's soul had been trapped in the mirror.'

'And this Alice girl never turned up?'

'No. But the mother kept the bedroom just as it was. Locked herself in for days on end talking to the bally mirror, as if her daughter might hear. When she passed, the family cleared the room, but they kept the mirror and a few odds and sods.'

'And stored it in the barn? Makes a weird kind of sense.'

'Not to me.'

'I could never throw something like that out.' Ali aimed her next shot at her uncle's croquet ball. 'It's like a legacy thing, part of the family story.' She took a gentle backswing, then cracked her uncle's ball right off the playing green.

'Oh! A tad mean-spirited, but well played.'

'I mean … they had to keep the mirror, doesn't matter how crazy we think it is. If the mother believed it, you have to respect her wishes – kind of a family duty.'

'Well, I wish they hadn't. My poor dear Martha was obsessed with the story when she was a girl. I thought that was all in the past, but in recent months she's started talking about it again, even dreaming about it. Which is why she's in the damn wheelchair – she was sleepwalking to the barn.'

Ali didn't look up at her uncle. She focused on her croquet ball and kept her voice neutral, like this was a conversation that didn't matter. 'So you spun me a white lie to keep a family skeleton secret. No big deal. But why are you telling me now?'

'Because things got a bit foolish last night. Waxstaff claims to be a bit psychic – hogwash of course, but it's a straw Martha chose to cling to. She wanted to have a séance in the barn.'

'Oh, right.'

'Won't go into details, but Martha got worked up and made herself ill. Either that or she got food poisoning. So I might need your support.'

'How?'

'Need to nip all this nonsense in the bud. Talk the old girl out of another séance. Logic and science verses all that mumbo jumbo. What do you say?'

'I'll do my best.'

'That's the spirit. If your best is anything like your croquet, the mumbo jumbo is toast!'

Ali watched her uncle as he took aim and hit his croquet ball across the grass and, quite suddenly, she felt lost and alone. More than that, she felt adrift, as if the mooring rope that kept her safely bound to the shoreline had been cut.

She was on some vast new ocean with no stars to guide her home. She felt the tears welling up and there was nothing she could do to stop them. Her uncle had his back to her, intent on his next shot, so he didn't see her crying, nor see her raise her mallet and bring it down on her own foot.

'Shit!' Ali dropped the mallet and began hopping around theatrically.

'Hit yourself?' Her uncle laughed. 'You get used to it, especially playing after a decent lunch – never mix port and sport. Just give it a good rub.'

She did, and started to focus on the game to use it as a

distraction. And after a few minutes she had overtaken his score.

'Don't take prisoners, do you?' he said, as Ali lined up her final shot.

'Never,' said Ali, as she nailed it, straight through the hoop. 'So let's make the next game worth my while.'

'A wager? Excellent! How much?'

'Your share of the blue cheese tonight.'

'Ha! Or yours if I win. All right, give me twenty minutes. I'll go and check on Martha. Hearing that I've been completely thrashed will be a great tonic for her.'

'One question, uncle.'

'Fire away.'

'If the barn's not dangerous, if there are no toxic fumes, why was Aunty worried about my stomach pains? Why the blood tests?'

'Why?' Her uncle frowned as if the question surprised him. 'You know why, Martha said it wasn't up for discussion. Which I assume means it was "ladies' business." But all's good in that department, so onward and upward.' And away he went, back to the house to check on his wife.

Ali waited for him to disappear inside, then set off to the herb garden.

CHAPTER 30

DAY SIX

MUSHROOM CASSEROLE

———————

'I don't understand,' said Alice. 'It's dreadfully confusing!'
'That's the effect of living backwards,' the Queen said kindly:
'it makes one a little giddy at first.'

This time there was no one around and Ali spent a few minutes wandering up and down the paths that divided the raised beds. The beds themselves looked recent, but the flagstones covering the various pathways were older. The original flooring of the stables? A loose flagstone would have made a great hiding place.

But which one? There were dozens of them, fifty or sixty at least. It would take days to lift each one and check. Then a picture of Mrs King jumped into Ali's head. Why was that? She closed her eyes, waiting for her brain to join the dots.

'Sound.' Ali smiled to herself. There was no need to lift them, the blind woman could tap them! If there was a hollow space under one of the flagstones, she would hear it. She looked for something to tap with and found a spade in the far corner.

But if she was someone's lab rat, she had to be careful. Potts might be watching from the house, snapping long shots. And Waxstaff might be heading back from the village. Either she waited till dark, or she had to disguise what she was doing.

So Ali made a pantomime of surveying each bed, checking the plants and pulling the occasional weed. And she ambled down the paths, she tapped each flagstone with the spade, as if tapping along to a tune in her head.

She was halfway down the second path when she got a dull echo from one flagstone. She tapped it again, and the ones on either side. No mistaking the difference, this one had an empty space right underneath. Ali looked back along the path and counted.

Eight flagstones. North end. Second path. She made a mental note. There would be no more written notes, not now. Aunt Alice had gone to a lot of trouble to keep this a secret. So no digging till she could come up with a distraction, one that would keep the entire household busy.

'Running out on me?' Lord Grey was heading towards her, twirling his crochet mallet in one hand, and balancing a glass of port in the other. He raised the glass. 'A pre-lunch aperitif for my pre-match nerves. Don't tell Martha.'

The port didn't help. He was thrashed a second time.

Ali skipped lunch. She felt exhausted, not physically, but mentally. She'd been raised as a rationalist, her parents encouraging her to be open-minded but sceptical. And now this! She really believed a dead aunt was alive and kicking in another world. Her rational self was putting up a good defence; it was telling her to get her act together, but she couldn't. And the fight was wearing her out.

213

She grabbed a blanket from her room, spread it on the lawn in the shade of the giant cedar and lay down. She slept the entire afternoon.

'What a pair we make.' Lady Grey was still the colour of chalk, but she had insisted on coming down for dinner. Her remark was intended for Ali, but her husband assumed otherwise.

'We do indeed. But a pair of what, exactly? A pair of organ donors?'

'Who would want your liver, Bertie? No, I was referring to myself and Ali – we are both on our second bowl of mushroom casserole. One would think we hadn't eaten for days.'

'Well, I did skip lunch,' said Ali. 'And this is really good,' she glanced down the table at Waxstaff to see how the compliment had gone down. The woman simply nodded.

'I agree,' Aunt Martha turned to her husband and tapped the back of his hand, 'which means you have an apology to make. You were very critical of Miss Waxstaff's kitchen skills this morning.'

'I never apologise,' Lord Grey protested, waving the idea away. 'I make too many gaffes, I'd spend all day apologising. Not tenable. Best to deny everything, crack the odd joke and move on.' He beamed cheerfully at his wife, registered her expression, and changed tack. 'However, on this occasion, I apologise unreservedly – the stew is delicious.'

'Casserole,' Waxstaff corrected him, 'it's mushroom casserole.'

'Right, apology number two then. Delicious mushroom casserole it is.'

'Yeah, really good.' Ali glanced down the table at Waxstaff. 'Are these the ones the blind woman was picking?'

'Yes, they are,' said Waxstaff.

'And they're supposed to be medicinal, right?'

'So I understand.'

'Well, I feel a great deal better, whatever the cause,' said Lady Grey.

'Me too,' said Ali. 'Everyone okay if I have some more?' She reached for the serving ladle, then stopped when her aunt burst into tears. Lord Grey reached for his wife's hand.

'My dear, what's wrong?'

'I'm fine,' she lifted a napkin to her face and dabbed her cheeks.

'The devil you are. Last night and now this. What is it?'

'Memories, dear. Just a flood of old memories returning. Unbidden, but not unwelcome.' She smiled tenderly at her husband. 'I'm fine, really I am. Right now, all I need is a little night air.'

'A promenade. Excellent, I shall leave the port and cheese till our return.'

'No, the cheese you will leave altogether.'

'It's mine anyway.' Ali reminded her uncle. 'I won it at croquet.'

'Damn, you did indeed.'

'Good.' Lady Grey nodded with satisfaction. 'Then enjoy your port, Bertie, I'd like Alice to take me for a stroll. If that's all right with you, Alice?'

'Sure, yes. Of course.' Ali was on her feet immediately. 'A walk would be great, I think I need it after three bowls of stew.'

'Casserole,' Waxstaff corrected her.

'And it was four bowls,' said Lady Grey. 'Don't think I wasn't counting.'

'A double negative, Aunt Martha?'

'Fetch my scarf and don't be smart.'

Five minutes later, Ali was pushing her aunt down the driveway. Potts had insisted on joining them, but Lady Grey had insisted back. Ali was impressed by her strength of will; she weighed less than Potts' right leg, yet had voice-wrestled the giant nurse into obedience.

'I do love late summer evenings,' Aunt Martha said, gesturing at the pink sky. 'Twilight has an enchantment about it, don't you think? If science allows for the idea of enchantment …' Ali was almost shocked by the question. Talk about hitting the nail! Had her aunt been eavesdropping in Ali's head?!

'Depends what you mean by enchantment, I guess. If you mean fairy dust and magic? No, science has no time for that crap.'

'Language.'

'Sorry. But if you mean something we can't explain yet, something we can see but don't understand, then sure. Enchantment is as good a word as any.'

'I mean it as a metaphor, the gap between day and night, like the tideline on a beach, a halfway place where two worlds collide.'

Bloody hell! There she goes again. Two worlds collide! Was her aunt about to fess up about the door in the barn? Was she probing to see what Ali knew?

'I feel like that when I'm falling asleep …' Ali kept her voice flat and neutral, 'like I'm between two worlds – not quite awake, not quite asleep.' She was behind the wheelchair, pushing her aunt along, so couldn't see her face, but she saw her back stiffen. 'So I guess you could call dreams "enchanted".'

'Especially ours, Alice. Wouldn't you say?'

'Yeah, I would. Especially ours.'

'And how many times have you had our dream of the bluebell woods?'

'Three times.'

'And they left you feeling sick each time?'

'Yes. Stomach cramps. Like I've been kicked in the stomach. Not when I'm in the dream; when I wake up. Was it like that for you? When you were a kid?'

'Yes. Rather odd, don't you think?' She turned her head and peered up at Ali, the pink light of the sky setting her face aglow, like porcelain in firelight.

'I do. very odd.'

'How can sleep cause such a thing? How would science explain it?'

'I've got two theories,' said Ali. 'Do you snore?'

'I don't believe so. I would need to ask Bertie.'

'Ha! He wouldn't tell you even if you did, he loves you too much.'

'So perhaps I do.'

'And I definitely do, like a truck. Dad even had me checked out. Sleep apnoea, it's called – my throat relaxes and blocks my windpipe, so my brain gets starved of oxygen. Might explain the weird dreams.'

'And the nausea?'

'Could be the inner ear. Maybe lack of oxygen messes with that, like we get sea sickness and puke our guts out.

'Sounds delightful. I prefer it when you channel Jane Austen.'

'Ha! How would she say it?'

'She wouldn't. And the explanation's too drab anyway. When I was a young girl, I invented far more romantic notions for it.'

'Tell me.'

'I loved reading Jules Verne. His underwater adventures with the dashing Captain Nemo. He would walk the ocean floor in his dive suit. Air pumped in long pipes down to his helmet. I decided my dream world must work like that. I was a visitor breathing the wrong air.'

'So there's a bit of the scientist in you, too.'

'It was my childish attempt to rationalise it. So the next time I had the dream, I held my breath for as long as I could.'

'Did it work?'

'How could it? The notion was foolish. The air in my bedroom would have been the same, dreaming or not. So your rather drab explanation will have to do.'

'Unless the dreamworld is another place. Part of you thinks it might be.'

'As a child I did. Not anymore.'

'Then why did you want my blood tested? Because you're not sure, that's why. You think maybe the place is real; and maybe I paid it a visit.'

'And did you?'

'I don't know. The scientist in me says it was a dream. I saw your painting, I read the Wonderland books. Dreams are the brain making sense of the day, plugging things together, putting them in boxes. Kind of a tidy up.'

'Very romantic.'

They reached the end of the drive. Ali turned the chair in a gentle arc and set off back to the house. She walked slowly, waiting for her aunt to go into more detail, to ask more questions. She didn't. So Ali jumped in.

'How did you get out of your dreams? I was scared of getting stuck, like I might be falling into a coma and never wake up.'

'Pinching worked at first. But you know this – your little fight with the tree!'

'You knew?'

'More of a guess. I was worried. I had Potts bring me the keys after that.'

'Did you tell her why?'

'Heavens, no! Where would I begin? But am I right? Was that brush with a tree your way of waking yourself up?'

'Yep. Hard to stay asleep after a rush of adrenaline.'

'Quite so. And that's what ended the escapade for me.' Lady Grey gave a small sigh, her shoulders dropping. 'I started sleeping with a safety pin hooked into my sleeve. I would stick it in the back of my hand.'

'Ouch!'

'After a while, I needed a bigger jolt. Stop pushing me, dear. Come round here where you can see this. It's important that you do.' Ali walked to the front of the wheelchair and watched as her aunt peeled off one of her elegant lace gloves.

'Frack!' The frail, parchment skin was criss-crossed by a latticework of old scars. Cuts from a knife. 'You were a cutter?'

'Is that what they call it now? I was taken to Switzerland, to a clinic for the emotionally disturbed. Psychiatrists told my parents that the dreams were an escape from some inner misery; the cuts a cry for help.'

'And what did you think?'

'For a while I stopped thinking altogether, I was so devastated. I came to see my dreams as an addiction. They were taken away from me, and I went into shock. That's when I did the painting.'

'Of the bluebell woods?'

'Yes, the dreams stopped once I was away from this house. The doctors held it to be a sign of recovery. But I missed them terribly. I started remembering them onto canvas. My new obsession. But in time they made me stop that, too.'

Ali said nothing. She was feeling the same compulsion, the same pressure to get to the barn – to go back into that other world.

They carried on towards the house and were almost at the front steps when her aunt spoke again. 'I shall phone the school tomorrow. It's clear you can't stay here.'

'What … leave?' Ali stopped the wheelchair and walked round to the front again. 'But it's good for me here.'

'Clearly that's not correct.' Lady Grey's face wore an expression of rigid determination that Ali recognised from the mirror. Was this where her own stubborn streak came from?

'I thought you liked having me around.'

'We do, my dear, we do. You're a tonic for us both. That's not the point.'

'No, the point is to stop me punching more people in the face. And it's working. I've wanted to punch Waxstaff every day, and I haven't.'

'Ha! Progress indeed. Look, Alice, the only issue is your welfare. This place, the house and grounds, they seem to be hurting you. You may be offended by the term "enchanted," but I can't think of a better one. It's a place of enchantment and it has you in its grip. I've been hurt by it. I will not let that to happen to you.'

'Can we wait till Dad gets here? See what he says. If he agrees, then I'll leave. He can't be much longer, his shifts never last more than three days.' She could see her aunt wavering.

'Very well, we'll wait for your father. On two conditions.'

'Okay, what?'

'You will not discuss any of this with the staff.'

'You don't trust them?'

'It's not a matter of trust, it's a matter of respectability.

It has taken me a lifetime to regain mine, to cast off the stigma of being mentally unsound. Society has given me a wide berth.'

'Except for Uncle Bertie!'

'Yes, God bless the silly man. I believe he courted me just to snub his nose at everyone's pomposity. He was a moth to my histrionic flame.'

'You were exotic.'

'Oh yes, very. And secondly, you will never go in the barn again. I won't have your father arriving to find you in a coma.'

The front door opened and Potts stepped out. Lady Grey thanked Ali for the walk and allowed the nurse to escort her inside.

CHAPTER 31

DAY SEVEN

BACK AGAIN

———————

'I can't remember things before they happen,' Alice remarked.
'It's a poor sort of memory that only works backwards,'
said the Queen.

Back in the library, Ali lay down, her head spinning. Aunt Martha had been there. Multiple times. But she believed it was a dreamworld, a dangerous illusion that could enthral you and trap you into never waking up.

The pressure to go back to the barn had been building all day. Ali knew it was a compulsion, even though she'd never been addicted to anything, not even sugar. Maybe ice cream. It was hard to pass a van in summer without wanting a double cone with chocolate sprinkles. But was that a craving for ice cream, or for the memories that went with it? Running to the van with her parents on hot, long-ago afternoons.

Ali waited till midnight, then went to the kitchen and the

room behind the pantry. She shone her penlight across the jars of mushrooms, chose a small one and shuffled the others to hide the gap. Then she looked around for chillies. All she could find was small packet of chilli powder. It would have to do.

Moonlight lay like frosting across the lawn, as if the place was trying to live up to her aunt's description, dialling up the enchantment. Ali skirted the lawn and paused behind a tree, waiting to see if Waxstaff or Potts appeared. There was no sign of them, so she set off for the well.

In the barn she put the jar of mushrooms and her journal down in front of the dressing table, pulled the dust sheet off and folded it for a cushion. It wasn't much, but better than bare floorboards.

She kicked off her shoes, sat down and pulled her feet onto her knees, the full lotus position, copying the sketch her mother had made. Then she lifted the journal and jar of mushrooms onto her lap and closed her eyes.

'One small step,' she whispered, and began the breathing cycle she'd been taught at college. After six or seven cycles, a calm settled over her, and she gave herself up to the process and to the silence of the night. It brought memories of sitting with her parents round a bonfire, of watching the glow of the embers.

Then she felt sunlight on her face.

'I'm still awake,' she whispered. 'I know I'm still awake.' Very slowly, she opened her eyes. She was sitting in the bluebell meadow.

'Bloody hell!' The shock was intense. Ali felt her heart starting to pound, adrenaline kicking in. She resisted; keeping hold of her breath, trying to preserve the moment. Then she saw the inside of the barn! It didn't fade in, it slammed back. The transition was like a slap and she toppled over, gasping for breath.

For a while, all she could do was lie there staring at the ceiling, confused and exhilarated, stunned and scared, a cocktail of emotions racing through her. The place was real! The certainty of it was terrifying – and liberating. She hadn't lost her mind. This was too concrete to be part of a delusion she'd woven round herself.

Multiverse wasn't a cute mathematical theory. It was real.

And she didn't feel sick; no stomach cramps! For those few brief seconds she had held her breath. Ali sat up, and began the routine again. It took longer this time, longer to slow her breathing and to relax her body, longer for her racing pulse to settle to a gentle rhythm. Then she felt it again, sunlight on her eyelids. This time she kept her eyes closed and just listened. First to her own breathing, then to the sounds of crickets in the grass close by and to the rustle of leaves just above her. She could hear bees and birdsong, layer after layer of sound, and all of it natural, no hum of traffic, no droning of distant planes.

Still with eyes closed, she explored her lap with her finger-tips. Her journal was there, and the jar of mushrooms. They had made it through with her. What did that say about the physics of this? Would anything she carried come through? Even her backpack? Ali had taken a dozen breaths now, and knew she would be sick as a dog when she went back, but that was all right, the price of the ticket.

She opened her eyes. The large white rabbit was pacing in front of her.

'You're real!' was all she could think of to say. 'You're really real!'

'And you, young lady, are really irritating.'

'I thought this was a weird dream last time. Thought I'd made you up.'

'Apology accepted. Reality is a complex beast, according to one of the Queen's scholars, and who am I to argue? Why have you closed your eyes?'

'I'm trying to stay calm. If my adrenaline spikes it might rip me back.'

'Interesting.' The rabbit didn't sound interested, he sounded impatient. Ali heard him hop-step towards her. 'When do you plan to open them? I can't spend the rest of the day leading you by the hand.'

'Just give me a moment. I need to settle my heartbeat.'

'And why are you sitting all folded up like a frog?'

'No reason, just comfy like this. How long have I been gone?'

'Since just now when you flicked in and out? Or when you charged the tree like a small bull?'

'The time with the tree.'

'Let me see, this is my third turn looking out for you. There are four of us on a two-day roster, so … twenty-four days.'

'That's more than three weeks!'

'The child can do maths, ring the bells!' The rabbit came another hop-step closer and Ali could smell his breath, warm and salty, like the breath of a puppy. She opened her eyes and smiled up at him.

'It was just yesterday for me,' she said, 'which means time moves more quickly here – relative to the real world.'

'Meaning this one is unreal? A little bit presumptuous, don't you think?'

'Sorry. I meant relative to the other world.'

'And are you staying with us this time? Because if you are, my instructions are to get you safely to the palace.'

'Not yet.' Ali opened the jar and shook out a few dried mushrooms. 'I need to check some things out. Starting with how to get back.'

'Find the nearest tree.'

'Funny bunny. So how much of this do I need to take?' She opened her hand and showed him the dehydrated mushrooms.

'What are those?'

'Mushrooms.'

'Really?' The rabbit bent forward and sniffed them. 'They look dead. What do you plan to do with them? Bury them?'

'Eat them.'

'Revolting. Why?'

'To get back. I think I need to take mushrooms or get a slam of adrenalin. Or maybe it's a mix of both.'

'If only it were that simple,' the rabbit sighed. He bent forward and sniffed the mushrooms again. 'Scholars agree that mushrooms can ease the discomfort of crossing back. Fresh mushrooms, not dead ones, but they don't help you to go back, not in themselves. All they do is stop you from dying.'

'Dying?!'

'Correct.'

'That's a pretty crappy piece of news. So, they're medicinal?'

'As I understand it, yes.'

'Which means adrenaline is the key.'

'I couldn't say. I have no idea what that is.'

'It's a hormone, gets the body prepped for a fight.'

'None of that made sense. You might as well have waggled your ears.'

'It doesn't matter. I just need to find a safe way to get a big surge of it to push me back through the event horizon.'

'Event, I understand. Horizon too. Everything else? Ear waggles. You may explain as we walk, very quickly, towards those trees.' The rabbit indicated the woodland on the far side of the meadow.

'An event horizon is the … ah, the outer skin of our space-time bubbles, the place where they touch.'

'Bubbles I understand. Walk, now.'

'Where they touch is like a pore in the skin that lets things through. I sat in front of a mirror that seems to reflect the light from both sides. Right in front of it is one of these pores … or maybe the mirror creates the pore. I don't know yet.'

The rabbit just stared at her, his head tilted to one side.

'Just more waggles. Come along.' He reached down, took her by the hands and pulled her up. Ali didn't resist, she just stared at the soft white paws. Memories surfaced of a child-hood encounter with a TV character, an actor dressed as a teddybear. Suddenly, holding hands with a rabbit seemed the most natural thing in the world.

'You can ask the Queen,' said the rabbit. 'Getting back safely is the hardest thing imaginable. There's a great deal more to it than getting your heart racing. The scholars have been working on it for years. Getting back isn't hard. Getting back without dying – that's the tricky bit.'

'Okay, tell me what you do know. I'll make notes. I need to do this right or dad will kill me.'

'Your father will have you murdered?'

'Yes, if I don't make notes.' Ali opened her journal.

The rabbit looked bewildered.

'We can't dawdle here. And why go back anyway if your father is waiting to kill you? This is complete madness.'

'No. Madness is being swept up in random chaos.'

Ali tapped her notepad. 'This is the opposite. This is order and knowledge, this is science.'

CHAPTER 32

DAY SEVEN

FEAR

_____

The Jabberwock, with eyes of flame,
came whiffling through the tulgey wood,
and burbled as it came!

For the next few minutes, Ali wrote down her observations, which included how the rabbit was getting increasingly agitated.

'Please, we have to go, are you finished?'

'Nearly, I need a sample, something to take back ... a bluebell.' She picked one and pressed it between the pages of her notepad. 'Okay, I'm done for this trip.'

'You're going back?' The rabbit stared at her. Ali was amazed how much she could read from his expression, from his eyes and ears, even the twitching of his nose was easy to understand. He was confused, upset and very anxious.

'Yes. I need to investigate this in small steps, I can't jump in boots and all and imprint myself all over the place; it would mess up the observations. It's why NASA makes their landers and rovers sterile – not much point finding life on Mars if it turns out you took it there on a previous mission.'

'Waggle, waggle! Look, child, we've been waiting weeks now, ever since you spoke to the boys. The Queen will explain everything, now come on.'

'No. I can't leave this spot till I understand how this works. I always arrive here, exactly here, which means the barn is right here too. This is where the two worlds connect. It's got something to do with the mirror, maybe it creates a local field of some kind, enough to weaken the membrane.'

The rabbit reached up, pulled his ears down over his face and started to hop on the spot. His agitation was so great it was coming off him in waves.

'She's going to be very cross with me. So very, very cross.'

'Tough, deal with it. I need to find out if mushrooms really stop the pain when I go back through.'

'I told you, they don't stop the pain!' He released his ears, which sprang upright. 'They just stop you *dying* from it!'

'You telling me something isn't science. I have to field test,' she said, and she crammed a handful of the dried mushrooms in her mouth. They tasted like stale bread and were hard to swallow. Finally she managed it.

'I wonder how long they need. Five minutes maybe? Enough for my gut juices to work their magic?'

'What?' the rabbit blinked at her. 'You have magic juices in your gut?'

'Yes, Rabbit. I have magic juices in my guts. Now, let's sit down and chat for five minutes while you download every-thing you know about this place.'

'Firstly, how does one download? And secondly, no, we are

not sitting here for even a single minute. The patrols circle through here, and they want you as much as we do. We can't risk them finding you here.'

'Good start. Who's patrolling? Why? And what's the risk?'

'I think you should ask him.'

'Who?'

'Him,' the rabbit pointed behind her, 'the Hatter.'

Ali swung round and there he was, a few yards away, his eyes dark and deeply disturbing. She felt like a specimen in a petri dish.

'You're back,' said the Hatter. It sounded like he was thinking aloud rather than addressing her.

'Nice eyes, shame about the hat,' she replied with the same air of casual disinterest. The Hatter continued as if he hadn't heard.

'There are similarities, that's clear. Around the eyes, and the corners of the mouth. A relative perhaps?'

'Is that a question?'

'I believe it is. Did you bring the histories?' He pointed to her notebook.

'That's my journal. What histories?'

'Your journal? Very smart, be sure to write down everything that happens to you, and read it every day, cover to cover.'

'And why would I want to do that?'

'To remember yourself. This is a place of forgetting,' he warned, as his eyes continued to scan her face.

'Can you stop doing that please? I feel like a shop window.'

'Stop what, exactly?'

'Scanning each freckle like you're checking for sun damage. Tell me about the patrols, why is Bugs Bunny so agitated?'

'His name, as far as we know, is Theodore. And he's

agitated because bad people are looking for you.'

'Why?'

'You're news – a visitor who pops back and forth with little sign of damage …' the Hatter leaned in again, his face millimetres from hers, 'apart from the white skin and a little bleeding in the eyes. There are spiderwebs of red in both.'

'I know, broken veins. The people looking for me – what do they want?'

'They want the journals, the histories. A relative of yours was compiling them. We believe she hid them back there, back in your world.'

'My great-aunt Alice. She sent me a note. Where is she?'

'Lost.'

'You mean you can't find her?'

'Lost to herself, like the rest of us. She was compiling our true histories and made one for herself too, safeguarding her memories. We need you to find them and bring them here, she will have hidden them from the others.'

'Others? Over in my world? What others?'

'She didn't say, except that they wore roses. White roses.'

'They're coming!' The rabbit sniffed the air. 'We must leave right now.'

'Yes, I rather think we must. Young lady, can you get back to your world?'

'I think so.'

'We can't stay and fight them. Theodore and I are hopeless in that regard and must take to our heels. Are you quite sure you can cross back?'

'Yes.' Ali pulled the sachet of chilli powder from her pocket. 'Take bunny and go, I'll be fine.'

Then she smelt it; a rank odour drifting their way. 'What the hell's that smell? It's disgusting.'

'Putrefaction. You must leave now! Come, Theodore, are you ready for a little exercise?'

'Ready,' the rabbit nodded. He was trembling now as he pointed to the trees on the far side of the clearing. 'Over there, they're coming from over there.'

Ali tried to rip open the sachet of chilli powder, but the plastic wouldn't tear. 'Stupid fracking packaging. Can you believe this?!'

'Hurry, child.'

'I'm hurrying!' Ali used her teeth, biting a small tear in one corner. The bad smell was growing by the second. Ali wanted to hold her nose to stop it reaching into her lungs. The Hatter and the Rabbit waited.

'I'll be fine,' Ali said, waving them away, 'just go.' The Hatter nodded and set off into the woodland behind them, the rabbit hopping in his wake.

Ali looked in the other direction, out across the clearing. She couldn't see the others yet, but she could hear them – yelps and cackles of laughter, and an odd sound, like dry sticks rubbing together.

'Come on, come on,' she pulled at the tear and the packet split open, the chilli spilling out across the grass. 'Shit!!' Ali dropped to her hands and knees and began licking anything with a hint of powder on it. She felt a slight heat on her tongue and gums, but no chilli burn, nothing to get her blood racing.

The yelps and cackles grew closer. Ali craned her head and stared across the clearing. A pack of small animals scampered into view. They were bouncing as they ran, jumping up to see their way through the tall grass.

Then a larger shape stepped from the line of trees. It was the height of a man, but moved like a beetle on grotesque, multi-jointed limbs. It spotted Ali and shrieked with delight. Then it charged towards her, the pack of animals bouncing beside it.

Ali tried to get up and run, but she couldn't move. Not since the day of her mother's death had she felt so overwhelmed. She couldn't think, couldn't act. Her mind had stalled, all she felt was raw fear, and the pounding of her heart as it tried to beat itself out of her chest.

And – SLAM! – she was back in the barn, toppling sideways like a ragdoll. The pain was excruciating, far worse than before. Ali wondered if she was dying. Was this how divers felt when they surfaced too quickly? Then the nausea struck … and with it something new. Violent tremors that set her limbs jerking about. She curled into a ball, hugging her knees to her chest as the cramping in her stomach grew tighter and tighter. Time lost all meaning. She was adrift in a sea of pain.

When it was over, Ali lay soaked in sweat and shivering uncontrollably. Her brain came back online, slowly at first, crawling out from the bunker it had taken refuge in. And she started to scream.

They were silent screams; her throat felt burnt and raw from the vomiting. That thing, that disgusting beetle thing, could it follow her through? That weird rat creature had – the one who'd chewed on the letter. She had to get out of the barn, but she couldn't move. And she was cold, right through to her bones.

'Move! Now!' For a moment, Ali imagined she was standing over her body, chastising it, trying to kick it into action. Then she was lying flat again, her shivering so intense that her heels and elbows were drumming on the floor.

She fought to move one arm, reached for the folded dust sheet behind her and pulled it over herself like a thin blanket.

Ali didn't remember leaving the barn. She remembered drifting in and out of a restless sleep filled with nightmare visions; remembered being on hands and knees, screaming to herself. Snippets of memory. Then she was lying on wet grass, the moon on her face. She pulled herself up and staggered to the house. All she the could think about was climbing into a hot bath and melting the ice from her bones. She had never in her life felt so cold.

Ali made no effort to be quiet; there was no point. Running hot water in the manor house set every pipe rattling. She poured shampoo under the running taps till foam crept like icing over the side of the bath, then eased herself in.

She tried not to direct her thoughts, tried to lie there and let the heat soak into her. But it was impossible. Every time she closed her eyes, the image of the creature was there, a deformed thing, more beetle than man, scurrying across the bluebells towards her. Limbs clicking.

Yet despite this, she knew she had to go back. The realisation stunned her. Despite the hideous creature, despite the agony of the return, she was determined to go back. Not that she'd be allowed to, her aunt would see to that. Ali had broken her promise the moment she'd made it. Aunt Martha would take one look at her face and know exactly what she'd done. Any chance of another trip would be over.

Ali watched as a peak of foam toppled from one of her knees. It joined the layer of bubbles on the water and lost its form. Would that be her fate, too? One moment a unique individual on a grand adventure; the next, lost in the seething mass of humanity.

Not that she was unique in doing this. First, there was her great-aunt, then Aunt Martha, then her own mother. Now her. Four generations of women. Was there something in the maternal line, a mutation in their DNA that let them cross through? A genetic abnormality?

Ali lay there a long while, soaking away the cold. The problem of how to lie to her aunt – what story might account for her terrible appearance – that could wait for tomorrow. Right now she was too exhausted to think clearly. Just getting out of the bath and down to the library felt like a mission.

When she did finally drop full length on the bed, she was asleep in seconds.

CHAPTER 33

DAY SEVEN

A SURPRISE GUEST

'This must be the wood,' she said to herself, 'where things have no names. I wonder what will become of my name when I go in? I shouldn't like to lose it.' She stood silent for a minute, thinking. 'And now, who am I? I will remember. I'm determined to do it!' But being determined didn't help much.

Morning arrived minutes later, or so it felt, and with a punch of sunshine. She'd forgotten to pull the drapes. Ali reached for a pillow, covered her head and groaned. Every part of her was aching. Two years ago, after running a marathon for charity, she'd promised her body she'd never do anything that stupid again. An apology was called for.

She turned her head and looked at the clock on the mantel. Half past ten, way past breakfast. Not that she was hungry. Empty, yes, from all the vomiting, but not the least bit hungry. She lay still for a long time, waiting to have the strength to get up; not just physical strength, mental too. She needed to write everything down, everything she'd seen last night. But she wasn't ready. Images of the grotesque creature kept flashing behind her eyes. Ali pushed them away. Later! She would write everything down when she was sitting on the lawn surrounded by commonsense trees and flowers.

First, she had to find a way to avoid the scrutiny of her aunt. She struggled out of bed, dropped a towel over her head like a veil and went to check herself in the bathroom mirror.

'Shit!' Her zombie look had gone from vaguely glamorous to completely disgusting. She couldn't believe the face staring back at her, it was like a slab of her uncle's blue cheese! Her skin was as white as candle fat, with thin blue worms running through it. No amount of make-up was going to hide this. Her aunt would know immediately, and that would be the end of everything.

'Shit, shit, SHIT!' Even if she could persuade her dad that some multiverse thing was going on here, even if he brought a squad of whitecoats to study it, the chances that he would let his daughter be part of it were a big fat zero. He would protect her. He would keep her as far away as possible.

'Think!' Ali almost slapped her reflection. 'It's what you're good at.' There had to be a way to stop her aunt seeing her face and going ballistic. There was! Ali laughed as the idea struck her. It would be embarrassing, but it would work.

Forty minutes later she was lying on a picnic blanket in the shade of the giant cedar. She had a jug of cold water by her side, a thick layer of yogurt on her face, and a slice of cucumber on each eye. With luck the yogurt would look like a face pack, so long as no cat came by and licked it off.

Time to plan the morning. She was exhausted, and desperately wanted to fall asleep, but first she had to relive the events of last night, every detail, before they began to fade.

Did the forgetting work both ways? It seemed to. Already the details were getting fuzzy. She needed to dig up whatever her great-aunt had buried in the herb garden. Either it was the 'true histories' the Hatter had told her about, or it was the secret to getting out safely. Or both.

Or was the secret hidden in the stories? Had the author been there himself and written up his adventures as a pair of kids' books? Written them so he could keep reading them and beat the problem of forgetting? Had he filled them with riddles to kept the secret safe from people like Waxstaff?

'That has to be it!' Ali wanted to read both novels again, immediately. But not with cucumber slices on both eyes. Damn it!

'God in heaven! What's with the face?' Ali lifted one slice of cucumber and blinked at the bright sunshine. Her uncle was standing over her.

'Face-pack, Uncle Bertie.'

'You look like a pavlova!'

'Thanks.' Ali grinned up at him. 'Good look, huh?'

'Not the look that's the problem, dear girl. it's the smell. I don't think the sun agrees with it. Best wash it off before you come in. Martha wants a word.'

Ali swore under her breath, went to the bathroom and washed her face. Her uncle was right, the yoghurt had turned rancid in the heat, like sour milk, and the smell had soaked into her pores. The deception had brought her a couple of hours. It was time for step two, and step two was going to hurt like hell.

'Sorry about this,' Ali said, apologising to her reflection, then set to work.

'Ah, there you are.' Lady Grey was sitting in the window, 'God in heavens girl! Did you fall asleep in the sun?' She stared at the crimson face of her niece.

'Sure did, pretty stupid, huh?,' Ali had spent ten painful minutes scrubbing her face with toothpaste. It had worked a little too well. Her face was red and raw – and burning like hell.

'Very silly. We'll see if Nurse Potts has a cream for it.'

'Okay ... but it might not be sunburn, it might be a chemical burn, a reaction to a face mask I used. The pack said twenty minutes, but I fell asleep in the sun.'

'And you left it on for how long?'

'Maybe two hours.'

'How utterly foolish. The chemicals they put in things today, you're lucky to have any skin left. I'll see what Potts has in her little black bag, while you go and see our guest.'

'Guest?' Ali felt a surge of excitement. 'Dad made it?'

'No, sadly, which is something else we will need to discuss. It's been six days now, and I understood he only went down into that research bunker for a few days at a time. Correct?'

'He does a double shift sometimes, but he always lets me know in advance. Have you called his work?'

'We have, dear. No response. Your uncle's trying to track down someone in your father's organisation, plugging into his 'old boy' network.'

'Thanks, so who's the visitor?'

'A young man from the village, the vicar's boy. Not strictly within the rules your school laid down, but I don't see the harm. If you want to see him.'

'Erm, okay, I think?'

'You think? I thought you'd be delighted. Someone your own age.'

'Face?' Ali pointed to herself. 'A girl likes to be presentable.'

'A girl shouldn't fall asleep with a cocktail of chemicals on her skin.'

'Fair enough,' Ali wheeled her aunt to the front parlour. Peter was sitting opposite Waxstaff who'd been left in charge of him, a babysitting Rottweiler. He was wearing in a smart pair of jeans and a linen shirt, crisply ironed.

'You scrub up well,' said Ali, and immediately realised her mistake.

'Have you two met before?' Her aunt frowned at them.

'Yes,' said Ali, her mind scrambling for an explanation that wouldn't get Peter in trouble for trespassing.

'I gave her directions,' Peter said, 'to the house. When she first got here.'

'And I gave him shit about his school uniform.'

'Language please!' her aunt cautioned.

'And five days later you decide to pay a visit?' Waxstaff wasn't buying it.

'Miss Waxstaff,' Lady Grey smiled and shook her head, 'have you seen the selection of young ladies in this village? Why would a young man ˆnot chance his arm with a visit?' She turned to Ali. 'Mind you, the chemical mistreatment of your face does you no favours.'

'Really?' Ali grinned at her aunt. 'So you're saying I'm not fetching enough?'

'Touché!' Her aunt laughed and then cautioned Peter, 'My niece has a fast brain and a mouth to match. You'll be sprinting for the gate within the hour.'

'Thanks,' Ali said, acting hurt, 'good to have team support.'

'You're welcome. Come along Miss Waxstaff, we'll leave them to it.'

'She's a piece of work,' whispered Peter when the door

had closed and they were on their own. Ali sat on the couch opposite him.

'Sure is. Ninety something and sharp as a dagger.'

'So, what's with the face?'

'Sunburn.'

'No. No way that's sunburn,' Peter leaned in for a closer look. 'Burnt myself enough times.'

'Lucky you. So what's happened, why are you here?'

'You happened!' Peter looked over at the door and lowered his voice, 'You know how I said everything was in your head? All that conspiracy stuff you were going on about?'

'Delusional. You said I was delusional.'

'I know.' Peter shrugged his shoulders. 'Sorry about that.'

'A basket case.' Ali folded her arms and pretended to glare at him. 'Those were your exact words. I was behaving like a basket case.'

'Well, you said some pretty weird shit! And you do weird shit too – I mean, look at your face! I totally bet you did that to yourself.'

'Yes, I exfoliated. A mix of toothpaste and sand.'

'You're kidding me?'

'No.'

'So convince me that's normal.'

'If my aunt sees how white my face is, she won't let me stay. Now why are you here. Either you believe me now, or you fancy me.'

'Yes.'

'Which?' She stood up and play-smacked the top of his head.

'Can it be a bit of both?' He grinned sheepishly and she grinned back.

'So what's changed your mind?'

'Nothing. I fancied you the first day.'

'Not funny,' She slapped the top of his head again.

'Last night I looked up your dad. Found his lab's website. This morning I called every number on the contact page, work colleagues mostly. Made a pain of myself; told them I knew his daughter from college, told them you were in a bit of trouble so could they send a message down to his lab and let him know.'

'Smart. Thank you. And what did they say? Bet he stayed for a second shift and couldn't get away.'

'He's not been there. He never turned up.' Peter dropped his eyes, unable to look at her. 'His team did the shift without him. They came up two days ago.'

'What! Oh my god! Something's happened.' Ali closed her eyes, trying to digest the news. Think! She took a deep breath, went to the door and peered into the hall. It was empty. She went back to the couch but couldn't sit. 'Dad was fine when I left for school, his usual self, talking about work. We'd gone out the night before and done a mega shop. I played the guilt card and scored a whole bunch of good food. After breakfast he started packing and I biked off to school.'

'The lab's in Wales? Driving there must add a day.'

'Half a day.' Ali fell silent as she did the maths. It had been mid-afternoon when she'd busted the boy's nose. Her dad would still have been on the road or else prepping his team before they went down to the lab. Either way, the school should have been able to reach him.

Ali started to pace, a cold dread building inside her that made it hard to breath. 'Who did you speak to?' she asked.

'Jenny somebody.'

'She's okay. Their office manager I think. What else did she tell you?'

'That the team had reported him missing to the company funding his research … Rossetti something.'

'Rosetti Foundation, the money people. Dad hates going to see them, says they're always pushing for results, things they can commercialise. So what else?'

'Jenny called the police for an update, but the cops hadn't heard anything. The Rossetti people never reported him missing.'

'That doesn't make sense.'

'That's what the Jenny woman said. So she drove to London and checked your apartment – says the place is empty, everything's gone.'

Ali's legs turned to jelly. She sat down heavily next to Peter, one hand on his shoulder to steady herself. 'I have to go to London,' she whispered, repeating it like a mantra, a way to stay in control, to keep the panic at bay, 'I have to go to London.'

'Yes,' Peter took one of her hands and held it. She snatched it away.

'I have to find him.'

'Good. I'm agreeing with you. What can I do?'

Ali didn't reply, she needed to move, needed to do something. She jumped up and went to the window. None of it made sense. How could everything have gone? Who would do that … and why? But it was connected, it was all connected. Had to be.

She stared out at the garden – the herb garden. She closed her eyes and focused on her breathing, slowing it down. Taking back control.

'Ali?'

'I'm thinking!'

'Just want to help, that's all.' Peter got up and joined her at the window. Ali opened her eyes and turned to face him.

'The two officials who came to your place – can you describe them?'

'The suits?' Peter shrugged. 'One man, one woman – dark grey suits, like bankers. Thirties ... forty maybe.'

'I think I've seen them.'

'Here?'

'No,' Ali closed her eyes again, recalling the scene, 'at my school. I was too wrapped up in myself to notice. I mean I saw them, but I didn't pay attention. They were background noise, just people to see the principal.' She pictured herself storming out; her teacher opening the door as she'd pushed past.

'It was them.' The visitors had been sitting to her right in dark suits. Like bankers. No one dressed like that, not even the school governors.

'Lot of people wear suits in London,' said Peter. 'Not that special.'

'Maybe, but there was something else ... something about their suits ... or their ties ...' Ali tried to bring the memory into focus. 'Brooches! They had tiny brooches.'

'That's them,' Peter agreed. 'Pins in their lapels. Small white roses.'

'White roses?'

'Yeah ... mean something?'

'Just one of the things my mum was fixated on in the novels. She wrote in the margin every time white roses got mentioned.'

'So who are they?'

'Don't know, but that's who's grabbed Dad.'

'Grabbed him? Like – kidnapped him?'

'Of course, kidnapped! He's missing! Our apartment's been cleaned out. What else can it be?'

'I don't know. Something.'

'Like what?'

'I don't know …' Peter waved his arms around. '… maybe a car accident?'

'A car accidentally came and cleaned out the apartment?'

'Don't get shitty with me. I came to help. How about industrial espionage? Russians or Chinese stealing your dad's work?'

'Maybe. Yes, that one makes sense.'

'They break into your apartment and steal all his research papers.'

'But why clean the whole place out – even my stuff?'

'To make it look like a robbery. Your dad walks in and disturbs them, so they have to grab him too. Then they cleared the place.'

'Doesn't fit. I went back in the afternoon to pack to come here.' Ali felt the growing panic. She wanted to race off to London. To leave now. 'I haven't thanked you.'

'What?' Peter looked surprised.

'Not once, that's shitty of me. Sorry.'

'It's fine.' Peter grinned at her. 'I get to hang out with a weirdo who scrubs her face with toothpaste – keeps life interesting.' He sat back on the couch and Ali sat beside him. Closer this time.

'I need to be smart about this, Peter.'

'How?'

'I can race back to London, get in the face of the police, and stalk everyone in a dark suit … or I can stay here and find out who's behind this. Who's messing with my dad. Because it's connected.'

'Losing me here.'

'The suits were at school the day I got thrown out. I was set up. They paid that dipshit to press my buttons. Then they turn up here. They're watching me. Or Waxstaff is. Or Potts. But they're definitely keeping tabs on me.'

'What for?'

'Don't know. But someone's taking pictures of me. Maybe to send to him, to show him I'm okay, all safe. Keep him under control. You know, like leverage.'

'Like blackmail? To keep him working for them on his secret stuff?'

'Something like that.'

'Shit.' They sat quietly for a while, neither talking. Ali could feel her brain churning, crunching data, looking for threads of sense in all this. She got up and pulled Peter by the elbow. 'I need you to do some digging.'

'Sure, I'll call that Jenny woman again.'

'No, *real* digging.' She steered him to the window. 'Out there in the garden. I found the spot marked on that second treasure map.'

'How does that help your dad?'

'I'm sure they're connected – Dad's kidnapping and the gateway in the barn. The Suits are trying to figure it out.'

'So they're government people? Like MI6?'

'Don't think so. Or this place would be buried in barbed wire. Whoever these people are, they don't want to share. They want the secret to getting out safely. They want to own that world.'

'That's ...' Peter stared back at her, hesitating.

'More of my stupid conspiracy theory?'

'No,' he said, shaking his head, 'I was going to say fucking scary. '

'Yeah, and that's why they've taken my dad. They need to control me.'

'That's a leap! Why do they need you?'

'Some genetic trait. Great-aunt Alice made it through, so

did Aunt Martha when she was a kid. Maybe my mum. There's something different about us.'

'Like how some people don't get bitten by mosquitos?'

'Exactly like that. Now I'm their lab rat. Waxstaff wants to get her hands on my blood tests. I need to get into her room, see if there's a London address, a place they're holding Dad.'

'We should go to the police.'

'And say what – my dad's been kidnapped? There's a gateway to another world in the barn? They'll look at me exactly like you did. A basket case.'

'I guess.'

'And you need to be careful, Peter. They don't want you around, obviously, which is why they've been trying to scare you off. They think you're a distraction.'

'Distraction,' he grinned. 'Good to know.'

'To them, not me.'

'So, Waxstaff's room. You'll need the master key. Sometimes called a butler's key. Our church house has one, I found it when I was a kid. It was like my super power,' he grinned. 'No door could stop Peter Powerboy.'

'Seriously. Powerboy?'

'I was seven. So, what am I digging up in the herb garden?'

'Aunt Alice buried some notebooks.' Ali told him about the loose flagstone, and which one. 'I'll get everyone into the dining room, it looks out the other way.'

'Now?'

'Yes, now.'

'In my best shirt, excellent. What will you tell them?''

'That I was worried about not hearing from Dad. So I skipped out yesterday to find a phone, met you, made some calls, discovered he was missing.'

'And what do I do with whatever I find under that path?'

'Hide it someplace safe. Then we'll meet up in the village, in the open where no one can put bags over our heads.'

'No … I'll hide up till I know you've got it sorted.'

'Hide up where?' There was a knock on the door and they jumped up from the couch, stepping apart as the door opened. Peter leant towards her.

'Peter Powerboy,' he whispered, 'where I hid as a kid.'

CHAPTER 34

DAY SEVEN

PUSH BACK

————

'What a thick black cloud that is!'
Alice said, 'why I do believe it has wings.'
'It's the crow!' Tweedledum cried out, and the two brothers
took to their heels and were out of sight in a moment.

Lady Grey wheeled herself into the room. 'So, young man, which version of my niece did you get?'

'The nice me,' Ali answered for him. 'No biting or swearing.'

'Pretty much,' said Peter.

'I'm glad to hear it. And this will be the last visit for the near future. I hope Ali explained her situation.'

'Some of it.'

They saw Peter to the front door, Ali pushing the wheelchair, her aunt making small talk about the village. Ali gave Peter a curt goodbye, closed the door on him and turned to her aunt.

'We need to talk.'

'What about, dear?'

'Something Peter just told me. It was the reason he came here.' Lady Grey frowned and tilted her head to one side, regarding Ali closely.

'So Waxstaff was correct – you did know him.'

'Yes.' Ali didn't elaborate, she just held her aunt's gaze.

'I see. That's ... disappointing. Very well, your uncle's dozing in his chair, but we can rouse him if it's important.' They started back to the parlour just as Nurse Potts was coming down the stairs.

'Ah, good, did you find something for Ali's face?'

'Perhaps,' said Potts, 'depends what caused it.' She bent and inspected Ali's face. 'Hmm, looks like a chemical burn.' She gave Ali a tube of ointment, saying, 'Try it on a small patch first. If it stings, wash it off immediately.'

'Thanks,' said Ali. 'But first, I need to talk to everyone. Can we all meet up in the parlour?' Potts looked at Lady Grey for acknowledgement, got a nod of approval, and went off to get Waxstaff.

'Why does it involve the staff?' asked Aunt Martha. 'You're not going to tell them about our dreams? I don't care to be the village laughing-stock again.'

'Nothing about the dreams,' Ali promised, as they entered the parlour. Her uncle was in his favourite chair, snoring like a chainsaw. It took a full minute to rouse him properly, by which time the others had arrived.

'Well?' Potts planted her feet and folded her arms. 'What's the big fuss all about?' Ali ignored her and focused on her aunt.

'Peter told me something. If it's true, I need to go back to London – today.'

'Peter?' Her uncle was confused. 'Who's this Peter fellow?'

'A young man from the village,' said his wife. 'Alice has breached our trust and is going to give us a very good account for it.'

'Oh, dear.' Her uncle shook his head. 'Smells like confrontation to me. Don't like confrontation, especially when romance is involved.' He started to get up, saying, 'I'll leave that to you ladies. May I be excused?'

'No,' said his wife.

'Please stay, Uncle. It's about Dad,' said Ali. 'He's missing.'

'Missing?' Her aunt looked confused. So did her uncle. Waxstaff's face gave nothing away; Potts just looked irritated. Was she a good actress, or was she out of the loop?

'Not just missing, Aunty – our apartment's empty. Everything's gone, even the furniture.'

'Good grief!' Lord Grey got out of his chair and turned to his wife. 'We must contact the police immediately.'

'They already know,' said Ali.

'They do? That's very odd, why the devil weren't we informed?' He strode to the sideboard and drummed his fingers on a decanter as if contemplating an early drink. 'It doesn't make sense!'

'Exactly,' said Ali, 'something's not right. They should have called you.'

'It doesn't surprise me in the least,' said Waxstaff. 'In my experience, the police are next to useless.'

'I know someone at the Met,' Lord Grey said, turning his back on the decanter, 'he'll tell us what's what.'

'Clearly this is a personal matter for your family,' said Waxstaff. 'If you'll excuse us, we'll get back to our duties.' She turned to leave. Damn! Ali had to stop her; Peter would still be digging. What would keep her in the room? Losing her little lab rat back to London? Would that do it?

'I'm leaving,' Ali said, 'right this minute. I have to get to London.'

'Why?' Waxstaff turned and locked eyes with her. 'To what end?'

'That's a personal matter for my family,' said Aunt Martha, throwing Waxstaff's words back at her.

'Of course,' Waxstaff dipped her head, a small nod of apology, 'but I don't imagine you'll be letting your niece travel on her own. If you plan to accompany her, Nurse Potts and I will have a great deal to arrange.'

'Right, let's have it from the top,' said Lord Grey.

'That's all I know,' said Ali. 'Our apartment's been cleaned out. Dad never showed up for work. Which means something's happened to him.'

'It's very odd,' said Lady Grey, 'but let's not jump to conclusions. There could be any number of explanations.'

'He would never take off without me. I know I've been a real pain, but he wouldn't just sell everything and wash his hands of me.'

'Well of course he wouldn't, I wasn't suggesting that. But money was never his strong suit. Perhaps the bailiffs came and repossessed everything.'

'Doubt it. We're okay for money; a new company's funding his work.'

'No point standing here guessing,' said her uncle. 'I'm with you, Alice, best we drive to London right now and get to the bottom of it.'

'All in good time, Bertie. We'll start with the local police, get them up to speed. They can speak to their colleagues in London. If we hit a wall, you can call your club and get them onto it. They've reached out to you for help often enough.'

'I'd better start packing your things,' said Potts, 'just in case.'

'Not yet,' said Lady Grey, 'but you can leave us now,' and she dismissed the two women with a wave of her hand. Waxstaff gave a curt nod and followed Potts from the room. Ali hoped she'd bought Peter enough time.

'Right, ... Lord Grey fussed through his waistcoat pocket. 'First, the local bobbies, yes?' He pulled out a cell phone.

'You do have a phone!' Ali scolded him. 'You lied to me.'

'A little white lie ... your teacher thought it for the best, he said you'd pester me all day until I let you use it.'

'He was right, too,' said Aunt Martha. 'You're soft as a sponge cake, Bertie. Ali would have had it off you in a blink. Now, find that number.'

Ali watched her uncle open the sideboard and pull out a copy of the local directory. This was going to take forever! She had to get out of there.

'Try to be patient,' her aunt said. 'I know this is difficult, but we'll get to the bottom of it. Go and pack your bags – keep yourself busy.'

'Pack, yes!' Ali leapt on the excuse and hurried out. She had no intention of going to London – any clue to finding her father would be in Waxstaff's room, she was sure of it – but she packed anyway, for appearances' sake, stuffing clothes in her bag without making any effort to fold them.

Then she went to find the master key.

CHAPTER 35

DAY SEVEN

NOTHING

———————

*'You're thinking about something, and that makes you forget
to talk; I can't tell you just now what the moral of that is,
but I shall remember it.'*

If Peter was right, if there was a master key for the house,
where would they keep it? A bedside drawer?

As Ali headed down the hall, she could hear her uncle
lecturing at full volume into his cell phone.

'We will do nothing of the sort, quite the contrary, you will
drop whatever you are doing and present yourself here within
the hour, or I shall be phoning our mutual friend to discuss my
disappointment. Are we clear? ... Excellent.'

'Go, Uncle,' thought Ali. At the top of the stairs, a window
overlooked the herb garden. Ali looked down. Peter had left in
a hurry. Flagstones lay upended, the spade beside them, dirt
scattered everywhere. Had someone caught him in the act?

'Frack!' Ali hurried on to her uncle's bedroom.

'What do you want?' Potts looked up as Ali walked in. She was folding Lord Grey's large blue dressing gown.

'Just grabbing something for Uncle Bertie.' Ali wanted to kick herself; that was dumb. Grabbing what? What would her uncle send her up for? 'Are you packing for London?' she said quickly, hoping to distract the nurse.

'You tell me, Miss Alice, everyone seems to be dancing to your tune.' Then suddenly, surprisingly, the woman softened. 'Sorry, that was unfair. Is it true your dad's missing?' The change of tone threw Ali off balance; it felt genuine.

'Can't see any reason for Peter to make it up.' She crossed to the bedside unit. What could her uncle have sent her up for? Think!

'London it is, then,' said Potts. 'Haven't been back since I finished my training at Great Ormond Street Hospital,' – for a moment she looked almost wistful – 'my glory days. Before I joined.'

'Joined?' Ali pulled open the top drawer and rummaged around.

'Armed forces – medical corps – got to see a bit of the world.'

'Really? I didn't know.' The drawer was a mess, full of kinds of junk.

'How would you? So, what does he want?'

'It's here somewhere,' Ali said, stalling. There were cuff-links, coins, two broken watches and a small notepad. And one key! She slipped it between the pages of the notepad.

'Here it is!' She waved the pad. 'Phone numbers! Uncle's going to call in a few favours.'

'Best he does ... and he should give the police a kick up their whatsits. First thing they should have done is call the school and ask for you. Find out when you last saw him. That's what they do on every cop show I've ever seen.'

Ali shrugged. Potts was right, that's exactly what they'd do. So where did Potts fit in? Ali paused for a moment, staring at the nurse, weighing up the risks, then dived in. 'You're right. Doesn't make sense unless the police have been told to look the other way. When did you know I'd be coming here?'

'Last week.'

'When last week?'

'Does it matter?'

'Just curious.'

'Early in the week. Miss Waxstaff was told to get a room set up for you.'

'Told by who?'

'I guess it was the school.'

'Clever of them, knowing in advance like that before I was even suspended.' Ali watched the puzzlement register on Potts' face. 'I think someone's gone to a lot of trouble to get me here. What do you think, Miss Potts?'

The nurse said nothing for a moment, her expression going from confused to one Ali couldn't read. 'What do I think?' Potts tapped her nose. 'I think I'll keep my thoughts to myself. Suggest you do the same.'

Ali nodded and left the room. She almost ran downstairs, took the key from the notebook and tested it in the kitchen door. It turned. She tried the library door. Yes! It was the master key. Ali slipped it in her pocket and wondered what to do with the notepad; should she risk putting it back now? Would her uncle miss it? Maybe, depending what was in it. She flicked through the first few pages.

'Ha!' Ali laughed out loud. It was a ledger of his horse betting, a history of all the losses and a few wins. The bets were small hobby bets. No serious money. But as she read on, the amounts grew, and so did the losses. At the bottom of each page was a tally. Ali flipped to the last entry and winced.

'Holy crap, what are you doing, Uncle?' The tally of losses was over 300,000 pounds. How could he feed a gambling habit on that scale? What had he done to get hold of that much?

Ali closed her eyes. How clean was he? She wanted to believe in him, she wanted it with all her heart. In just a few days she'd come to love him – love them both – two relatives she'd never known before.

She had to know, would have to talk to him, but first she had to decide what to tell the police when they arrived. Not the truth! They'd react like Peter, dismiss her as a UFO nutter. Safer to play the worried daughter; push them to do their jobs.

'They're on their way,' her uncle announced as Ali stepped back into the parlour. 'We'll soon find out what's what.'

'Try not to fret, my dear,' said her aunt, 'we'll get to the bottom of this, whatever it is. We're family; families take care of their own. Right, Bertie?'

'Damn right!' He gave Ali a big thumbs up. Then they heard the sound or tyres on gravel outside. 'Excellent! I'll let them in.' He set off to greet them and returned a moment later with someone else entirely: Doctor Cherabics.

'Good morning, Doctor, how lovely to see you.' Lady Grey gestured to the settee. 'Please sit down. Ali, be a dear and wheel me a little closer, would you?'

'I tried to call, but your phone was engaged.'

'Yes, all kinds of busy right now,' said Lord Grey, 'but plonk yourself down and I'll find Waxstaff – rustle up some tea and biscuits. I'll leave you three to chat. For the best I think. Yes indeed.' And with that he bustled out.

'Do excuse him,' said Lady Grey, 'he thinks you've come with the results of a pregnancy test.'

'Ah! Right, understood.' The doctor settled himself at one end of the settee as Ali took the other. 'Hello again, Alice. What on earth happened to your face?'

'Did it to myself and feel a bit stupid. I'll tell you another time.'

'Meaning when I'm not in earshot,' said her aunt. 'So, can we assume Ali's blood tests are back?'

'They are.'

'And?'

'Alice?' Doctor Cherabics glanced at Ali, seeking her permission.

'Go head, happy to share.' She grinned at her aunt. 'We've been swapping a few secrets recently, current face job excepted.'

'That's good because I'd like to take samples from everyone.'

'From all of us?' Aunt Martha frowned at him. 'Staff included?'

'With their permission. Alice, your white blood cell count is through the roof, the kind of response we see when someone has an aggressive infection.'

'What kind of infection?'

'That's the issue. You don't have one. Not one I can find. There are no markers in your blood. Your body has a rallied a huge army to fight an enemy it doesn't recognise.'

CHAPTER 36

DAY SEVEN

KNIGHT OR PAWN?

———————

Alice began to feel very uneasy: to be sure, she had not as yet had any dispute with the Queen, but she knew that it might happen any minute.

'I don't follow,' said Lady Grey.

'I do.' Ali reached forward and patted her aunt's hand. 'We have blood cells that wander round with mug shots for every bug they know, so they can fight back. Whatever I've got, my white blood cells haven't seen it before. They're flying blind.'

'Essentially correct,' said Doctor Cherabics, 'with some artistic licence, which is why I'd like to take samples from everyone in the house.'

'No.' They all turned. Waxstaff was standing at the door. 'No one will be sticking needles in me, thank you very much ...' she said bluntly, setting down a tray of coffee on a small table beside Lady Grey, 'unless I know what it's for?'

'Alice?' Doctor Cherabics looked to Ali for permission.

'Sorry Doc, no sharing this time.' Ali kept her eyes on Waxstaff, and was rewarded with a look of open contempt.

'But, surely under the circumstances ...'

'No,' Ali said, getting to her feet, 'but I'll find Uncle Bertie and tell him.' She turned at the door and smiled. 'Thanks for bringing the results yourself, Doc.'

Waxstaff pressed her lips together and began pouring the coffee, focusing on the task as if it were the most interesting job on the planet.

Ali couldn't find her uncle at first. He wasn't in any of his usual spots. The need to speak to him had been building like a pressure cooker. The idea that he could be involved in what was happening here, in what might have happened to her dad, was like poison in her soul. If he couldn't be trusted, she would grab her things and hitch back to London. It would be business as usual: Dad and her against the world. Everyone else could frack off. She could feel the slow burn of resentment stoking its fire inside her, fuelling the anger that had sustained her all these years. And she felt stupid for letting her guard down.

Then she spotted her uncle. He was heading to the garage and she hurried to catch up. It took a second for her eyes to adjust to the dark. He was sitting in the Bentley, his hands on the wheel like a child pretending to drive. He saw her and stuck his head out of the window.

'Care for a spin down the drive?'

'Sure,' Ali opened the large barn-like doors as her uncle started the engine. The Bentley coughed, then purred like an old tiger as Ali hopped in.

'Have you still got your licence?'

'Certainly not,' he waved the idea away, 'never give a licence to old bones like mine.' He put the car in gear and drove from the garage. 'The day you can't tie your laces is the day you throw away the car keys.'

'I need to ask you something.' Ali didn't want his small talk; she'd worked herself up for this, for whatever bad news was thrown at her.

'Fire away.'

'How can you afford my school fees? I'm grateful, but I'm sure I'd survive in a state school.'

'Absolutely not. Wouldn't hear of it. Brain like yours would go mad without a teacher like that Kepler fellow.'

'Not if you can't afford it – and I teach myself anyway. Science moves way too fast for schools to keep up. I follow a dozen websites and even they struggle – so many new papers coming out every day …' She paused. 'Can you slow down? You're scaring the trees.'

'We're barely crawling,' he protested, but slowed anyway, 'and there's a great deal more to school than keeping up with science. Like English, for instance. Science does not move too *fast*, it moves too *quickly*. Let's hear no more about it. We are fine for money.'

'How fine? This place must cost a fortune to repair.'

'It does. Old buildings are leeches, they suck every last penny out of you, and it never stops – each generation feels obliged to keep the family home in good fettle for the next. It costs an arm just to reroof the damn thing.'

Ali put her hands on the dashboard to brace herself as they drove through the main gates and made a tight turn onto the road.

'No licence, remember!'

'I know.' He beamed at her and carried on. 'Just once round the perimeter – no one comes down this road anyway. Where was I?'

'The house, it costs the earth.'

'Oh yes, so Martha and I decided this money pit ends with us. The last of the Greys – her family of course, her lineage, I'm just the lucky bastard who swept her off her feet. I changed *my* name; did you know that?'

'I guessed.'

'Such a bunch of tosh having the family name follow the male line. Ha! We showed them, caused a scandal back in the day. I'm not even a Lord! Your aunt's a Lady but she has no Lord beside her, I'm still a wastrel son as far as the village is concerned. Bertie Wainwright. We made wheels.'

'Times change, no one cares about that stuff anymore. And you haven't answered my question. How can you afford this place *and* my school fees?'

'No one can. Death duties force families to sell. First it was oil magnates, then rock stars, now it's internet types, hardly out of their nappies and making squillions doing Lord-knows-what.'

'Are you saying you've sold the place?'

'Sort of.' Lord Grey squinted as the road curved and sunlight angled onto his face. Ali reached across and pulled down his sun visor.

'Sort of? How does that work?'

'Reverse mortgage. We held out for as long as we could. I tried everything, stock market, sold half the furniture, even had a go at the horses. But it's a mug's game, gave it six months, no one wins except the bookies. I kept a record of all my losses, didn't want to fool myself.'

He sighed and shook his head, 'I keep my tally book by the bed and look at it when I get itchy fingers. That sobers you up, I can tell you. Hey, what's wrong?'

'Nothing,' Ali rubbed at the tears rolling down her cheeks.

She slipped an arm round her uncle's and snuggled in as close as she could. 'For some reason I keep blubbing. Never used to cry, not since Mum died. Now I'm a broken tap!'

'Let them roll. I cry all the time, keeps the eyes in good nick.' They had come full circle round the property. Lord Grey pulled up just short of the front gates and gave Ali's arm a squeeze.

'We'll find your dad. That's a promise. We'll find him together. Look how fast we solve the crossword!'

''You mean how *quickly*.'

'Yes,' he laughed, 'and we'll make damn fine detectives. I'll be Watson to your Sherlock Holmes.'

'That's a deal, Watson.'

'And forget about the money and the school fees. The bank owns the house now, but pays us a good chunk of cash each month till we slip our clogs.'

'What bank?' Ali let go of his arm and sat up straight.

'Not one of the high-street chains. Very established. You should have seen the grounds a few weeks ago. The bank paid for a massive clean-up, gardeners and builders everywhere, spring cleaning like you wouldn't believe.'

Ali did believe. The Suits owned this place. No wonder it had felt like a film set when she first arrived. They'd set everything up for her visit.

'When did they do all that, uncle?'

'Three or four weeks ago. Very impressive people, must have been a dozen or more, busy as bees for days. Timing couldn't have been better though –you got the best of it, what are the odds?'

'Pretty high I think,' Ali said, trying to keep the sarcasm out of her voice.

'Tell you what, you drive her round the block.'

'What?'

'The old girl.' Her uncle patted the dash. 'Have a go.' He opened his door and climbed out. 'Piece of cake, aside from the dodgy gear stick – slide over.'

'You know I'm fifteen, right?' Ali slid over to the driving seat as her uncle walked round the car and got in the passenger side.

'So was the Queen when she was crowned. And this road only goes round the manor. Martha's ancestors paid for it, so in effect, we own it. No more arguments young lady, start driving.'

'Two arguments from me ...' Ali crunched the gears and stalled. 'First, Elizabeth was twenty-five when she was crowned; and second, I'm sure the council pays for the road these days.'

'Correct on both counts. Now, more throttle and less back chat.'

Ali slowly got the hang of it, though she didn't go faster than a slow walk and never got the car beyond second gear.

'Thanks.' Ali parked up outside the gates. 'You'd better drive to the house. Aunt Martha will bark if she sees me driving!'

'Righto!' They switched places, her uncle put the Bentley in gear and they pulled out from the kerb.

BAARRPPPP! A car horn blared from behind and they both jumped in their seats.

The police!

CHAPTER 37

DAY SEVEN

AN INSPECTOR CALLS

'You may look in front of you, and on both sides,' said the Sheep: 'but you can't look all round you—unless you've got eyes at the back of your head.'

Ali shrank down in her seat as they drove in ahead of the police car, her uncle laughing so hard his eyes were watering.

'I wonder if they serve port and cheese in prison!'

'Great start, Uncle. We're after their help, remember? So don't bully them like you did on the phone earlier.'

'Bit firm, was I? Old habits. Always struggled with authority. Martha says I turn into a pompous clown. Best behaviour today, I promise.'

They parked in front of the main door. The police car pulled up behind and an officer climbed out. She was alone, tall and lean, and out of uniform. Ali took an instant liking to her; she had ebony skin, kind eyes and a mass of red hair scrunched up on her head and tied like a bundle of corn.

'Superintendent Dovecot,' she said, extending a hand. Ali shook it.

'Good,' said her uncle, 'let's get inside,' and he led them back to the parlour where his wife had organised a fresh round of coffee and biscuits.

'So, straight to it,' said Lord Grey, 'what have you dug up so far?'

'Nothing at all.'

'I don't understand,' said Aunt Martha, 'you must have something. A case number at the very least?'

'No case and no case number. Nothing's been entered in the national data base. There's no missing-person's report for Mr White.'

'Professor White,' Ali corrected her.

'How can that be?' asked Aunt Martha. 'A valuable government scientist goes missing, a colleague reports it – and there's nothing in police records?'

'Correct. But if his work's classified, other agencies might have stepped in to keep it under wraps.'

'*Might* have?' asked Ali. 'Or have they already told you to back off?'

'Not yet.' Dovecot didn't seem put out by the question. 'I called his work; he never showed up. I asked a colleague in London to check your apartment. She confirmed it's empty.'

'So what more do you need?' Ali tried to keep the anger out of her voice.

'I need evidence of misadventure. People are free to quit their jobs. Free to pack up and move house.'

'Without telling their kids?!'

'You'd be surprised, sadly.' Dovecot paused and took a sip of her coffee.

'So you sit back and do nothing?'

'Certainly not. You're in my district so you can report this to me. I'll treat it as a new case – open my own file. The same issue might arise, but until then I'll do what I can.'

'Excellent,' said Lord Grey. 'More, we can't ask. Right, Alice?'

Ali took a deep breath and nodded. Then she spent the next ten minutes alone with Dovecot, who used her phone to record the interview. Ali answered every question, recalling her dad's mood the day he set off for work, his plans for when he got back, his social life, his colleagues and friends. She only bristled once.

'What about his romantic relationships?'

'Dad? No! None. Married to his work.'

'Are you sure? No one you can think of – not even this Jenny?'

'He would have told me.'

'That was quite an undertaking on her part.' The super-intendent waited for Ali to join the dots. She chose not to. So Dovecot continued, 'Jenny travelled from Wales to London to check the apartment. How? Did she have a key?'

'No! Like I said, he would have told me.'

'Why?'

'What do you mean, why?' Ali didn't like where this was going. 'Dad tells me everything. We're a team, that's how it works between us.'

'When someone goes missing, very often there's a close family member involved ... or a lover.'

'No!' Ali felt a surge of anger.

'Listen up young lady. You see this face?' Dovecot tapped the deep black skin of her cheek. 'My dear husband, John Dovecot, is a smart, intelligent and very loving man. But he kept me a secret from his sisters for three years. Some of us keep secrets from the ones we love out of misplaced kindness.'

'I guess it's possible.' A memory rose up: Ali's dad bringing someone home to dinner. It hadn't gone well. 'I was shitty to him once when he tried dating.'

'So maybe he's more discreet now – he doesn't want to upset you.'

'Maybe.' Ali knew the officer was right, there could have been someone, but it was the wrong path to go down. A distraction. She had to bring the focus onto Waxstaff.

'Alice, we have to be open to all possibilities, however painful or irrational.' Dovecot reached over and switched off her cell phone.

'Okay,' Ali nodded. 'But just how irrational are we talking here?'

'Why, do you have a theory?'

'Maybe.' Ali liked Dovecot, but not enough to tell her the whole truth; her credibility would be trashed. 'I don't know if I trust you yet.'

'Well, when you do, I want you to call me.' Dovecot stood and fished a card from her pocket.

'Police carry business cards now?'

'At my rank we do.'

'Okay.' Ali slipped it in her pocket and wondered what she could tell this woman, something to hook her interest. 'Look, there is something.'

'Tell me.'

'Better if I show you. There's a bedroom you should look at.'

'One your father uses when he comes here?'

'No, the housekeeper's.'

'I'll need her permission.'

'Ask my uncle, it's his house.'

'But it's her room. I'll ask for her permission, but only if you give me a good enough reason.'

'All right.' Ali decided to double down on her lie. 'I think she poisoned me.'

'What?'

'And Aunt Martha, too. I think Waxstaff poisoned both of us.'

CHAPTER 38

DAY SEVEN

MORE RIDDLES

Alice sighed wearily. 'I think you might do something
better with the time than waste it in asking riddles
that have no answers.'

'That's a very serious allegation, Alice.'

'I know.'

'Do you? Really? You just accused someone of attempted murder.' Ali felt the officer reassessing her, and not in a good way. 'How does attempted murder tie back to your father's disappearance?'

'Dad and I are the only family left. It's an inheritance thing. A scam.'

'Alice ... please stop.'

'Maybe she's pretending to be a long-lost love child or something, heir to the estate when everyone else is dead.'

'Alice, sit down and listen. Right now.'

'You don't believe me, do you?'

'I interview suspects every day, Alice. I recognise the truth when I hear it, and lies, too. I also know when someone's spinning me a mix of both. You don't believe someone's trying to swindle the estate off you, but you do believe you're in some kind of danger.'

'Am I that obvious?' Ali felt six years old again; small and foolish.

'To me, yes. So just tell me; what do you really think?'

'I think he's been kidnapped.'

'Kidnapped?'

'Yes.'

'Good.' Dovecot smiled. 'Very good. That's something you really do believe.'

'Yes. And don't do that!'

'Do what?'

'Talk like I'm a good puppy. I don't need a pat on the head.' Ali folded her arms, doing her best to look pissed off.

'I disagree. We all need a pat on the head sometimes – my boss does it with tea and biscuits.' Dovecot broke into a smile and so did Ali, and wanted to kick herself for it. This woman was an expert; she could probably get a lump of rock to do back flips.

'So, kidnapping? How did you arrive at that?'

'Dad works on cutting-edge stuff; it's valuable, so he's valuable.'

'Industrial espionage?'

'Yes, but Dad wouldn't share anything, unless he was forced to.'

'Go on.'

'Waxstaff's photographing me. I think it's to show my dad they can get to me if he doesn't play ball with them.'

'Or she might be an amateur photographer. We're not

talking about shots through the bathroom window, I hope?'

'No, nothing pervy, just walking round the garden.'

'All right, let's go talk to her. Taking pictures without your consent isn't a crime, but she might agree to show us her room. If nothing else we can put your mind at rest.'

They found Waxstaff in the kitchen, peeling potatoes. She glanced up as they walked in. 'Still here, are we?'

'Almost done.' The superintendent scanned the room. 'Big kitchen! I've barely enough room to fry an egg. I'm jealous.'

'Wouldn't be if you had to clean it. What do you want?'

'I'd like to see your room.'

'My bedroom?' Waxstaff finished a potato, tossed it in a pan, and reached for the next. 'What for?'

'Curiosity.'

'Don't you need a reason, and maybe a search warrant?'

'I do,' said Dovecot, 'or I need your permission.'

'Go ahead, knock yourself out.' Waxstaff grinned at them, and Ali knew there would be nothing to see. They followed Waxstaff to her bedroom. The only picture on the walls was a watercolour of three horses. There was no desk, no computer. It was two doors along from the bathroom. The wrong room.

Dovecot's phone rang, she glanced at the number. 'Excuse me, ladies, I need to take this.' She stepped out of the room, leaving Waxstaff and Ali alone.

'So, here we are,' Waxstaff's voice was a whisper, 'just the two of us – the stupid girl and the evil housekeeper.'

Ali fought the urge to shiver. She folded her arms and tried to look belligerent; tried to hold Waxstaff's gaze. 'I know what you're doing,' she whispered back.

'And yet you're whispering.' Waxstaff grinned and shook her head, 'I find that interesting, don't you? Why not tell the pretty police lady all about it?'

'I will.'

'It might go badly. A disturbed girl with a history of violence and delusions of grandeur.'

'Not going to happen.' Ali tried to sound convincing.

'You really are the most frustratingly stupid little creature. You think you know everything.'

'Not everything …' Ali realised she was letting her anger surface, using it as a tool to mask her fear of Waxstaff, 'but enough to get you arrested.'

'Poor me.' Waxstaff put up her hands in mock horror. 'It would be funny if it wasn't so depressing.'

'Where's my dad?' Ali tried to keep her voice down.

'I've no idea. My god, you really can't see what's staring you in the face. The time I've wasted on you. The effort. And for nothing!'

'What does that mean?' Ali took a step towards Waxstaff.

'You're the smart one, you figure it out.' Waxstaff's smile was a thin gash across her white face.

'Where … is … he?' Ali paused between each word. She was ready to hit Waxstaff. Ready to punch the truth out of her.

'Listen carefully,' Waxstaff said, lowering her voice still further, 'I'll say this very slowly so even you can understand. I … don't … know.'

Ali gave in to her anger and hurled herself at Waxstaff.

'Where's my dad, you frackin' bitch?'

Arms grabbed her from behind. Huge arms. Ali hardly noticed. Through the red fog of her rage all she could see was Waxstaff's smirking face; all she wanted to do was smash her fists into it. But her arms were pinned, her body wrapped in a vice. She heard screaming … someone in pain? Was it Waxstaff? Ali screeched in triumph, and started to laugh.

'Alice,' a voice broke through. Firm and gentle. It was good to have it there. Something to focus on. Massive arms released their pressure. She could breathe again.

'Please stop. You're fine, dear. You're perfectly safe, everyone is trying to help, please do stop kicking out like that.'

'Aunt Martha?' Ali blinked, trying to clear the fog.

'Yes dear, it's me. We're all here.'

'Waxstaff?'

'No, Miss Waxstaff is with the officer in the next room.'

'Good.' Ali blinked again, bringing the room into focus. She was on a couch in the parlour, Potts sitting next to her like a mountain. 'Is she arresting her?'

'We'll talk about that later. All that matters now is that you listen carefully to me before the officer comes back in.'

'Sure, okay.'

'That's my girl.' Her uncle's voice, close by. 'Listen to your aunt – I always do – life's much easier that way.'

'Thank you, Bertie,' sighed his wife, 'so very helpful as usual. Ali, when the officer comes back in, I want you to listen quietly to what she has to say. Do not make a fuss of any kind, and promise her you will do whatever she suggests.'

'Why would I promise that?'

'Because, my dear, it's in your interests to appease her, you assaulted her. You had a temper tantrum.'

'Crap! I lost it.'

'Yes, and now you're going to listen to my advice while you drink an entire pot of tea. Nothing soothes the nerves better than hot tea with sugar.' Her aunt paused, clearly weighing up her next words: 'The superintendent has had a call from her London colleague. There's been a development.'

CHAPTER 39

DAY SEVEN

THE NOTE

———————

Here the conversation dropped, and the party sat silent while
Alice thought over all she could remember about ravens and
writing-desks, which wasn't much.

'What! What's happened?' Ali tried to stand. It made her head spin and she felt a hand on her shoulder.

'Steady,' said Nurse Potts, 'best not to be racing about just yet.'

'Tell me!' She fixed her gaze on her aunt. 'If it's bad news, I don't want it from police, I want it from family.' Ali knew she was being hostile. Bad news was an attack; the death of her mother had left her vulnerable. Her aunt knew this, Ali saw it in her eyes.

Aunt Martha absorbed the aggression without flinching. 'Of course, dear. Miss Potts, would you leave us? We'll see to it our niece doesn't do any gymnastics for a while. And let the super-intendent know we're ready for her.'

'Will do. Potts left and Lord Grey took her place on the settee.

'Don't fret', he said, 'it's not bad news, just rather odd. Seems your father left you a note saying he needed time to sort a few things out.'

'A note?' Ali felt a wave of relief. 'Where is it?'

'Police chap in London read it over the phone to Dovecot.'

'He never leaves me notes, we always text.' Ali tried to clear her head; this didn't make any sense. Then suddenly it did. The Suits made him write it; a way to stop the police from investigating. No abduction, just a man with a midlife crisis gone off to find himself.

Superintendent Dovecot came in. Her whole demeanour had changed, Ali saw it immediately. Telling her about Waxstaff had been a stupid mistake and the tantrum had sealed it. Nothing she said would be taken seriously now.

'Did I hit Waxstaff?'

'Don't you remember?'

'Things go misty when I lose it like that.'

'Miss Waxstaff is fine, she stepped out of your way and won't be pressing charges. Luckily for you.'

'Yes, lucky, lucky.' Ali shuffled down the couch, a silent invitation for the officer to sit beside her. She didn't.

'You've been told about the note?'

'Yes, how come it just turned up?'

'It didn't, it was on the table the first day.' She turned a chair to face Ali and sat down. 'Another agency has taken charge of the investigation.'

'Who?'

'MI6. The Met were told to stay out of it; now I've been told the same.'

'To stop sniffing around?'

'Correct,' the superintendent pulled out her phone. 'They scanned your father's note and texted it to me by way of closure.' She tapped the screen and handed it to Ali.

Dear Ali,

So sorry I've created a gap between us. We've been living in different worlds for some time now and I need some space to sort myself out. I'm going to be away for a few weeks. I will be able to explain everything when I get back. Please, please do not do anything foolish.

I have put some cash in the usual place, and I will keep paying all the online bills so just use our normal stores when you buy stuff. I have decided to switch my phone off – work won't understand and I don't want the distraction. No doubt you will think this has something to do with you, that I am unhappy. I am not, you are the most amazing thing that has ever happened to me.

The truth is, I'm trying to resign from this job, the research angle is a dead end, and I can't in all conscience keep taking their money, nor can I spend more valuable years on this approach if I know it won't deliver. But this is a big decision and I need the time to really figure it out, and what to do next. Be tolerant with me, I should have told you all this but I don't want my decision to be clouded by your concern for me.

See you very soon,
Hugs, Dad

It took only one sentence for Ali to know it was a fake. He didn't write like that. Or speak like that! The Suits must have been standing over him, dictating.

'It's total shit.'

'The truth can be messy,' Dovecot said, taking her phone back, 'some things can be hard to accept at first.'

'No,' Ali interrupted her. 'I mean the note is total shit. It's not from Dad.'

'Alice, please …' Her aunt raised a hand to silence her.

'Sorry Aunty, it's not from him. Dad's a lazy writer, shortens everything. And he's got a pet name for me – Newt – he uses it whenever he's trying to reassure me.'

'He's under stress.' Dovecot got to her feet. 'People under stress never sound like themselves. Is it his handwriting?'

'Yes.'

'There we are then.'

'His kidnappers dictated it.' Ali watched Dovecot's face. She wasn't buying it; Ali was on her own.

'Come on,' said Aunt Martha when the officer had left. 'It's good news of a sort. Your father's alive and well. And whatever demons he's grappling with, the thing to understand is that you are not responsible. Let's be crystal clear about that, children always blame themselves. And drink that tea, don't stare at it.'

'Yes, Aunty.' Ali sipped the tea.

'And we can still put our heads together,' said her uncle, 'do our Holmes and Watson routine. A spot of sleuthing.'

'You will do no such thing,' his wife scolded, waving a finger at him. 'Her father was very clear in his note, he wanted space to work this out.' Aunt Martha wheeled her chair closer to the settee. 'Now, let's talk practicalities, shall we?'

'Later Aunty, okay? I need to make sense of this, be on my own for a bit.'

'Of course, we'll talk it through at dinner.'

Ali went straight out into the garden. What was she

missing? The note was wrong, obviously. But it was *so* wrong; wrong in every way. Too complicated, too long, too detailed. If the kidnappers had dictated it, why would they bother with so much detail? And how would they know about the 'usual place' Dad used to leave money for her?

The afternoon had turned grey and cloudy, matching her mood. She set off down the drive at a slow jog, then broke into a sprint.

'What?' she panted. What was she missing? Ali knew her mind would be working on the problem, quietly crunching the data.

When she came to the gates she slowed back to a walk and stepped into the trees. Waxstaff and the Suits had played her brilliantly, and she'd delivered for them. But not what they wanted most – not the secret source for getting out of Wonderland safely. It was the only leverage she had to get her dad back.

She had to find Peter before they did, but first she needed space for her subconscious to pull up whatever it was trawling around for. She followed the path to the back of the main lawn, stepped out from the trees – and there was Waxstaff.

The housekeeper was sitting twenty paces away on the lip of the well. Had she been waiting for her? Were her movements that predictable?

CHAPTER 40

DAY SEVEN

CONFRONTATION

'What matters it, how far we go?' his scaly friend replied,
'there is another shore, you know, upon the other side.'

As she crossed the lawn, Ali could feel Waxstaff's eyes cutting into her. The housekeeper didn't blink once, and the comparison to a snake was unsettling.

'So here we are,' said Waxstaff, her voice soft, almost conversational.

'Where is he?' Ali stopped a few feet away.

'I told you, I don't know where he is.'

'But the Suits know, right?' Ali held Waxstaff's stare. 'They know where my dad is?'

'Suits?' Waxstaff nodded to herself. 'As good a name as any. They call themselves Knaves.'

'Like in a pack of cards?

'I imagine so.'

'Why?'

'I don't know,' Waxstaff shrugged, 'and I don't care. Maybe it's like calling someone a pawn. So, what did you tell the pretty police lady?'

'Everything.' Ali knew it sounded lame even as she said it.

'I doubt that. But go ahead and tell them if you want, no one's going to believe you. I tried that a long time ago. Doesn't work.'

'They might.'

'No, not when they hear about a bottle of painkillers gone missing from Potts' medicine bag. Police meet spoilt kids like you all the time, kids who can't tell the real world from their drugged-out hallucinations.'

'Smart.'

'Thank you. Contingency planning – I do a lot of it these days.'

'So what happens now? I help you, or Dad gets hurt?'

'We'll know soon enough,' Waxstaff said, patting the well beside her, 'so stop hovering like a school bully and sit down. They want us to have a little chat.' She patted the bricks again as if coaxing a puppy. 'Play nice, they might be watching.'

Ali scanned the trees opposite. She couldn't see anyone, but she sat down. 'A chat?'

'Yes.' Waxstaff began clasping and unclasping her hands. 'We have to get a few things clear if we're going to work together.'

'Ha! You've got to be joking.'

'Here you go again, being belligerent for the sake of it. Have you any idea how boring that is? It's been painful watching you strut around the house shooting your mouth off like a spoilt princess.'

'Not a member of your fan club either.'

'There! Again! You can't help yourself, no matter what's at stake, you have to prove how smart you are. Stop it and focus on what matters.'

'And what would that be?'

'No more games between us – you *know* what!' Waxstaff rolled her eyes, and Ali saw how red they were at the edges – a mess of small broken veins.

'You've been through.'

'Give the girl a biscuit ... of course I have ...' Waxstaff leaned in, her face almost touching Ali's, 'and look what it did to me.' Her skin was so thin it seemed translucent. 'I was a pretty young thing before that place got its hooks into me. Want to see a picture?'

'No thanks,'

'You will in a minute.' Waxstaff gave a snort of laughter. 'I was half dead when the place spat me out. Months in hospital, left me a poisoned wreck.'

'And you want to go back?'

'Everybody does. You do! White as a sheet and puking your guts out and still you want to go back.' Waxstaff took a deep breath. 'It will kill us in the end, unless we find how your aunt did it. She went back and forth without a bruise.'

'So you set me up. Got me sent out here to be your dumb explorer?'

'Not me.' Waxstaff almost spat the words out, a flash of rage contorting her white face. 'They own me – now they own you.'

'So who *are* they?'

'Bad people with lots of money.'

'And what do they have over you? What stops you walking away?'

'You're smart, you'll work that out for yourself.'

Ali stared at the ground, her mind spinning. Was Waxstaff still playing her, trying a new approach to get what she wanted? 'You could escape. Go back through and stay there. It only damages you when you come back. If you love it over there so much, go ... and stay there.'

'When I can, I will.' Waxstaff paused and closed her eyes. 'It's not that easy for me, not with all the damage. Not like you, slipping through like it's a stroll in the park ... just like your mother.'

'What?' Ali reached out instinctively, grabbing Waxstaff's wrist. It was like grabbing a broom handle. 'What do you mean?'

'Oh, interested now, are we?' Waxstaff reached into a pocket. 'Ready to see that picture?' Ali nodded, her throat suddenly dry. Had her mother gone through? She'd been fascinated, obviously, even obsessed, but had she done it herself? There was nothing in her notes about succeeding.

Waxstaff pulled out a photograph and handed it to Ali. Two girls were laughing into the camera, arms round each other's shoulders, close friends in their early teens. Waxstaff ... and Ali's mother.

'Lady Grey called us her little pixies, like we were a pair, and I guess we were. Naughty pixies and thick as thieves, right up until our stupid adventure.' She paused, her thin smile almost wistful. 'You're a lot like her. Not just looks, the same self-confidence. Same arrogance.'

'Dad says that too.' Ali's mind was churning. Why hadn't her aunt told her any of this? 'Do my folks know who you are?'

'They do now. They didn't when I knocked on their door again two years ago. The playmate from the village who went missing for ten years.'

'Ten years! You were stuck over there for ten years?'

'No, most of that time I was back on this side – in a psych ward. I don't know how long I was over there; time didn't seem to move the same way.'

Was she for real? Ali didn't know what to say. Better to say nothing, just keep Waxstaff talking. If this was bullshit, she'd hear it soon enough.

'I hated your mum for what happened. She was the brave explorer, I was the little puppy tag-along; and she left me there to rot.' Waxstaff paused, and pointed to the pendant round Ali's neck. 'I thought she'd forgotten all about me.'

'What do you mean?' Ali didn't get it. Then understanding hit home like a hammer blow. 'Oh my god! You're Jack!'

'Yes, its Jackie. Your mum called me Jack – her pet name for me. So she told you about me?'

'Once, maybe, well not exactly. Back when we were moving house, I was five and screamed the roof off. I didn't want to leave the kid next door, my best friend. Mum calmed me down, talked about how she had to leave a best friend once, how hard it was.'

'And she told you my name?'

'Not then. Later. But I didn't connect it.' Ali lifted the St Christopher. 'She always kissed this before she went on one of her missions.'

'Save the Children?'

'Yes …' Ali nodded, staring at the pendant as if seeing it properly for the first time. 'She'd say, "For you Jack." I thought Jack was an old flame and thought that was a bit rough on Dad. I even got shitty about it once. Mum smiled and said Dad knew all about Jack. So I guess she'd told him about you.'

CHAPTER 41

DAY SEVEN

JACKIE

———

The rushes had begun to fade, and to lose their scent and beauty;
and being dream-rushes, they melted away like snow as they lay
in heaps at her feet.

For a while, neither spoke. Ali felt completely derailed by the conversation, unable to get a fix on Waxstaff. Was she a victim? The enemy? Both. And did it matter, as long as she knew who'd taken her dad? Keep her talking; just keep her talking.

'So what happened? How did you go through?'

'It was an accident. We snuck into the forbidden room, the bedroom where your great-aunt Alice disappeared. Your mum had heard the family stories: how it was haunted, how your great-aunt's spirit was trapped in the mirror. The room was kept locked, but your mother got hold of a key. We did it for a dare, wondered if we could last a night sleeping in there.'

'And woke up in Wonderland?'

'Yes, but the shock was so intense, your mother bounced straight back.'

'Adrenaline.'

'Yes, we didn't know that, not then. But I didn't bounce back, too sleepy, I think, so the shock didn't register. I wandered about over there looking for your mum ... next thing, there she is, back again. She'd spent days reading the books, figured some of it out, and came back with a pin. We gave ourselves a good jab and she disappeared again.'

'Not you.'

'No. I've studied it since. Seems I'm slow to anger. I don't have the same short fuse as you or your mother, no volatility. But I got myself fired up in the end.' Waxstaff pulled up her sleeves.

'Shit!'

'Yes.' Waxstaff's arms were disfigured by swathes of scar tissue. 'This got me back. Not even deliberate, just a stupid accident.' The housekeeper fell silent for a moment, as if the memory was burning her again.

Ali waited, watching as Waxstaff continued to clasp and unclasp her hands.

'I made camp in that clearing, praying every night Gillian would come back. She was trying, I know that now, devouring all your great-aunt's notes, reading the novels and making her own notes. Turns out she made three more trips back, but never when I was at the clearing. I'd be off finding food. Once, I got back and found this hanging on the birch tree.' She reached into the neck of her blouse and pulled out a St Christopher, identical to Ali's, except for the inscription – Gill.

'You each had one?'

'Your Uncle Bertie had them made, they were his pet names

for us, Jack and Gill, because we were always getting into scrapes. We never wore them back then, thought they were a bit childish. But your mum hung it on the tree with a note telling me to stay put, stay in the clearing and wait for her. So I did. But she never came back.'

'She wouldn't have given up.'

'What you want to believe, right?' Suddenly Waxstaff was her grim self again, her face setting into a scowl. 'But how would you even know? You never knew her.' The spite in her voice was like a slap, and Ali shrank back.

'I knew her!' Even as she said it, Ali realised she was defending her mother without any grounds for it. She'd spent years blaming her for disappearing, for her choice of work, for leaving her behind. Now Waxstaff comes along and … Ali froze, eyes wide, hardly able to breathe, pinned by a flash of insight that had suddenly crashlanded in her head.

'You!' she stammered. 'You're the reason.'

'Excuse me?'

'You're the reason she's dead. You're the reason I lost her!'

'What?' The scowl vanished from Waxstaff's face, replaced by surprise. 'What do you mean by that?'

'Her job with the UN, going into all those war zones to rescue children, it was one big guilt trip.' Even as she said it, as she pulled the threads together, Ali knew she was right. The simple truth of it was an unwanted revelation, clear and simple, stripping away all the fantasies she developed over the years for her mother's motives. 'She couldn't rescue you, couldn't bring you back, so she saved all these other kids. She kissed this St Christopher before every trip, said "For you Jack." Oh fuck, FUCK! I hate you! You killed my mum!'

Ali jumped down from the lip of the well; she wanted to run off, to scream, to fight someone, anyone. Instead, she ripped the pendant from her neck, threw it on the ground and collapsed beside it. Then she did what her mother had taught her so many years before; she lay on her back and hammered the lawn with feet and fists, screaming out her rage at the top of her voice.

No tears, just white-hot rage pouring from her as memories came flooding back, good memories and bad, and a nightmare she'd had every night in the weeks after her mother's death. It came again now, with a brutal ferocity.

She was running through a field of long grass, searching for her mother. She spotted her – far away across the field. Ali waved and shouted, but no words came. She ran as fast as her small legs could go. Her mother turned, spreading her arms to scoop her up. Then she blew apart. No blood – she simply shattered into tiny pieces of wood, a thousand jigsaw puzzle pieces flying across the field.

Every night Ali would search and search, desperately trying to find all the pieces, trying to put her mother back together again.

She sat up, gasping. Drenched in sweat. The tantrum had taken her over, blacking her out. She looked around. Waxstaff was still there, sitting on the lip of the well. Her stiff posture had gone; she was doubled over, her body heaving as she wept a lifetime of tears.

Waxstaff was grieving! Ali pulled herself up and sat on the well beside her.

'That was unspeakably cruel,' said Waxstaff.

Ali didn't reply, and surprised herself by putting a hand on the housekeeper's back. She expected Waxstaff to shake it away but she didn't. She remained hunched over while her sobbing turned to sighs and then deep, shuddering breaths.

'And she did keep trying.' Waxstaff straightened up. 'You

were right about that. Your mother made herself so sick, your aunt took her to hospital. Then they cleared the room out; packed everything up and put it in the barn.'

'Like nothing had happened?'

'Families are good at that. It's how they keep going.'

'Aunt Martha doesn't know the truth,' said Ali. 'She thinks it's a dream world that traps your spirit in mirrors when you sleep.'

'She's found her own way to make sense of it.'

'She told me she had dreams of the place when she was a kid. She got a bit obsessed and then painted that picture.'

'Did she? I always thought it was painted by that missing Aunt Alice.'

'Who's still stuck over there.'

'Or dead,' said Waxstaff.

'Maybe,' Ali nodded, 'maybe not, I mean she sent me a note, but then you know all about that, right? I saw a copy pinned up on your wall,' Ali paused and felt stupid as a realisation struck home, 'crap! You wrote it! Just another bit of the puzzle to sucker me in.'

'Not me. Where did you find it?'

'It was with all the stuff in the barn. An ugly beaver thing was chewing it.'

'When?'

'First day I was here. It was like a giant mutant rat.'

'So it came through? Into the barn?'

'Must have.'

'Was it sick? Vomiting?'

'Not sure, I was too busy being scared of it. So tell me the rest. You got out by setting fire to yourself?'

'It was an accident. I waited in the clearing, day and night. Two young boys started bringing me food.'

'How long?'

'No idea, it all fades. A few weeks, perhaps. In the end I forgot why I was there. Everyone forgets. I carried on camping in the clearing, the folk over there started calling me the Bonfire Girl. They would gather by my fire, tell and retell their stories – pieces of them anyway – stitched together from threads of memory. We were mad, all of us. Barking mad.'

'And you fell in the fire?'

'Yes, dancing round it like a crazy druid, I tripped and fell. Went up like a torch. Suddenly I was back in the real world, writhing in pain, my clothes melting to my body.'

Ali listened as Waxstaff told her the rest of her story. How she was found in the village, wandering around and scream-ing. No one recognised her, partly because of the burns, mostly because five years had passed back in this world. The Jackie who returned had aged only a few weeks.

She told how she was taken to a burns unit in London, then to a psychiatric hospital. She couldn't remember much, not till years later. Her parents had never given up looking for her, but they died without knowing she'd been found. Waxstaff was in her thirties when the memories started coming back, slowly at first, then a flood, and she discovered that her child-hood friend, the one she wanted to blame for all her suffering, had been dead for years. So all she wanted was to go back through, back to Wonderland. There was nothing more she wanted in this world.

'So I came back here – tried my luck with your aunt and uncle, just knocked on the door. They were very gracious and gave me a job looking after the place.'

'When did the Knaves show up?'

'Long before. They'd started watching the place when your great-aunt Alice went missing. They'd watched your mum and me disappear. Turns out they paid my hospital bills. They've been keeping tabs on me since I came back as a flaming torch.'

'Then what?'

'Then the real person behind all this turned up.'

'And who's that?'

'You'll be meeting them soon enough. Anyway, they knocked on the door one night and gave me a lecture, all smiles and promises, told me how things were going to be from now on. I showed them where they could stick it.'

'And?'

'And your aunt fell down a flight of stairs.'

'Aunt Martha! But I thought …' Ali fell silent as the pieces dropped into place. She stared at Waxstaff, seeing the woman properly for the first time: the dreadful pain she was carrying, the responsibilities. Ali wanted to punch herself. How did she get everything so wrong, so completely back to front?

'Aunt Martha wasn't sleepwalking?'

'Oh, she was sleepwalking right enough, but usually it would wake your uncle, he would get me and we'd guide her back to bed. Not that night. He was sedated.'

'By Potts?'

'No, she wasn't here then. But the broken hip became an excuse to hire her. She's one of their foot soldiers.'

'Does Potts know everything? About the doorway … my dad being kidnapped?'

'No. She's all red meat and no grey matter. She's here to keep me in line, and give your aunt a shove if I don't play along.'

'Frack!' Ali sat forward and covered her face with her hands. Something she'd always done as a child when she'd made a fool of herself. She didn't know what to say. No wonder her aunt had blown up in a fit of anger the night Ali made fun of Waxstaff at the dinner table. Waxstaff was her broken angel.

'They own this place,' said Waxstaff. 'Did you know that?'

'Uncle Bertie said he had a reverse mortgage deal from the bank.'

'He did a deal with a bank, right enough. Just not a regular bank.'

'God, I'm an idiot.'

'No argument from me,' Waxstaff stood up, took a deep breath and wiped her hands on her sides. 'So now you know as much as I do. They told me to bring you up to speed, let you know what's at stake for your family, for all of us. Now go and get the package from that boy.'

'I'll need a day or so to find him.'

'Not possible,' Waxstaff shook her head. 'Find him now, get whatever he dug up, and bring it here.'

'I'll try,' Ali started to walk off.

'Trying doesn't work, Alice. Fast as you can. I'll wait for you here.'

CHAPTER 42

DAY SEVEN

TICK TOCK

_____

'I can't explain myself, I'm afraid,' said Alice,
'because I'm not myself, you see.'

THINK! Ali ran back to the house. Her plan to get the documents and to negotiate seemed stupid now. That wasn't a plan, it was just wishful thinking. She had to find a way to keep everyone safe, not just her dad, but her aunt and uncle too. And Peter. Even Waxstaff. What that poor woman had been through!

And I was such a shit to her, she thought. Sorry, Mum!

Pictures from the last few days scrolled through her head; the cruel things she'd said. She got to the library and flung herself on her bed. The calm and calculated serenity had gone, replaced by churning confusion. And under it all, her subconscious was still nagging away at her, rapping on the door to get her attention.

'What?' She almost screamed the question. 'What the hell am I trying to remember?'

It had to be important to be plaguing her like this. Something about her dad and riddles. She closed her eyes and tried to picture the scene when the Suits had grabbed him. He would try to get a message to her, she was sure of it, and if they were watching him, he would have to do it in code.

Woah! Ali's eyes snapped open. Obvious! She jumped off the bed and started pacing. She and her dad had written a note to her mother every year after her death. A ritual to celebrate her birthday, a way of keeping her alive in their hearts, as if she were still out there, travelling in some faraway country.

They would write the note, then take it into the garden and burn it, their words of love turning to smoke, carried to wherever her mother might be in the universe. The note was written in code, one they'd made up together. They would hide the note in a much longer letter.

If you knew the code you could pick out the scattered words of the love note hidden in the letter. It was impossible to break unless you knew the code, but easy once you did. Her mother's name, her dad's name and her own were the sequences, each letter standing for a number.

That's what her father had done now, she was sure of it. He'd have sent a note to her buried inside the fake letter. That's why it had sounded so weird, like he'd been forced to write it. He hadn't. He'd asked to write it! And the Suits had happily played along because it threw the police off the scent.

Go, Dad! She raced from the library and went to find her uncle. She didn't need his help decoding the letter, she just needed the letter. But if they solved it together, then he'd believe her – he would know her dad had been kidnapped.

She found him dozing in a chair on the patio, a straw boater angled over his face. He was snoring, and he was alone. She bent and tapped him on the shoulder. He stirred but didn't wake. She tapped again.

'Badgers!' said Lord Grey. He sat up, the straw boater falling to the floor.

'Just me, sorry.' Ali picked up the hat.

'No badgers?'

'Nope. Had to wake you. Sorry.' She handed him his hat. 'I need your help.'

'Of course.' He stretched and rubbed his eyes. 'Might need a coffee to kick-start the old brainbox.'

'I'll get that, you get your phone and a notepad – we're going to do a spot of Holmes and Watson.'

'Sleuthing! Excellent.'

Five minutes later they were back on the patio. Her uncle sipped his coffee as Ali opened the text from the police.

'I'm going to read out the note dad left.'

'What's this to do with sleuthing?' He didn't look happy. 'Your father made his wishes very clear.'

'Just trust me. You know I'm good at riddles and crosswords, right?'

'Too good!'

'Because I've been doing them all my life with Mum and Dad. We made up secret codes. So just play along; pretend there's a message hidden in this letter and we're going to Sherlock the crap out of it.'

'Hardly fair. I go along with this, knowing it's nonsense, encouraging you. Then I have to watch your disappointment when it all comes to nothing.'

'I'll risk it if you will.'

'Rather have another game of croquet and do the disappoint-ing myself.'

'Just the first few sentences. If I'm wrong, I'll quit and beat you senseless at croquet. Deal?'

'Deal. And we don't tell Martha about these shenanigans.'

'Unless there's a message.'

'Okay. What's the code sequence?'

'It's our names turned into numbers.'

'Like one for the letter 'a', two for 'b' and so forth?'

'Exactly.'

'Bit obvious.'

'You have to know all three names, and put them in the right order.'

'Which is?'

'Me, then mum, then dad.' She watched him write them out on his pad with the corresponding number under each letter.

'Ok, all set.' He tapped the pad with his pen. 'Read away.' Ali read slowly, just the first three sentences. It was enough.

'I'll be damned!' Her uncle looked up, his expression a mix of bewilderment and anger. Ali burst into tears. It really *was* there, a message from her dad. She had been decoding it in her head: *Newt. You are not safe there.*

'Newt. Wasn't that his pet name for you?'

'Yes, shall we dig out the rest of it?' Her uncle nodded and they set to work. It only took a few minutes, then he read the hidden message aloud:

'Newt. You are not safe there, get away. Folk will use you. I will be fine if I know you are safe. Trust no one, not school, not police. Only family. Go now. Love Dad.'

Her uncle shook his head. 'I fell for it, just like that police-woman.'

'But you believe me now, right? Dad's really been kidnapped.'

'By who – foreign types? After his research?'

'Who knows?'

'And he thinks they'll grab you, too.'

'Dad wouldn't hand over his work, except to keep me safe.'

'Right!' Her uncle pulled himself up from his chair. 'Come on, we must call that superintendent right now, tell her what's what.'

'No! You heard Dad – trust no one, not even the police. We have to get away from here. Get to London.'

'Potts and Waxstaff?'

'Only *family*, like Dad said. Grab some stuff and get Aunty in the car.'

'What if she doesn't believe us?'

'Show her the note. And if she still digs her heels in, tell her it's about the sickness – our sickness.'

'*Our* sickness? What the devil does that mean?'

'The dreams she had when she was a kid – she told you about them, right? And you believed her. Only you.'

'And she told you?'

'She had to, Uncle Bertie, I've been getting them too.'

'The devil you have!'

'That's why I've been getting so sick, just like her.' She watched this sinking in, watched him putting the pieces together.

'That séance thingy the other night – that all part of it?'

'Yes. We can talk about it in the car, but we need to get away from here.'

Ali raced back to the library to check the clock. Twenty minutes before she had to be at the well and meet the person behind all this – the person Waxstaff was so terrified of. So what next? Should she get in the car and go? She stared around at the room. Her clothes were packed in her suitcase.

Everything else was in her backpack: the novels, her scribbled notes, the bizarre letter from her missing great-aunt. She took it out and read it again.:

Dearest Alice, my great-grandniece to be,

I pray these books survive undisturbed until your arrival so many years from now. I will explain all when we meet, for meet we must. I entrust my safety to you. Everything you need to know is hidden in these books, penned as childish tales of distraction. The books hold the key to finding me. Forgive their cryptic conceits; I have to protect access to this peculiar world from dark hearts who are set on destroying it.

Dear child, please find me. More is at stake than my survival or I would not send this bottle across the tide of years to your future shore.

With hope and affection,
your great-aunt, Alice.

She read one line again, as if seeing it properly for the first time: *I have to protect access to this peculiar world from dark hearts who are set on destroying it.*

Were these 'dark hearts' the same people she was about to meet at the well? How long had this been going on, this war?

'I won't give it to them!' Ali said it aloud, as if making a promise.

CHAPTER 43

DAY SEVEN

DING DONG DELL

———————

'I beg your pardon?' said Alice.
'It isn't respectable to beg,' said the King.
'I only meant that I didn't understand,' said Alice.

Waxstaff was already at the well as Ali jogged back across the lawn. She was pacing back and forth and talking to herself.

'You took your time,' said Waxstaff. 'Did you find Peter?'

'Not yet.'

'Heaven help us!' Waxstaff's almost collapsed. She sat on the lip of the well and started to shake. Ali sat beside her.

'Maybe it's for the best,' Waxstaff whispered. 'Not for us, of course, but for the poor sods over there. Heaven help me, I'm so tired of fighting her.'

'Her? Who is it?'

'You've already met her,' sighed Waxstaff, straightening

up and doing her best to control her trembling hands, 'and here she is.'

Ali looked up and saw the huge figure of Nurse Potts step from the cover of the trees opposite ... and trotting beside her, skipping like an excited child, was the blind Mrs King.

'Glass eyes!' It was the last person Ali expected to see.

'Hello!' Mrs King shouted the greeting when she was halfway across the lawn. She made a beeline straight for them, as if her eyes were the real thing. 'I do hope Jacky has filled you in on the essentials?'

'Do everything she asks,' Waxstaff whispered, 'and don't be smart.'

'Sound advice,' laughed Mrs King, who was still a dozen paces away. Ali stared at her – there was no way she could have heard that. Not from there.

'Nothing wrong with your ears then?' Ali shouted back, and felt Waxstaff stiffen beside her. Mrs King didn't seem to take offence, she kept on smiling as she skipped over and stopped in front of them.

'On the contrary, young lady, there's a great deal wrong with my ears, but I get by.' She turned to Potts, who was a few paces behind. 'This will do perfectly. Set the table up here.' The nurse was carrying a wicker basket in one hand, and a folding table and chair in the other.

'So, where is it?' Mrs King directed the question to Waxstaff.

'We're still looking,' said Waxstaff, her voice wavering.

'That won't do at all,' said Mrs King. 'Made myself perfectly clear.'

'See, that's the problem,' said Ali. 'I don't have a good track record with being told what to do. Doesn't work.'

'How very modern of you. In my day, children did as they were told or were severely punished.'

'In your day?'

'Yes.' Mrs King opened the basket and began laying the contents on the table, placing every item with meticulous care. Ali watched in disbelief. The old lady wasn't using the tongue-clicking she'd talked about in the tea shop; and yet she was laying the table as if her vision was perfect.

'I thought your clicking only worked inside?'

'Which is why I'm not clicking.' The blind woman looked into Ali's face, the glass eyes staring straight at her. 'You look dreadful, young lady. We must find the secret to crossing back without all this damage.' She sat on the folding chair and clapped her hands. 'There, all set. Only a single chair, I'm afraid, but you two look cosy on the well.'

'I'm not hungry,' said Ali.

'Nonsense, every cell of your body is screaming out for repair. And I made it all myself – tea and mushroom quiche. We have a lot to discuss.'

'Like, who you really are?'

'We can start there.'

'Not just a weirdo with spooky eyes, right?' Ali almost spat the words out.

Waxstaff stifled a groan beside her. Why was she so terrified of this person?

'Hear that, Potts?' Mrs King laughed. 'I told you I'd found a new warrior for the cause. So yes, Alice, let's start with me. I run a team studying the gateway in your barn. If you join my project, I'll tell you a great deal more about it.'

'And if I choose to run a mile the other way?'

'You won't.' She gestured to the table. 'Pour the tea, would you, my dear?'

'Sure.' Ali felt a strange detachment from the scene. It was like the calm she'd felt earlier, except this time it was icy cold.

Her senses were on high alert. Was this how a hunted deer felt – cold and detached, alert for the smallest detail that might save its life?

She reached forward and poured the tea, observing her arm as if someone else was doing the work, impressed at how steady her hand was. Unlike Waxstaff who was trembling beside her.

'Let's start with a little Q and A, shall we?' King lifted her teacup and took a sip. 'According to Jackie's notes, you've been through four times, correct?'

Ali didn't reply. She picked up her own tea and took a sip, then another, letting the silence stretch.

Waxstaff broke it, answering for her. 'It was four times.'

'Thank you, Jackie, but I'd like Alice to confirm that.'

'Three or four,' Ali agreed, 'maybe five. What's the difference?'

'You're alive, that's the difference. To the best of our knowledge only your great-aunt has been through more than twice without suffering all kinds of brutal damage. Most die, and the few who don't are wretched and broken. We have a facility where we do our best for them, but it's scarcely more than a hospice.'

'Is that right?' Ali took another sip of tea. She knew exactly what Mrs King was up to. Her teacher had tried the same tactic on the drive from London: try to draw her out by appealing to the scientist in her. Not going to happen. She wouldn't let this freak befriend her. Or intimidate her, though that was harder, with the glass eyes boring into her and Waxstaff trembling so much. And what was Potts up to? The nurse had moved behind Mrs King and was undoing the back of the woman's floral dress.

'Enough crap.' Ali put her cup down. 'Get to the point. Where's Dad?'

'Working hard on his research, I hope.'

'Your lot kidnapped him.'

'We relocated him ...'

'Like I said.'

'... to a new facility, better equipped and with its own apartments, more like a university campus. Everyone can focus on the work.' She smiled and gestured to the table. 'Do have some quiche.'

'Stick your quiche.' Ali folded her arms and did her best to glare at the glass eyes in front of her.

'I see.' The woman gave a little sigh. 'How very disappointing.' She leaned forward and cut herself a slice. 'I thought better of you. Anyway, your father is hard at work figuring out the mechanics of the doorway.'

'Not his field – he's researching gravity waves.'

'And gravity wells and how they can bend time. Essential for understanding multiverse theory.'

'You fund him?' It wasn't a question; it was a sudden realisation. Pieces of an old puzzle falling into place, things her dad had said about the cost of funding; how hard it was to keep research clean of industry pressures.

'Yes ... that is to say, I bought the company that's funding him.'

'Does he know about you? About what you're doing?'

'Not at first. But he's a clever man.' Mrs King paused to wipe pastry from her chin. 'He tested us: two weeks ago he wrote a paper and tried to have it published. We blocked it; he dug his heels in. I was forced to get creative. Now your father will do as he's told in order to keep you safe.'

Ali didn't reply. What was there to say? Everything was on the table.

'You were just an insurance policy to begin with, until you

went fossicking around in the barn. You surprised us there. Delighted us, in fact. So we instructed Jackie here to keep track of your adventures.'

Potts eased open the back of King's dress, revealing a bandage. It looked moist and discoloured. The nurse peeled it away.

'Shit!' Ali reeled back and covered her nose. The smell from the wound was disgusting, almost overpowering. Waxstaff started to gag beside her.

'Yes,' Mrs King nodded in agreement, 'the smell of putrefaction. Something you can look forward to if you continue to trot between the worlds without your great-aunt's secret recipe.'

'You've been through?'

'Many years ago. It left me with a plague of wretched boils. I didn't take a tumble in your garden the other night. I was here to see Potts. The boils must be drained or the poison builds up and takes the edge off my mood. The mushroom quiche helps too, of course.'

'How many times?' Ali barely got the question out before she had to look away. Potts had started squeezing the edges of the boil and a glutinous mass of grey pus was oozing out like coil of toothpaste.

'Three.' Mrs King reached up and slapped Potts' wrist. 'Don't be so ham-fisted. I'm not a corpse. If you can't be gentle, I shall give the job to Alice.' Potts adjusted her fingers and began squeezing again. More pus coiled out. The nurse did her best to catch it in a tissue, but some fell like grey cream onto the dress.

'I intend to go through many more times when I can do it safely. There's so much to learn over there. A whole universe of strange and wonderful things.'

'Like a large talking rabbit?'

'He was human once, then underwent metamorphosis at a cellular level.'

'Not possible.'

'Not here, no. But over there, it seems commonplace, like manifesting a wish – a process of self-induced mutation.'

'That's completely stupid.'

'Says the girl who walks between worlds. Let me show you what stupid can look like. Remove this dreadful head wrap, would you, Potts?'

The nurse grunted disapproval, but complied, unwinding the gypsy turban from the old lady's head. What the hell was going on? Then the band of cloth fell away revealing two gigantic ears. They were grotesque: two flaps of gristle, the skin translucent and laced with blood vessels.

Ali stared, too shocked to say anything.

'That's better,' said King. 'It's rather painful keeping them strapped in, but we can't go around drawing attention.' She stood up and tapped one shoulder. 'Dress too, if you please, Potts.'

'I'd rather not,' said the nurse, 'they're the devil to fold back.' But she did as she was asked, unfastening more buttons. There was a crack of air, and a pair of bat wings unfurled, snapping open like tightly sprung umbrellas.

'For fuck's sake!' Ali jumped to her feet and moved around the other side of the well, putting it between her and the freakshow. 'What *are* you?'

'I'm not sure,' the woman said, and she spread the wings, flapping them briefly, 'but it's definitely happening at a cellular level. Some form of mutation that is, as you can see, transformational.'

'Does it hurt?'

'Yes. One day I'll go back and stay there till the transformation's complete. Like the rabbit. But this hybrid state gives me no end of pain.'

Ali stayed where she was, leaning on the lip of the well, almost squeezing the bricks as she stared across at Mrs King, at her deformed ears, her sinewy wings. Her glass eyes.

'Is that how you lost your eyes?'

'No. I was born blind. I taught myself to see with the clicking, just like a bat. I suppose I identified with them at some level. So when you go back, Alice, as you will I'm sure, do be mindful of an old and very wise expression.'

'Like, don't talk to strangers and freaky bat people?' The insult was out before Ali could catch herself.

'No. I meant, be careful what you wish for. You need to stay in charge of your thoughts at all times over there.' King flapped her wings to underscore the point. 'But enough chitchat – you know what you have to do. Find that young man and whatever he uncovered in the herb garden. There's a great deal at stake. Jackie explained all this, I'm sure.'

'Yeah ... I do as I'm told or you'll hurt my dad. Right?'

'Hurt him? No, dear' – she paused for a heartbeat – 'I shall kill him.' The woman kept talking, but Ali could no longer hear her, there was so much noise in her ears, the roaring of her own blood.

'So, Alice, are we clear on this?'

'On what?' Ali tried to focus.

'Pay attention. I won't tolerate one of your famous tantrums. Bring me the secret to safe passage or watch everyone you care about suffer very badly.' She pointed at Waxstaff. 'If you please, Miss Potts.'

'With pleasure.' The giant nurse stepped towards Waxstaff.

'Wait!' Waxstaff stood up, holding her arms out to fend Potts off. 'What are you doing?'

'A little demonstration for young Alice here,' said Mrs King.

'Nothing personal,' laughed Potts, 'but some jobs are more satisfying than others.' And without breaking stride, she reached out, grabbed Waxstaff by both shoulders, and with no effort at all, lifted her off the ground.

'Let go of her!' Ali sprang at Potts, grabbing one of her arms as Waxstaff started kicking out.

'I won't beg,' Waxstaff said, glaring at Potts, 'not from you.'

'Shame,' said Potts.

'Put her down!' Ali screamed. She let go of Potts' arm and began kicking the nurse's legs. Potts hardly noticed. She extended her arms and dropped Waxstaff down the well. There was a brief moment of silence, then a sickening thump as her frail body hit the bottom.

'NO!' Ali leaned over, peering down into the shadows below.

'Point made, I trust,' said King. 'Now go and find Peter.'

Ali couldn't see her mother's old friend, but she could hear her ragged breathing. It sounded wet, the air gargling from lungs filling with blood.'

'She's dying!' Ali started climbing into the well, her feet scrambling to find the rungs of the iron ladder.

'I hope so,' said Potts. 'That was the plan.' She grabbed Ali round the waist, hoisted her up and set her down in front of Mrs King.

'Consequences ...' King leant in, her glass eyes inches from Ali's face, 'do we understand each other?' Ali could see twin images of her own reflection staring back at her.

'That was sick!' Ali screamed. 'You're sick!'

'Very possibly. And what have we just learnt? Hmm? We have learnt that I won't hesitate to kill your father; and that you are the prime suspect in a murder. The girl with the anger management issues; the girl suspended from school for assault; the girl who attacked Waxstaff in front of a police officer.'

Ali stared at the grotesque parody of a woman in front of her. She wanted to feel rage, wanted the simple blind heat of anger to fill her up, to give her the strength to reach out and slam her fists into those glass eyes. But all her anger had evaporated. Only dread remained.

'One hour?'

'What?' Ali's voice was barely a whisper.

'One hour to find Peter. Not a minute more, or your aunt joins our dear friend down the well. Potts will be sure to look after her till then.'

Ali ran.

CHAPTER 44

DAY SEVEN

APOLOGIES

————

'Tell me, please, which way I ought to go?'
'That depends on where you want to get to,' said the Cat.
'I don't much care where,' said Alice.
'Then it doesn't matter which way you go,' said the Cat.

Ali raced across the lawn. It was like running in sand, or running with the Red Queen – faster and faster, just to stand still. The master key was where she'd left it, taped under the desk in the library. She tore it free and ran to the stairs.

'Alice, is that you?' She caught a glimpse of her aunt through the open door of the dining room. Ali didn't reply, she took the stairs two at a time, up to Potts' bedroom. The key worked and Ali almost fell inside.

The room was sparse and tidy, no frills. Sitting on a bedside table was Potts' medical bag. Ali grabbed it and raced out.

'What have you got there?' Her aunt had wheeled herself

into the hall and was parked at the bottom of the stairs, blocking the way.

'No time, Aunty.' Ali didn't break stride, she used the end of the banisters for leverage and vaulted sideways over the handrail.

'You will bloody well make time!' Lady Grey tried to stand, her frail body shaking with the effort.

'I'll explain later. Please sit down.'

'I will not!' Her aunt raised her voice. 'Bertie, come here this instant!'

'Don't shout.' Ali was already halfway down the hall and could see through the dining room to the lawn beyond. Potts was striding back to the house.

'Give me that bag, young lady. Now!'

'I can't Aunty, and you have to get out of here, right now.'

'Bertie just spun me the same line, he's a terrible liar. What is going on, tell me now – right now. What is really going on?'

'Potts just pushed Waxstaff down the well.'

'What! Don't talk gibberish.'

'These are for her.' Ali hugged the bag to her chest. 'She's in terrible pain; and you have to get out. Potts will hurt you too, Aunty. Go! Right now.'

Lady Grey said nothing for a moment, she simply stared at her niece, her eyes scanning Ali's face. Then she sagged back in her chair, her face tightening into an expression Ali couldn't read.

'Jackie ... is she badly hurt?'

'I think so. Get on the road to London, then call an ambulance. Potts won't do anything, not yet. Play along as if nothing's happened – but get out.' Ali heard the garden door to the kitchen open. She ran to her aunt, planted a kiss on her forehead and disappeared through into the dining room.

Twenty seconds. Ali ran out through the French doors. It would be twenty seconds before Potts came out of the kitchen and down the hall. Twenty seconds to get to the brick wall and through the ivy before Potts wheeled her aunt into one of the rooms and had a clear view of the back garden.

She counted the seconds as she ran, pushing through the ivy on eighteen, and slowing as she raced through the tangled mess of the orchard, then dropping to a crouch at the door of the barn. She pulled out the master key. Please let it fit ...

It didn't.

'Damn it!' Ali dropped to the ground and crawled around the barn till she found boards that looked weathered and rotten. She lay on her side and kicked out. The impact sent a shock wave back up her leg, but the plank seemed to give a little. She kicked, and kicked again – and again – until it splintered. Then she kicked the one above. That gave way too, and she squeezed into the barn.

There wasn't time to think, only to act, to follow a plan that was rolling out in front of her. Gut instinct.

'No such thing as instinct, Newt.' Her mother's voice, a dislocated memory from long ago. 'Instinct is merely a name for data crunching before computers were invented. The brain's a powerful thing, lining up options. Sometimes we have to get out of the way and let the brain do its thing.'

Ali crossed to the bed, grabbed the dust sheet, kicked the stacked boxes clear of the trapdoor and climbed down. The moment she was in the tunnel she could hear Waxstaff's ragged breathing; it was faint, but the tunnel seemed to amplify it. Ali wanted to call out, let her know she was coming, but the blind woman might still be in the garden above, sipping tea. So she shuffled down the passage as quickly as she could, the bag in one hand, the bundled sheet in the other.

Waxstaff was a mess. There was blood on her chin and blouse, her nose looked broken, bent to one side, and the side of her face was swollen, the skin puffed and purple. Ali bent down and whispered, 'Don't cry out.'

Waxstaff didn't move, but her breathing faltered slightly.

'I've got Potts' bag.' Still nothing. She wanted to nudge her, but Waxstaff might cry out. Ali glanced up at the circle of blue sky. If Mrs King had left, it would make things easier. What to do? Climb up and check?

Then Waxstaff's eyes drifted opened. 'Stupid girl,' she whispered, the words barely audible.

'Shush.' Ali knelt down, put a finger to her lips and pointed up. Waxstaff nodded and Ali lifted Potts' bag into the light. The housekeeper looked confused for a second, then relief flooded her face.

One by one, Ali took out each packet and sachet of drugs, holding them steady as Waxstaff read the labels. She shook her head each time until Ali held up a small glass vial. It took a lot of whispered instruction, but Ali managed to fill a syringe and give the injection. The effect was instant as a powerful painkiller flooded Waxstaff's body.

'Must get you to the barn,' Ali whispered. She spread the dustsheet on the ground beside Waxstaff, lifting her onto it as gently as she could. She knew there was no time for this. But what else could she do? Leave the poor woman to die in a dark tunnel? Her mum's childhood friend? She picked up two corners of the sheet and started dragging Waxstaff back towards the barn.

'They can't have it,' Waxstaff whispered, her voice just audible above the quiet swish of the sheet on the brick floor.

'I know,' Ali whispered back.

'Your great-aunt …' Waxstaff could only whisper a few

words at a time before needing to take a shallow breath, '...
she kept it safe from them ... for all these years.'

'I know. Once batwoman has it we're history. You, me, Dad.
They'll cover their tracks and kill anyone who knows anything
about them. I won't let them have it.'

'Good ... it's why she wrote the books ... I'm sure of it.'

'Her journals?'

'Not journals ... the two novels ... your great aunt ... wrote
the novels.'

'What?!' Ali paused to rest; they were halfway along the
tunnel, and it was hard work walking backwards at a crouch
pulling her mother's friend.

'Lewis Carroll ... was your great-aunt Alice.'

'Bloody hell! I'm an idiot!'

'We already ... agreed on that.' Waxstaff chuckled, then
groaned at the pain it caused. Ali started hauling on the sheet
again, and played the riddle out in her mind. It was obvious,
now it had been pointed it out. Lewis was an anagram for
'wiles', an old-fashioned word for a devious strategy; and
Carroll was Alice Grey's middle name. But why bother?

'Why? What was the point?'

'Insurance ... if she stayed over there ... she'd forget everything ... I think the books ... are full of secrets.'

'But why leave them here? She could have taken them with
her.'

'No ... the dates ... don't match.'

Ali crunched the numbers. Her great-aunt disappeared
before the books were published. Something forced her to go
back early.

They reached the trapdoor and Ali climbed up. She pulled
a drawer from the dressing table and took it back down to use
as a step. Lifting Waxstaff into the barn was painful for both

of them, but Ali managed. She settled Waxstaff on the bed and injected her with another vial of the painkiller. The housekeeper gave a deep sigh and closed her eyes. Ali watched her face, watched the lines soften as the pain eased.

'I have to go,' said Ali.

'Yes, you do.'

'There's so much to ask you.'

'Another time ... find the secret ... and destroy it.'

'Yes,' Ali nodded, but didn't move. She couldn't.

'What is it?'

'Nothing.'

'Tell me.'

'I can't. It's selfish. I'm being selfish, even now in all of this.'

'Helping me? No ... this is brave.'

'No,' Ali shook her head, 'it's selfish, I want ... I so want ...'

'What? Tell me.'

'I want ... I want Mum to be proud of me.' Saying it aloud like that, a simple declaration of something so honest and heartfelt, was too much. Ali felt a wave of anguish rising up from her chest. She clamped a hand over her mouth to stifle it. She had no idea what it was, she'd had no experience of it – the inconsolable grief of the bereaved.

Ali crumpled forward, her head dropping onto Waxstaff's lap; a child again, seven years old, desperate for a kind word, for a mother's gentle caress, for the quiet assurance that everything will be all right. But it wouldn't be. Monsters existed, and no one was coming to make it all right. Only she could do that.

Ali found it hard to leave. There was a glass jar on the sink. She washed it as best she could, filled it with fresh water from the tap and set it on a packing case beside the bed, along with everything from Potts' bag.

'Go,' Waxstaff seemed to sense Ali's hesitation, '... and destroy it.'

'First I have to stop Potts.'

'How?'

'I'll think of something. Maybe push her down the stairs.'

'No.' Waxstaff shook her head, then nodded towards the black bag. 'Empty that ... show me ... what's left.'

CHAPTER 45

DAY SEVEN

BREAKING POTTS

———————

See how eagerly the lobsters, and the turtles all advance!
They wait upon the shingle; will you come and join the dance?

Tick, tock. Ali rolled out of the hole she'd kicked in the barn, and sprinted through the orchard. How much of her precious hour had she spent looking after Waxstaff? Half? More? How long before Potts carried out the threat to punish Aunt Martha.

She reached the kitchen door without seeing anyone, and heard angry voices coming from another room. She looked at the syringe in her hand. Waxstaff had found a vial of sedative in the bag. Ali had filled the syringe with it, but would it be enough? Potts was twice the size of a normal person. But then it only had to slow her down, just enough to get Aunt Martha safely into the car.

The raised voices were coming from the dining room. Ali tiptoed down the hall and peered round the open door. Her aunt and uncle were at the table and Potts looked to be lec-turing them. She was parading back and forth by the French doors and waving the whisky decanter around. She was drunk and slurring her words.

'An' another thing, gonna enjoy puttin' Miss Fancy-pants cross my knee, needs a proper thrashin', gonna enjoy that ... oh yes, indeedy.' The nurse staggered a little, grabbed the drapes by the French doors to steady herself, and pulled them from the wall. 'Oopsie, sorry 'bout that!' She giggled, raised the decanter to her lips, took another swig, burped and held it out with a straight arm to Lord Grey like a salute. 'Nice li'l drop.'

'Very pleased you like it,' he replied, with no hint of sarcasm in his voice. 'I should hate to see it go to waste.'

Then he caught sight of Ali peering from the doorway. He didn't react; instead he looked back at Potts, who was weaving her way towards him. 'Please do go on, you were telling us about Waxstaff.'

'Ha! Yes, don' yous worry 'bout ol' bony.' She started moving her hips in a parody of dancing, and began to sing a nursery rhyme: 'Ding dong dell, Bony's in da well, who put 'er in, Li'l Missus King, who pulled 'er out ... no one!'

She cackled with laughter, tripped, grabbed the end of the table and stood swaying like a barge as she took another swig from the decanter.

Ali stepped back from the doorway, out of sight of Potts, but still able to see her uncle at his end of the table. Could she march straight in there and jab the syringe in Potts? What if she missed? As if he was reading her mind, Lord Grey started turning an imaginary steering wheel and made loud revving noises, play-acting driving the way a child would.

'Ha! No, no ... no drivin', lordshippyness, not never. Down the well, all o' yous.'

'I'm not planning to drive off, you ridiculous woman. I plan on parking the Bentley on your head.' He nodded to the French doors as he said it, taking care not to glance at Ali. 'Straight up the patio steps and through those windows and to hell with the furniture. Right on your head, you wretched woman!'

Ali didn't hesitate. She took a few quiet steps down the hall, then raced to the front door and out onto the drive. The Bentley was parked up and ready to go, keys in the ignition.

What were you thinking, Uncle Bertie? Ali quietly cursed her uncle. She had told him to be discreet, to take their bags and Aunt Martha to the garage, not announce their departure by bringing the car to the front door! No wonder Potts had stepped in and corralled them in the dining room!

Ali jumped in and tried to remember the driving lesson her uncle had given her the other day. She turned the key and the engine purred into life; then she stamped down on the clutch pedal and threw the car into gear, released the clutch and applied some throttle. It stalled. She looked round to see if anyone had heard, couldn't see anyone, and tried again.

The car lurched forward at a gentle crawl. One gear would have to do, slow and sure. The throttle lever was attached to a sleeve on the steering column, and she pulled it down a notch. The car went from its slow crawl to a stately walking pace. Ali rounded the corner of the house, drove onto the grass, and turned the car in a wide arc, lining it up with the dining room.

Potts was standing with her back to the French doors. She was still waving the decanter and had started dancing again, swaying her massive hips to a tune Ali couldn't hear. The Bentley, solid and reliable, reached the terrace and began to judder up the shallow steps like a turtle pulling itself up a beach, the front wheels twisting at every step so that Ali had to fight to keep a straight line.

Over by the dining table, Lord Grey saw his beloved car shaking its way up the steps towards him; his pride and joy of more than fifty years, his Betty. But if he was worried, it didn't show; his expression gave nothing away.

Aunt Martha tried to do the same, but something in her eyes betrayed her and Potts turned to face the window.

The Bentley was on the terrace now, and Ali had to fight the urge to hit the brakes. Just a few feet away, on the other side of the glass, Potts was staring at her, a look of utter confusion on her face. Then her eyes widened, her intoxicated brain suddenly making sense of the scene. The giant nurse staggered back as the car struck the French doors. She didn't get far. Just one step.

The doors gave way in a shattering of glass. They didn't open, they fell inward, complete with their oak frames. They toppled down over Potts, one of the square windows lining up over her head, the glass shattering on her skull before the window frame came down over her shoulders and pinned her arms to her sides.

'Wha' th' fuck!'

The Bentley stalled. Ali jumped out and stepped up onto the French doors, which now lay like a kid's climbing frame, propped at one end on the hips of Nurse Potts, one of its square windows around her waist like a life belt.

Ali began to walk up the frame, stepping round glass splinters that poked from the rims of putty, her weight adding to the pressure of the frame on Potts' hips. Blood trickled from multiple wounds where shards of glass bit into her flesh like tiny teeth.

'Hello,' Ali hissed, waiting for the nurse to come to her senses, to shake off the concussion of the falling door. Potts stared at the car, then at Ali.

'Yer li' shit.'

'That's me,' said Ali, and she stabbed the nurse with the sedative, pushing the plunger and emptying the syringe. 'Waxstaff sends her love.'

'Was that necessary?' barked Lady Grey as Ali scooped her up from her wheelchair and carried her round the fallen doors.

'Yes!' We can't risk her waking up and calling that King woman.'

'Nice driving,' said her uncle, stepping ahead of them and opening the passenger door.

'Don't encourage her,' sighed Aunt Martha as Ali leaned into the car and settled her into the passenger seat. 'I hope the car can still get us to London after all this!' She paused. 'How is poor Jackie?'

'She'll be okay,' Ali lied, wanting to spare them. 'We'll call for an ambulance when we get on the road.'

She leaned back in to fasten her aunt's seat belt, then looked out across the lawn. There was no sign of Mrs King or the Suits. Not yet, but they must have heard the crash.

'You too, Alice – get in,' said Aunt Martha, as her husband climbed into the driving seat and started the engine. 'We go together, or not at all.'

'I'll ride in the boot. They're looking for me, Aunty, they think I've found the secret to coming back safely from the bluebell woods.'

'And have you?'

'No. But they think I have. If they see me in the car, they'll stop us. They might try anyway, but you keep driving till we get to the next town. Stop where there are lots of people around, outside a police station if you can.'

Her aunt said nothing, scanning Ali's face, searching her eyes, then nodded. 'I hope you've thought this through.'

'What about Potts?' Lord Grey pointed at the nurse who had started to collapse under the weight of the doors. With her arms pinned at her sides, she couldn't lift the frame off her hips. All she could do was surrender to its weight, and she fell backwards onto her rump, her legs stretched out in front of her on a bed of broken glass. Her eyes were closed, and she was whimpering.

'We can't leave her,' he said. 'We'd be leaving her to die.'

'Like she left poor Jackie,' said his wife, her voice cold as ice.

'We'll tell the ambulance,' said Ali. 'They can deal with it.' Moving to the back of the car, she popped the boot latch. Grabbing the luggage, she moved it to the back seat, then climbed into the boot. She didn't close the lid completely, and scanned the grounds as her uncle reversed off the patio.

CHAPTER 46

DAY SEVEN

PETER POWER

———————

Alice said nothing; she had sat down with her face in her hands,
wondering if anything would ever happen in a natural way again.

She crouched on hands and knees, tore a page from her notebook, held her penlight between her teeth, and started to scribble a note. Then face-planted as the car turned sharply out into the street.

'Ow!' Ali spat the penlight from her teeth. 'Slow down!' her voice was thick and muted and she guessed right away they couldn't hear her. The old Bentley had been built to last, a solid, reliable machine with thick insulation, even in the boot. Which meant her aunt and uncle wouldn't expect to hear her, or try to talk to her, and wouldn't know she'd jumped out till they stopped in the next town to let her out.

But where to jump out? Ali finished her note, pushed the lid of the boot up a fraction more, and peered out. Damn it! They were through the village already, and her uncle was picking up speed.

Then suddenly, amid a squeal of breaks, she rolled forward as the Bentley slammed to a stop. Ali didn't hesitate, she lifted the boot, grabbed her backpack and scrambled out, pressing down on the boot as she dropped to the road.

She rolled sideways into a verge of long grass and lay there for a moment, keeping her head down. She could hear her uncle arguing with another motorist, his language rich and eloquent ... and extremely rude. Then he blasted his horn, ending the conversation, and drove off.

A dog started yapping right behind her.

'Are you all right?'

Ali looked up over her shoulder. A young woman was staring down at her. She was dressed in designer jogging gear and had a small dog on a lead and a large child in pushchair.

'I'm fine,' Ali jumped to her feet, 'just fell over.' No one else was about, only the jogger, but a car was turning into the road a few blocks ahead.

'Fell over? You were in that old Bentley!'

'Yes. And I fell over – getting out of it.'

'Out of the boot! I saw you. Why were you in the boot?'

The approaching car was black. A limousine with tinted windows.

'Hitched a lift ...' Ali started walking backwards and made a pantomime of scanning the cottages behind her. 'Oh good, this is me. Bye!' She finger-waved at the barking dog, opened a low picket gate and raced up the path. To the side of the cottage was a line of rose bushes. Ali ducked behind them.

'Who the hell *are* you?' The young mother caught the gate before it closed, steered her pushchair and dog through, and stepped into the garden. 'This is *my* house! I live here.'

Ali didn't reply, merely pressed herself against the wall of the cottage and watched the road from the cover of the roses. The black sedan cruised by; its tinted windows closed.

'Stay where you are.' The mother began rummaging around in the front of the pushchair. 'I'm calling the police right now.'

Ali didn't stop to argue, she sprinted down the side of the cottage to the back garden. It was neat and tidy, except for an aging brick wall at the end. On the far side was a thicket of yew trees, their trunks gnarled and twisted with age, their outstretched branches sheltering gravestones that tilted from the ground like grey teeth. The church cemetery! Ali felt a small surge of relief; she could just see the church spire rising above the trees, a broken finger cradled in scaffolding.

'The police are on their way, right now!' the mother came marching round the house. 'Don't do anything stupid.'

'Can't promise!' Ali ran to the wall, clambered over and raced between the gravestones to the back of the church. There was no point in discretion now. The Suits had bugged Peter's cellphone; they might be listening to every phone in the village. And the police radio.

She slipped into a line of shadow on the northern wall where the steel scaffolding rose like an overgrown climbing frame. It rattled as she pulled herself up, but it was an easy climb and in less than a minute she had reached the top. The uppermost platform was lashed to the bell gallery where a series of open arches allowed the peal of the bells to ring out across the village.

But not anymore. One arch had been bricked in, two were propped up with steel piping, and a fourth was boarded over with planks. Ali grabbed the end of one plank and pulled. It fell away easily and she squeezed through into the bell gallery.

Over by the far wall, a brass bell half the size of Ali sat on a wooden pallet. Another bell hung right above her head, it's pull rope hanging through the gallery and down to the church below.

'Took your time.' Ali spun round. Nobody! The space was empty.

'Peter?'

'Sure. And for my next trick ...'

And suddenly there was Peter, as if he'd walked out of the wall.

'Okay, how did you do that?'

'Come and see. Oldest trick in the book.' Ali stepped past him. The wall wasn't one wall, it was two overlapping walls with a narrow gap between them like a short corridor.

'Neat hiding place. So what did you dig up? Anything?'

'Yeah, it's in here.' He stepped back between the walls. Ali followed. The space beyond was small and cramped – too low for them to stand – and decked out like a kid's treehouse, with maps and pictures pinned to the walls. Light streaked in like torch beams through gaps in the floorboards.

'I was seven when I found this place. Kept it my secret.'

'Peter Power's secret lair?'

'Exactly. Turns out loads of churches built secret rooms like this, places to hide stuff when towns got attacked – gold crosses, statues, that kind of thing.'

'Did they come looking for you?'

'Yea, a couple of Suits searched the whole church, and the bell tower. Got any food, I'm starving?'

'No, sorry, everything went to shit like we thought it would.' Ali told him about Mrs King and what she'd done to Waxstaff. Peter didn't say anything, just stared at her, as if she was talking in a foreign language. 'So you have to stay hidden for a few days. My aunt's going to tell the police about it.'

'Will they believe her?'

'Doubt it. Do you?'

'Old Mrs King – with bat wings! Are you serious? It's mad. She wouldn't hurt a fly.'

'Just stay hidden, okay?'

Peter nodded, reached behind him, and handed her a large package. It was damp, and bundled in newspaper. 'Hope it's worth it.'

'Did you wrap it in this?' Ali peeled off the wet sheets.

'It was soaked, newspaper was all I had.' Inside was a large canvas bag, wet through and half eaten with mildew.

'What was she thinking!' Ali felt a burst of irritation at her aunt.

'She was thinking it was under a dry floor. Not your aunt's fault the stable got pulled down.'

'But a canvas bag!' Ali tested one strap. The bag fell to pieces. Inside was another bag, leather this time, and inside that was a parcel bound in paper and string. 'How many layers? It's like pass the parcel!'

'It's waxed paper – keeps water out. Looks like your old aunt had a brain.'

Ali kept going, unwrapping more layers. Inside was a set of notebooks with leather covers. They were old and yellowing, but they were dry. She opened one. A title was written across the first page in her great-aunt's handwriting: *The White Knight – his lost history.*

'It's her research. The Hatter asked me to find these.' Ali glanced at the other books. They were all histories. 'It's not here.'

CHAPTER 47

DAY SEVEN

FINAL SPRINT

―――――――

*'It was such a thunderstorm; part of the roof came off
and ever so much thunder got in. I was so frightened
I couldn't remember my own name!'*

'Not what you were expecting?'

'No.' Ali tried to think. Her whole focus had been to find the instructions for safe passage and do as Waxstaff suggested – destroy them. But only after she'd read them and committed the secret to memory. Destroying them forever would condemn all the people stranded over there, the Hatter, the boys – all of them. The secret was their chance to get back safely, which is why her aunt had chosen to hide it, not destroy it.

'So where is it?' Ali closed her eyes. 'Where did she hide it?'

'Not your problem now. Get away and let the police do their thing.'

'I guess.' Ali put the journals into her backpack with the other books. 'And you have to stay hidden till they get here, okay?'

'Okay.' He squeezed out of the secret room. Ali handed her bag through, and followed.

'Very clever.' King was standing in the bell tower, grinning at them; her face lit by a shaft of light, her glass eyes shining. She was dressed in her head scarf again, and her floral dress; a picture of old age and innocence.

'All these years I've been looking after the church and I never knew this hidey-hole existed.' She extended a hand. 'Give me the bag, Ali, your part in this little adventure is over.'

'Take it!' Ali swung her backpack at King, striking her in the chest. King fell backwards with a surprised yelp. Peter tried to catch her, acting out of instinct to help a frail woman he'd known his entire life. He was too slow, but his hands grabbed her head scarf as she fell past him and her large, gristled ears sprang upright.

'What the shit!' He jumped back, staring at her in shock. King laughed and sprang at him, agile as a teenager, slapping him across the face, the tips of her nails raking his cheek. He fell back and King leapt on his chest, pinning him to the ground.

It seemed to Ali as if time had slowed to a snail's pace. She watched Peter as he struggled on the floor, his movements slow and ponderous, as if he were fighting in treacle. She looked about for a weapon, something to strike King with. Nothing! Just the bell rope hanging down through the room from the tower above. She grabbed it and pulled, felt the bell begin to rock, and pulled again.

King was climbing off Peter and reaching for the fallen backpack. Her head jerked up and her glass eyes looked from Ali to the bell swaying above them.

Then it rang. A soft, weak chime. Ali released the rope,

letting it rise back up, pulled by the bell as it completed its arc. Then she grabbed on again and heaved.

'BONG!' The chime was louder this time, vibrating round the small room, bouncing off the walls. King shrieked and launched herself at Ali, grabbing her neck. Ali pulled on the bell again as Peter struggled to his feet and tried to pull King away.

King flexed her wings under her dress. It ripped and the wings sprung free, snapping open and hurling Peter cross the room. He landed beside a set of steps leading down to the church below.

'Suits!' Peter yelled the warning to Ali. Two men were scrambling up into the narrow space. Peter kicked out at the head of the first. His foot struck home and the man swore and ducked back down. Ali hardly noticed; King's hands were tight around her throat and she felt threads of blood where the yellow fingernails were biting like claws into her skin. Ali put all her weight on the rope, hauling the bell above into its full arc.

'BONG!' this time the noise was unbearable, even to Ali, a thunderclap in her skull. King screamed, lifting her hands to her ears, releasing her hold on Ali's throat. Ali pulled again and felt something give above her. The bell chimed again, but it was dull this time. Dust was everywhere, falling like grey snow. Ali looked up and saw the bell had dropped on one side, the iron crossbeam that carried its weight had fallen free of its housing.

'Ali,' Peter yelled, kicking out at another Suit, 'he's got a gun!' A second man lifted his head into the room and aimed a gun at Ali. He fired just as the steps gave way beneath him. The bullet tore into the roof and he fell from view.

'Let's go!' screamed Ali, leaping over King who was writhing on the ground and whimpering like a child.

Ali grabbed her backpack and ran to the gap in the arch where she'd climbed in. Peter scrambled after her, out onto the scaffolding which had shifted dangerously to one side. Small squares of weathered slate fell past, shattering as they hit the gravel path below. The whole tower was groaning around them.

Ali hitched her backpack over her shoulder, grabbed one of the vertical poles of scaffolding, and launched herself clear. Using the bar like a fireman's pole, she slid down to the next working gantry of planks. The ground was still ten metres below and more than just roof tiles were falling now; the whole spire was shaking itself to pieces.

A police siren wailed in the distance. Ali swung herself over the gantry rail and grabbed the next pole.

Peter followed and they slid down one more level.

'It's going!' he yelled as the scaffolding tower pulled free of the wall and started to topple. 'Jump!'

'No!' Ali screamed. 'Hold on!' She pulled herself tight against the pole, clutching it to her chest as four stories of scaffolding began a slow-motion collapse around her, the steel bars shrieking and groaning. The frame twisted as it fell and she found herself staring back at the church, watching as sections of spire tumbled down through the building, the brass bell dropping out onto the path where it cracked open like a giant egg.

The scaffolding held together as it toppled, the upper sections dropping into the yew trees that bordered the cemetery. Ali and Peter were left dangling just above the ground. They stared at each other, relief flooding through them, then dropped to the ground. Ali hit grass and rolled. Peter landed badly, one foot catching the edge of a grave-stone.

Ali looked up at the church. The spire and bell tower were gone, they had fallen through the main roof where a plume of dust now rose like a miniature mushroom cloud … and tumbling slowly through the dust, almost invisible in the roiling cloud, a small figure was flapping its wings to break its fall.

'Look!' Ali turned to Peter, but he was staring white-faced down at his foot It was poking sideways at the wrong angle.

'Get going,' he whispered. Ali grabbed him under one arm and tried to pull him up, but Peter shrugged her off.

'Go, Ali! I mean it. I'm good. Doesn't get much safer than being arrested by police in broad daylight for causing all this.'

'You'll be locked up!'

'Not when they find a guy with a fucking gun buried in the rubble, right?' He grinned up at her. 'Dad will be here any second – he'll be so happy to see me, everything else will just be noise to him. Go find yours. Find your dad.'

Ali hesitated, then bent and planted a kiss on his upturned face. 'You taste like shit!' She hoisted her bag and sprinted into the shadow of the yew trees.

Nobody paid her any attention as she stepped out onto the street; they were too busy running towards the church, pointing their phones at the settling dust and dictating breathless commentaries. She fell in behind them, one face in a growing crowd. They came to the village green. Similar crowds were converging from other streets.

And then Ali saw the black limousine. It was weaving through the growing crowd and finally pulled up by the village shops. Two Suits jumped out – one man, one woman – they left the engine running and marched into the teashop. To get King? Ali didn't wait to find out; as soon as they disappeared inside, she set off at a slow jog towards the manor house.

The backpack was heavy, but she hardly noticed, focusing instead on her breathing, on the rhythm of her run. She tried to clear everything from her mind. Nothing mattered but getting to the barn ahead of King and her Knaves. Ali could hear different sirens now, fire, police and ambulance. She glanced back as she reached the gates. No one was behind her.

As she ran up the drive, Ali picked up speed. The closer she came to the barn, the stronger she felt the compulsion ... like an elastic cord was stretched to breaking point, an umbilical cord pulling her back to the other universe. Her mind was oddly silent, it had crunched all the data and was content with her decision to go back; it was the only option for keeping everyone safe. King had survived the collapse of the spire. She thought Ali had found the secret to safe passage, so Ali was sure King would come for her; she would follow Ali through into Wonderland, and everyone on this side would be left in peace for a while.

As she neared the house, Ali began worrying about Potts. She wanted to go to the barn, but if the sedative had worn off and Potts had pulled herself free, things could turn very ugly. She had to find out .

She heard Potts before she saw her. The woman was yelling curses at the top of her voice. Ali slowed to a walk and circled the house at a safe distance till she could see into the dining room. Potts was still wearing the doorframe like a giant tutu, her arms pinned where it girdled her waist. Blood was everywhere, her uniform more red than white, with stains blooming where the shards of glass bit into her. Then her eyes snapped open.

'You!' Potts spat the word, raw hatred blazing from her eyes.

'Your people are coming,' said Ali, 'you might still make it. More than you deserve.'

And she walked away, down the terrace and onto the lawn.

'Get back here!' The nurse roared her frustration, rage giving her a surge of strength. Ali glanced back. Potts was expanding her chest, pushing out against the wooden frame that pinned her arms. The effort drove the splinters of glass still deeper into her arms. She roared with agony, feeding off the pain, turning it into a furious strength that finally snapped the wood.

'You're dead!' she screamed. 'I'll rip your fuckin' face off!' She fell forward and began crawling on hands and knees over the splinters of glass. Ali ran, not looking back till she reached the wall of ivy. Potts was on the terrace, staggering to her feet. Ali raced to the barn, found the hole she'd kicked in the rotten boards, threw her bag inside and crawled in after it.

Waxstaff was curled up on the bed like a child; eyes closed, skin like wax, her breathing a soft wheeze. Ali climbed up, hitched her bag onto her back, and sat cross-legged at the head of the bed. As gently as she could, she eased her hands under Waxstaff's head, cradling it onto her lap. Waxstaff didn't stir.

'Please, please,' Ali whispered. 'Please, Mum.' Even as she closed her eyes, Ali knew it couldn't work. Her heart was hammering too hard, adrenaline flooded her system.

Then she felt a hand on hers, and opened her eyes. Waxstaff was looking up at her with a smile of such gentleness, such contentment, that it broke Ali's heart to see it. A wave of sadness swept over her, a desolation so complete that it carried with it an odd sense of peace, as if a long fight was finally at an end.

Waxstaff smiled again, and squeezed Ali's hand. 'She'd be … so proud,' she whispered.

Ali could hear Potts screaming outside, hammering at the door of the barn. It didn't matter. Not anymore. All that mattered was this ... sitting with her mother's friend, the warmth of her smile flooding through her like words of forgiveness.

Across the barn, the door gave way and Potts barged in. Ali barely noticed. She was looking past her to a line of trees where a huge moon hung in a sky of deepest turquoise. Lying in front of her on a carpet of bluebells, was Waxstaff.

Neither spoke. They squeezed hands and watched the huge moon as it rose clear of the silver birch trees.

POSTSCRIPT

———————

The journey to the next town had been without incident. Lord Grey drove as best he could, sticking to one side of the road and keeping below the speed limit. From time to time he would shake a little, but his wife would lay her gloved hand on his elbow till the trembling stopped. They kept their word, driving without a break till they came to the next town, a twenty-minute drive from the village.

They found a quiet street on the outskirts where tall hedge-rows lined a municipal park. Lord Grey climbed out, opened the boot and felt his heart drain though his shoes. He picked up the note and climbed back into the car.

He didn't say a word; he didn't need to – his wife had read his expression the moment he got back in. He handed her the note, and they read it together.

Thank you for making me fall in love with you. Please keep
driving and don't be angry. I know where the secret is, and
I know how to keep it from them. When Dad gets hold of you,
and somehow he will, tell him I found Jackie and I'll take care
of her for Mum. Tell him I love him with all my heart and I'm
sorry I was so angry all the time. It was never him. Never.
Now keep driving, and don't stop till London.

They sat in silence, holding hands, trying to decide what to do. Then turned the car around. Alice was family, and family stuck together, no matter what.

OTHER TITLES TO COME IN THE SERIES

———————

Printed in Great Britain
by Amazon

34881998R00192